CRIMSON &

CARIUS

REAL TRAP

LOVE

WRITTEN BY:

NIKKI NICOLE

Acknowledgments

Hi, how are you? I'm Nikki Nicole the Pen Goddess. Each time I complete a book I love to write acknowledgements. I love to give a reflection on how I felt about the book. I've been writing for almost three years now and this is my 17th book. When I first started writing I only had one story I wanted to tell and that was Baby I Play for Keeps. Three years later and I've penned a total of 17 books. I appreciate each one of you for taking this journey with me. I'm forever grateful for you believing in me and giving me your continuous support.

I don't know where to begin, but I'll start here. Crimson and Griff were originally supposed to be a Christmas Novella. I have never written a novella before. I don't think I could tell a story with 20,000 words or less because I talk too much. I decided to just make it a novel. I have Angela, who buys every paperback the day it's released, and the last thing I want to do is sell her a book with 90 pages or less. I've had so many setbacks with this release its crazy, but I kept pushing because I knew it was the devil trying to throw me off. He'll never win with me.

The cover didn't come on time and when it did come, I didn't like it. I felt like a motherfucka was trying to play me, so I had to order another one. I could've moved on to another release, another project that I had the covers for, but I didn't. It's reason why I had to sit on this one. I'm glad I trusted my instincts. I never forget the day I was on my way to work. I was on I-285N, it's raining and I'm listening to **Kevin Gates Find You Again**.

I put this on my OG, may he rest in peace. Griff came to me and sat on my shoulders pouring out his words. I'm literally crying because I can feel it. Tears clouded my vision. I don't even know how I made it to my exit. I couldn't wait to get to my desk to pen it. As soon as I got to work, I pulled up my document and got to writing. I knew then I had a serious masterpiece on my hands.

I've never wrote about a man like Griff. I'm so in love with him. This is the longest book that I've written to date. I love Crimson Rose Tristan. She's different than any female I've ever penned. I haven't written a book that flowed like this since Journee & Juelz. I've experienced a lot of setbacks, but I know it was because I had a major come back coming. I don't do patience but these past 60 days I've had plenty.

I want to Thank God for giving me this gift. I can't thank him enough because for years I've always wanted to know what my purpose was. I can do anything with my hands, their golden. I've always had a way with words.

I'm a creator. If I'm not creating, I'm a mess. I'm an author, and I love to write. I don't give a fuck where I'm at. I'm always writing, and it doesn't matter. I want to thank my supporters for backing me and believing in me. I love y'all to death. I wouldn't trade y'all for nothing. I promise y'all the wait was worth it. If I haven't dropped a book in 60 days, do trust I'm coming with some major work. In my absence I've been cooking my ass off.

I want to thank my supporters that haven't left me or had a conversation with. I appreciate y'all too. Please email me or contact me on social media. I want to acknowledge you and give you a S/O also.

I dedicate this book to my Queens in the Trap **Nikki Nicole's Readers Trap**. I swear y'all are the best. Y'all go so hard in the paint for me it's insane. Every day we lit. I appreciate y'all more than y'all will ever know. The Trap is going the fuck up on a Sunday. I can't wait for y'all to read it.

It's time for my S/O **Samantha, Tatina, Asha, Shanden (PinkDiva), Padrica, Liza, Aingsley, Trecie, Quack, Shemekia, Toni, Amisha, Tamika, Troy, Pat, Crystal C, Missy, Angela, Latoya, Helene, Tiffany, Lamaka, Reneshia, Charmaine, Misty, Toy, Toi, Shelby, Chanta, Jessica, Snowie, Jessica, Sommer, Cathy, Karen, Bria, Kelis, Lisa, Tina, Talisha, Naquisha, Iris, Nicole, Koi, Drea, Rickena, Saderia, Chanae, Shanise, Nacresha, Jalisa, Tamika H, Kendra, Meechie, Avis, Lynette, Pamela, Antoinette, Crystal W, Ivee, Kimberly, Yutanzia, Seanise, Chrishae, Demetria, Jennifer, Shatavia, LaTonya, Dimitra, Kellissa, Jawanda, Renea, Tomeika, Viola, Gigi, Barbie, Erica, Shanequa, Dallas, Verona, Catherine, Dominique, Natasha,**

If I named everybody, I will be here all day. Put your name here_____ if I missed you. The list goes on. S/O to every member in my reading group, I love y'all to the moon and back. These ladies right here are a hot mess. I love them to death. They go so hard about these books it doesn't make any sense. Sometimes, I feel like I should run and hide.

If you're looking for us meet us in **Nikki Nicole's Readers Trap** on Facebook, we are live and indirect all day.

S/O to My Pen Bae's **Ash ley, Chyna L, Chiquita, T. Miles,** I love them to the moon and back head over to Amazon and grab a book by them also.

Check my out my new favorite Author **Nique Luarks** baby girl can write her ass off. You heard it from me. I love her work! Look her up and go read her catalog!

To my new readers I have five complete series, and three completed standalones available. Here's my catalog if you don't have it.

Cuffed by a Trap God 1-3

I Just Wanna Cuff You (Standalone)

Baby I Play for Keeps 1-3

For My Savage, I Will Ride or Die

He's My Savage, I'm His Ridah

You Don't Miss A Good Thing, Until It's Gone (Standalone)

He's My Savage, I'm His Ridah

Journee & Juelz 1-3

Giselle & Dro (Standalone)

Our Love Is the Hoodest 1-2

Join my readers group **Nikki Nicole's Readers Trap** on **Facebook**

Follow me on Facebook Nikki Taylor

Follow me on Twitter @WatchNikkiwrite

Like my Facebook Page AuthoressNikkiNicole

Instagram @WatchNikkiwrite

GoodReads @authoressnikkinicole

Visit me on the web authoressnikkinicole.com

Email me authoressnikkinicole@gmail.com

Join my email contact list for exclusive sneak peeks.
http://eepurl.com/czCbKL

I made a playlist https://itunes.apple.com/us/playlist/crimson-carius-real-trap-love/pl.u-mJy81XJTKLej4p

Table of Contents

REAL TRAP
SHIT

PROLOGUE

Chapter-1

Crimson

I didn't have any plans today. The house was quiet as a mouse because everybody was gone. I could smell the aroma of sausages, biscuits, and hash browns and maybe some grits or oatmeal depending on the cook's attitude. The aroma was creeping underneath my door and my stomach was growling. Yeah, Mother Dear was in the kitchen throwing down. It's time to eat! Anytime it was just my grandmother and I alone she will cook us a big breakfast. It's the first of the month and the bills are due. Every tenant that's occupying a room here is long gone. They've cashed their checks and got the fuck on.

This is the only time that it's peace and quiet around here. I never get to sleep in late on any of my off days but today.

Whenever the bills are due everybody disappears for a few days because they don't want to help contribute to anything. As soon as their funds are exhausted, they'll reappear with their hands out like nothing's happened. I'm glad they're gone because I could help Mother Dear clean the house, do laundry and prepare us dinner.

Maybe I'll treat her out to Red Lobster or Pappadeaux for lunch. I've never seen a bunch of grown ass people who didn't want to work, but constantly wants to free load. I take that back. I have seen it. I've been around it my whole life. I vowed to never be that way. My grandmother worked her ass off her whole life to make sure she could provide for her family, but somehow her children lost that trait.

I stood to my feet and pulled my covers back. I walked to my bathroom to grab a face towel to wash my face. It's a little after 9:00 a.m. and for someone reason, the sun was shining through my curtains. I had black blinds and extra dark curtains in my room because I hate for the sunlight to wake me up. It's always been that way for as long as I can remember. I didn't like the sun shining on me and I didn't like being in the spotlight. Maybe that's why I stay to myself.

Mother Dear took me in when I was a new born baby and I'm forever grateful for that because I could've been lost in the system. Mother Dear's child was my creator. I will never say her name. Fuck her because it's always been fuck me. The moment I was old enough to provide for myself I made a promise that I would help Mother Dear with her bills and groceries. So far, I've been making that promise. She gets two checks a month. Social Security and retirement. Her income can barely cover the bills.

After she pays for everything, she barely has enough money for food and to pay for her medicine. I work part time at Walgreens, and I go to school full time. The money that I get from work I buy groceries and help her with other living expenses. Whenever I get a lump sum on my school check I make mortgage payments. I always treat her to a girl's day out because it's just the two of us.

"Crimson Rose Tristan, can you go to the store for me?" She yelled and asked. I was making my way downstairs any way. My stomach was touching my back. I took a seat at the kitchen table. Mother Dear slid a plate in front of me and it was loaded with all my favorites. I said grace quick and started devouring my food. Mother Dear knew I would go to the store for her. She knew she didn't have to ask me to do anything.

She's all I have in this world and I cherish her. I would be lost without her. Even with her daily struggles and unable to make ends meet, she made sure I had everything I needed. Yes, I wanted a lot of stuff, but she couldn't afford it, so I didn't dwell on what she couldn't do. I was thankful for what she was able to do.

"Of course, Mother Dear. What do you need?" I asked talking with my mouth full. I knew she had a ton of things she wanted me to do.

"I need you to pay the Georgia Power Bill for me. I also need you to run to the Farmers Market. We're running low on meat and vegetables. I need some fresh fruit too. I want to jar some strawberries. They cut my food stamps down to $17.00 per month. Crimson Rose, I can't feed you or my damn self with that. I might have to pick up a second job just to have a little cushion. I appreciate everything you do here Crimson. I added everything up and after I pay my bills. I should have about $200.00 left. When you go to the Farmers Market get beef and fish. Check the prices too.

It's August and it's 31 days in the month we'll have to make the food stretch. If you can, get some Flour and Corn meal too." She explained. Mother Dear also gave me a list of things she needed from the corner store.

"Mother Dear, I got you! How come Jermesha won't help with food around here? Damn, she has three kids and I know for a fact she gets over $400.00 worth of food stamps? Her kids eat up every damn thing! Uncle Tommy gets a check too and he blows it as soon as he gets it. What about Auntie Sherry? She gets stamps and a check. It doesn't make any sense." I argued. I swear I get so mad because they're so selfish. At least you could help or do something?

"Watch your damn mouth, Crimson Rose. I know it's not right, but God, he sits high, and he looks low. I will never treat people how they treat me no matter what, despite my current struggles. When I leave this world, I'm leaving everything to you, and they'll be lost without me. I know you won't tolerate anything that I'm going through, but I'm proud of the woman you've grown into." She argued.

"Mother Dear don't talk like that. I hate when you do that. What will I do without you?" I asked. Living without my Mother Dear is out the question. I wouldn't be able to take it, she's all I know.

"You'll live Crimson Rose Tristan, and you'll remember everything I taught you. I want you to get out of this house and meet your husband. You've never had a boyfriend that I know of and you're too damn old for that. I want some great grandbabies who I can cherish and adore. I can't complain because you don't have a shit load of kids running around."

"Mother Dear why do you always call me by my government name? You're always trying to put me off on somebody. I'm not thinking about a man. I'm trying to finish school and get my associates degree as a medical assistant. I want my own clinic to help my community get decent healthcare and treatment." I pouted and whined.

"I think you like hearing me talk. I love your name Crimson Rose Tristan! Crimson is the prettiest shade of red I ever laid eyes on. The moment I laid eyes on you, your little cheeks were red as a rose. You were smiling at me. You're my beautiful rose in the flesh. You can do all that Crimson Rose, but I want you to experience love. You have a beautiful soul, and someone deserves to experience that." She explained. "Don't roll your eyes at me." Mother Dear gave me pleading eyes and a very stern look. I wanted to bust out laughing. I hear her loud and clear, but I'm not listening.

"I'll pass Mother Dear. Being in love comes with pain and heart ache. My own mother and father didn't love me, so how can I love someone else?" I asked. I hate to say it, but it's the truth.

"Crimson don't do that. Your mother is my daughter true enough but fuck her, don't let what she did to you define you. I LOVE YOU. I taught you how to love. I raised my children the same way I raised you but look how they turned out. Let me tell you something and you can take it however you want too. Your mother, she's living her life how she sees fit but Crimson Rose, she'll have to pay for how she treated you. Trust me she'll get hers. She may be getting hers now, who knows. Excuse my language.

Karma is one bitch that always comes back around when you least expect it."

I heard everything she was saying, and I appreciated her for that. I grabbed the keys to Mother Dear's car and left. I was able to pick up a few extra hours at my job, so I can pay the Georgia Power and cable bill for her and she can keep her bill money as pocket change.

I paid the Georgia Power bill online. I didn't have the time to be standing in line to pay a bill. The only thing I had left to do was grocery shop. I took my shower early this morning. I threw on a pair of distressed Gibaud Jeans and a white Gibaud t-shirt. I threw on some white old navy flip flops. My hair was braided into two French braids that I braided last night.

I finally made it to the Farmers Market on East Ponce De Leon. I hated coming to this place because it was always packed. I pulled my list out of my purse and scratched off everything I would need as I went. I stocked up on ground beef, turkey wings, chicken, and steak. I also grabbed a variety of fruit. I couldn't wait until she jarred the strawberries with sugar and strawberry jam. Yummy! I'm currently in line waiting to get a few pounds of shrimp and fish. I noticed this guy would appear everywhere I would. I was ready to get out of here because he was making me uncomfortable.

"Hey, you, I know you see me following you? What's a man got to do to get your attention or a moment of your time," He asks. I wasn't even about to turn around to see if he was talking to me. His cologne invaded my nostrils and he smelled good too. I ignored him and continued to wait on the guy to take my order for seafood. I felt a tap on my shoulder. I looked over my shoulder to see who it was, and it was him.

Damn, he was fine as fuck. His skin was the color of a fresh jar of peanut butter. He had dark brown hazel eyes and two gold fangs. I could tell he was a dope boy. His swag was on a thousand. What did he want with me? I didn't have anything to offer him.

"What's up Shawty? What's your name? I'm Griff and it's nice to meet you. My eyes have been getting acquainted with you. I've done enough looking so I'm trying to see what's up with you?" He asked.

"Hi, I'm Crimson Rose. It's nice to meet you, Griff." I beamed. I didn't even extend my hand for him to shake it. I turned backed around as fast as I said Hi. I hope he takes his ass on and minds his business.

"Damn Crimson Rose, what's the rush? You're trying hard to hush a nigga up? You didn't even give a nigga the chance to speak up? I'm trying to get to know you. I know you don't have a man. You're beautiful as fuck and I don't see a wedding band shinning some light on your beautiful ass hands." He stated. I turned around and grilled him.

"Why do you want to get to know me? Just because I don't have a ring on my finger doesn't mean anything. I could have a man and just maybe I don't want to conversate with you. Did that ever occur to you?" I argued. He stepped in my personal space. I backed up a little bit because he was too damn close to me. I needed some space in between us. He didn't give a damn about my personal space. As soon as I stepped back. He closed the gap.

"You could have a man Crimson Rose, but you don't. If you did have a man, he's a dumb motherfucka because I would never let you roam these streets alone." He argued. We were in the middle of the Farmers Market going back and forth. I don't have time for this shit. I heard the store clerk speak. I looked over my shoulder to see what he wanted.

"Excuse me Ms., what did you want again," The store clerk asked. I gave him my order. Saved by the bell. My heart was beating fast as fuck. I don't know what this Griff man wanted with me, but he needed to go on. I grabbed my items from the clerk. I tried to walk away but Griff was standing right in front of my buggy. I'm beyond frustrated at this point.

"Excuse me, can you move, please? I'm trying to check out." I explained.

"Yeah, I'll move under two conditions. Can I ask you a question? Crimson, are you grocery shopping for yourself or someone else? Give me your phone number.," He asked.

"I'm grocery shopping for my man and I don't have a phone. Excuse me." I laughed. He didn't find that shit funny at all. I politely tried to move around him. My phone started ringing and I refuse to answer it. I started walking fast and he was right on my heels.

"I like playing this game with you, Crimson Rose." He walked up on me and grabbed me by the waist. Damn, he smelled good. I tried to break free from his embrace. He had a hold on me, and I didn't like it.

"I need you to back the fuck up," I argued and sassed.

"I knew you had a phone. You're to fine and feisty not to have one. I guarantee you, your man ain't coming like this CRIMSON." He argued. He tugged on the back pocket of my jeans where my phone was. He grabbed my phone. I turned around and popped his ass.

"Look I don't know you and you don't know me. Give ME MY DAMN PHONE BACK." I argued. I wasn't playing with his ass. My day started out perfect until I ran into his ass.

"Damn Crimson your ass is soft and fat as fuck. I know you don't know me, but I'm trying to get to know you. I'm not trying to waste your time. I'm trying to make you mine. Damn Crimson let a nigga shine. I'm taking your phone today and you can take mine. I'll call you later around nine." He explained. He gave me a sneaky ass grin and smile. He walked off.

"GRIFF, GRIFF!" I was yelling his name. People were looking at me like I was crazy. He looked back at me and laughed jogging out of the store. This man is crazy. I finished paying for my things. He can keep my phone. I need a new one anyway. His phone went off. He was texting me from my phone.

678-266-9247-I heard you yelling my name. I want you to yell it in other ways

I wasn't even about to respond. He can keep that phone. I'm going to toss this one. Thank God I didn't have any nudes on my phone, just a couple of selfies, that's it. Who was this man? Griff was his name? What did he want with me and why was he so fuckin' persistent? I finally made it to the car and stacked the groceries in the trunk nice and very neat. Mother Dear had a shit load of stuff in her trunk. As soon as I slammed the trunk and slid in the driver's seat. His phone went off again. I grabbed it and it was another text.

678-266-9247-I would've helped your mean ass with groceries, but I'll see you later

I looked all around to see if I saw him. I don't like this shit at all. Hell, he could be trying to kill me. I couldn't wait to make it back home, so I could tell Mother Dear about my day.

Chapter-2

Griff

Crimson Rose! Shawty has my nose wide open. I could still smell her scent on my clothes. She smelled like sugar. Brown sugar to be exact. I couldn't wait to bake and cake on her mean ass. Her skin was the color of cinnamon. She had big brown eyes. She was a natural chick no make-up, no hair weave, no fake ass or tits. Her lips were perfect. Two French braids to the back. She had to be at least 140 pounds. Her breasts sat up and her ass stuck out. She had me mesmerized. I wanted to see her again. We haven't even gotten acquainted yet. I can't think of one female that I've chased in my twenty-five years of living. Keondra doesn't fuckin' count. Shawty's phone was blowing up too. She thought I was playing with her ass but I'm not. I'm a man of my word and I meant everything I said. I'll see her later. I put that on everything. Shawty's phone was ringing off the hook. D Elle was calling her phone. I swear if **D-Elle** was her nigga, they were breaking up today because I'm staking my claim. I answered.

"Yeah, can I help you with something?" I yelled. My tone was aggressive. I could feel my blood pumping.

"Oops, I think I dialed the wrong number," she said.

"Okay." I chuckled and hung up. D. Elle called back again. I answered and she hung up. This is my phone now. Another call was coming through by the name of Mother Dear. I knew off top Mother Dear had to be her grandmother or her mother, so I had to answer.

"Hello."

"Who is this answering Crimson Roses phone?" She argued and ask. Oh shit, I done fucked up now. I shouldn't have answered.

"Hi I'm Griff, Crimson's man." I chuckled. Yeah, I was putting that out there.

"Crimson's man, you a Gawd damn lie young nigga. God don't like ugly. Since when Griff? If you've done something to my grand-daughter I'm going to light your ass up. Come to my house and let me meet you?" She argued. Oh shit, her grandmother is off the chain. I see where she gets it from.

"Hold up Mother Dear, I'm a good guy. I wouldn't do anything to Crimson Rose. I just want to love her, that's it. If she allows me too. Okay, I'll come over to meet you. Crimson and I have a date later. I had plans to meet you then. I don't know why she's been keeping me a secret. What's the address? Its lunch time, have you eaten yet?" I asked. I had to make a good impression in front of Mother Dear if had any chances with Crimson. Mother Dear gave me the address along with her lunch order too. Thank God I had a pen in the car because I didn't want to fuck this up.

"How do you know my gawd damn name? I want a fish plate from Maxine's with Fried Green tomatoes and sautéed onions. Make sure she puts extra hot sauce. TEXAS fuckin' PETE, mustard and ketchup in the bag. I want two large seasoned fries with two slices of wheat bread and a cold motherfuckin' drank. I'll take two of those. My girl Gladys needs lunch too. Do you hear me, YOUNG MAN," she asked and yelled? I almost choked on my fuckin' drink this lady was crazy. I had to pound my chest to stop from laughing.

"Yes, ma'am! I'll see you in about thirty minutes." Mother Dear hung the phone up in my face. Rude ass.

Maxine's was my family's business. I called up there to place the order.

"Griff, who are you ordering this food for? I know this order like the back of my hand." She asked and explained. I couldn't get shit passed my cousin Maria. She knew everybody and every damn thing. She was my eyes in the streets.

"Mother Dear, why?" I laughed.

"I knew it, Griff! She doesn't fuckin' play. What time will you make it hear? She likes her food cooked to serve. I'm not trying to get cursed out about selling her no cold ass food," she argued and laughed.

"I'm in route. I'll be pulling up in about twenty minutes. I got to scoop Rashad."

"Okay. Griff." She sighed. I could tell she was rolling those bug eyes of hers. Maxine's was the spot. The restaurant was popping in the day for breakfast and lunch. At night they had the club Maxes right next door.

It was the hood spot. That motherfucka goes up every night from 10:00 p.m. until 3:00 a.m. Maxine was my auntie; may she rest in peace. My daddy and she were brother and sister. My cousin Maria was running the spot. She could cook her ass off.

Rashad was already waiting for me. I pulled up at the spot-on Glenwood and sent him a text from my other phone. He stepped out on the porch observing his surroundings. Everything looked good. I checked shit out before I pulled up. Rashad hopped in and we slapped hands then I pulled off.

"Yo what the fuck is up Griff? I've been calling your phone for the past hour. Keondra pulled up on some real hot ass shit looking for you," he argued. I busted out laughing. Rashad was so fuckin' serious.

"Chill out. I ain't got my phone. I told Keondra about that shit. I got a few moves to make and I need you to ride with me." Rashad nodded his head in agreement. I called Keondra on my car phone. I wasn't about to call her on my other phone. I knew Crimson wouldn't answer my phone because she hasn't responded to one text message. She answered on the first ring, sounding real ghetto and shit.

"Hello who this is calling my phone."

"It's me bitch. Didn't I tell you about coming to my spot on that hot ass shit? Keondra I don't put my hands-on women, but I'll beat your ass if you keep fuckin' with me. Stay the fuck away from my spots and I mean that shit." I argued. I don't know why she wants to keep fuckin' playing with me.

"I only came by there because you were supposed to go to the store for me, what happened? Griff, why are you talking to your WIFE like this?" She argued and cried.

"Nah cut that crying shit out. You're my EX-WIFE because I'm divorcing your trifling ass. Before you knew who, it was me. You were on your good bull shit. I thought you were sick Keondra. You can't be that sick if you're running around on some bull shit? Go to the store and get your own shit. I'm not anybody's flunky. Tell that nigga that you're fuckin' on the low to take care of you while you're sick." I argued and hung up the phone.

I pulled up at Maxine's to get the food. I pulled off a hundo for Maria and she bagged my shit up. I was heading to Crimson's house. It wasn't too far from here. She stayed off Snapfinger. A cute little house ducked off at the end of the cul-de-sac.

"Aye Griff, where the fuck is, we headed? Who do you know that stays down on this street," he asked?

"Just follow my lead." I pulled up to Crimson's house and it was two ladies outside on the porch. I assume that was Mother Dear and Ms. Gladys. Rashad looked at me. I motioned with my hand for him to come on. As soon as we made it on the porch Mother Dear didn't take any time asking questions.

"Which one of y'all young niggas is Griff?" She asked. Rashad looked at me and busted out laughing.

"That'll be me. It's nice to meet you Mother Dear and this is my partner Rashad." I extended my hand out for a handshake. I handed Mother Dear her food. She thumbed through the plate to make sure everything is on point. She looked at me and nodded her head.

"Tell me a little bit about yourself Griff. You're Crimson's MAN? How long and why am I just now meeting you? What are your intentions with my granddaughter? I don't want to ask around about you. I want you to tell me about you."

"I'm trying to be her man, but she's giving me a real hard time. We just met today that's why you haven't met me. My intentions are good and I'm crushing on her. I'm a business man and nobody ever gave me anything. I always had to make the best of what I had. I'm not a saint and I don't want to be."

"Gladys, do you hear Griff? You met her today and you want to be her man? Crimson Rose. She's a piece of work. I sculptured that work. It's more to her than the beauty that you see on the outside. If you're in it for the pussy you can take a bow now, she ain't gonna give it to you. She's pessimistic and hard to please. She's stubborn as hell, always have been. She has a lot of walls built up. If you can deal with all that I wish you nothing but the best," she explained and laughed.

"It's not about the sex with me. I'm trying to get to know her. I can work with that. I love a challenge. It'll be worth it in the end." Rashad and I finished kicking it with Mother Dear and Ms. Gladys. I had a few moves to make and I'll be back through here later.

"Griff, what the fuck was that back there," he asked and laughed?

"Look nigga, you heard what it was. I'm on to something. Shawty was bad as fuck and I'm determined to bag that."

Chapter-3

Crimson

I finally made it back to the house and Mother Dear was sitting on the porch with Ms. Gladys sipping her lemonade. I had a ton of bags and here she was sitting here relaxing. I gave her a faint smile.

"Crimson ROSE what's wrong with YOU? I haven't seen your face this flustered in years. I called your phone a few hours ago and some man by the name of Griff said he was your boyfriend." She laughed. I dropped a few bags on the porch and placed my free hand on my hip. No, the fuck he didn't. I'm sick of him and I don't even fuckin' know him.

"Mother Dear, I ain't got no boyfriend. He's crazy. He stole my phone." I argued.

"A few hours ago, you didn't have a man but within two hours you have one? Crimson Rose Tristan, I couldn't believe it. I had to meet this man. I spoke this into existence. I told him to come over so I can meet him since you've been keeping secrets. He was a gentleman. He asked me had I eaten, and I told him no. I was waiting for you to come with the groceries. He asked me what I wanted for lunch and I told him. I wanted me a fried fish plate from Maxine's. He asked me for the address. I gave it to him because I wanted to meet him. Honey, he pulled up a few minutes ago and brought Gladys and me some lunch." She beamed and laughed.

"Mother Dear, are you feeling okay? I don't know that man and you shouldn't have invited him over. He could be a serial killer." I asked and explained.

"I'm feeling fine Crimson Rose. I have a good judge of character. He might have some shit with him, but he's not a serial killer. Its men that do and men that don't. I've always wanted you to recognize the two. If a man wants something and he's persistent nothing or no one is going to stop him from getting it.

Not even the one he's trying to GET." She argued and explained and pointed her index finger at me. Ms.

Gladys and Mother Dear slapped hands with each other. I grabbed the groceries off the porch and headed straight to the kitchen. I made my last two runs to the car, gave Mother Dear her keys, and then I put the groceries up. I needed a nap.

I wanted to take Mother Dear to lunch but thanks to Griff she's already eaten without me. My phone alerted me I had another text.

678-266-9247- Your grandmother loves me. I just got to work on you now. I know you're reading my text. I'll be there at nine. Be READY CRIMSON.

He's crazy and he won't let up. I'll be gone way before 9:00 p.m. I don't know who he thinks he is, but I'm not with it. I needed a nap fuckin' with this crazy ass nigga. I had to call my partner in crime Danielle. I'm her partner minus the crime. Danielle and I have been friends forever. Our grandmothers were best friends so it's only right we clicked because we always saw each other. Her mother wasn't shit either just like mine. Damn. she probably won't answer because this isn't my fuckin' phone. Let me grab the house phone. She probably was still asleep. I knew she went out last night, but oh well. I'm waking her ass up. I called Danielle and she answered on the first ring.

"Mother Dear, where's Crimson Rose Tristan? I called her phone and some man answered the phone. Is she home because I'm on my way over there?" She argued. I had to pull my ear away from the phone. I pressed the mute button quick. I busted out laughing. I couldn't hold it in. Danielle is crazy. Damn she's crazy as fuck. I wouldn't trade her bougie ass for shit.

"Yo Elle, chill out it's me trick. Girl come over here right now." I laughed. The phone got quiet instantly. I could tell she was getting her words together.

"It's you? Crimson Rose, bitch, what's so gawd damn funny? Why are you calling me from Mother Dear's phone? What type of games do you have going on? No bitch, you come over here. You're to fuckin' sneaky for me. I knew you was a hoe on the low? What man stole your phone and answering it like it's his," she argued and ask. "Fuck that Crimson, I'll meet your big head ass HALF FUCKIN' WAY." She argued. I could hear her clapping her hands. I probably should've taken my nap first before I called her ass. She's extra for no reason.

"Bye Danielle, I'm on my way." I laughed. I slammed the phone down and went upstairs to grab my purse and his phone. As soon as I stepped foot on the porch. Danielle was already coming down the street with her crazy ass. "I hope you washed your butt and brushed your teeth." I sassed.

"You know me better than that! Spill it. bitch." She argued and sassed.

"Damn, can I get hey Crimson. How are you Crimson?" I beamed.

"Girl go on! All the formalities and casualties went out the window when I called your phone a few times today and the same nigga kept picking up. I knew I wasn't tripping. I've been dialing this number for years. Cut the bull shit and explain yourself." She argued and sassed. I gave Danielle the run-down of my day and I didn't like the way she's looking at me.

"Crimson, I'm going to be honest with you. I don't know Griff personally, but I've seen him around the way. His name ring bells in these streets. He's real deep in the them. He's a few years older than us and he went to

Columbia High School. Be careful with him please." She explained and begged.

"Girl, I'm not thinking about him. He's the least of my worries. He's crazy. He brought Mother Dear and Ms. Gladys some lunch. He seems like a stalker to me. I'm getting rid of this phone. Check out these text messages." I tossed Danielle his phone, so she could see. She held her hands over her mouth.

" Girl, he's crazy. I don't see you getting rid of him that easily." She laughed. Danielle and I finished kicking it. I walked back to the house because I was tired. I'm curious about this Griff and I shouldn't be. What♡ I going to do? He knows where I live, and he has access to a small glimpse of my life.

"Wake your ass up," she yelled. I know I wasn't hearing things. I wiped my eyes with the back of my hands. I left out a long yawn. I turned around on my side and looked at the clock. It was 6:45 p.m. I took a long ass nap. I guess sleep finally consumed me.

"I know you hear me talking to you Crimson Rose Tristan," she yelled.

"What are you doing here Danielle? You need to STOP sneaking in people's room and waking them up while they're asleep. I'm tired go away." I yawned.

"Bitch, you got a date tonight. I've been sitting here for the past hour watching you sleep. I've picked out you the perfect outfit for you to bag Griff's ass. He's texted this phone at least twenty times. I started to text back and act like I was you. What did you do to him? You had to at least let him smell the pussy or something today?" She laughed. I raised up from my bed and threw my pillow at her ass.

"Go home, Danielle. I'm not going on a date with him. I don't even know him and just by his actions, I don't want to deal with him. You know I ain't giving up no pussy. If he pulls up here, he'll get his feelings hurt. I just want my phone back and to go on with my life, that's all." I argued and yawned. I'm still tired.

"Whatever Crimson go brush your damn teeth. I don't want Griff to smell your funky ass evening breath."

"Whatever, Griff, won't be smelling shit over here. Leave me alone please." I argued and pouted.

"I'm not. Why are you so fuckin' difficult? Just go on the date. You ain't got shit to lose. If you don't like his ass and he doesn't like you, then the two of you don't have to see each other again. I know you Crimson, better than you know yourself. You're scared you're going to end up liking him and falling in love. Why are you scared to love and date? It's a lot of women out here and trust me, Griff can have any woman he wants too. A nigga like Griff ain't giving his phone to anybody to keep tabs on them. Just see where it leads too. You need your cat blown out. You're too old not to even had a sample of a dick."

"Yeah, whatever Danielle. You know a lot about me but not enough. I'm not scared to date. I haven't run across anybody that's worth dating. You think sex solves everything, but it doesn't. If Griff can have any bitch out here, good for him. He can go harass them and leave me the hell alone. I know I'm not going to like him. That's why I don't want to waste my time or his time." I argued. I needed Danielle to agree with me on this one.

"You got a lot of excuses. How do you know if you're wasting your time if you haven't had an actual conversation with him? You owe me one. You're going on this date if I got to drag your ass to the fuckin' car myself. I didn't want to go on a date with Rashad, but it was you bitch who pumped me up to give this nigga a shot. I liked his ass. Shit, I was in love with him. I can admit it now. I gave him the pussy a few times and never heard from him again.

I didn't let what he did to me stop me from dating. I kept it moving. Life is filled with pain, heart ache, lessons, and blessings. Yeah, we've been through a lot and we've been dealt a bad hand from the start, but damn Crimson, we didn't let that shit make us or break us. We beat the odds. We're not a product of our environment. We came out swinging every fuckin' time."

Danielle had tears in her eyes. I know talking about Rashad is a touchy subject for her. A few tears escaped my eyes too. I never got the chance to meet him. He was secretive and he moved differently. I feel so bad because I told her to give him a chance and she did. As soon as she let him in, he disappointed her. I wrapped my arms around Danielle.

"Okay, I'll go. I'm not scared, Danielle. I just don't want to get hurt. I've been disappointed my whole life and the last thing I need is to fall for this nigga and he disappoints the fuck out of me. I know everybody ain't the same and I can't compare Griff to anybody. I just play things safe." Danielle dried her tears with the back of her hands. She jumped up and showed me my outfit. I shook my head because I couldn't wear that. It was too revealing.

"Yes bitch, that's what the fuck I'm talking about," she laughed and clapped her hands. I looked at Danielle with wide eyes. She just did a 360 in less than two minutes. This is the shit I'm talking about.

"Bitch, did you just trick me to go out on a date? You ain't shit for that Danielle. You got me in here balling my eyes out and this was just a little pawn." I laughed.

"Fuck Rashad. His momma should've swallowed his goofy ass." She laughed. We slapped hands with each other. We finally found the perfect fit. A white see through Levi crop top and Levi blue jean skirt with my white Tory Burch thong sandals.

I took my braids down. My hair was natural and wild. Danielle tried to tie a knot in the back of my crop top, but I wasn't having it. She wanted to beat my face, but I don't wear make-up.

"You look cute Crimson." She beamed.

"Thank you. He said he'll be here at 9:00 p.m. but I don't want it to be like I was sitting around waiting on him to take me out." I looked at the clock and it was 7:30.

"I feel you. I'm sure he'll be here early since you're full of shit. I'm going to head up out of here. Have fun Crimson, even if it's only for tonight. I'll be able to see him coming before you. I'll call you if I see him pull up. You can walk toward my house to act like you're going somewhere else instead of waiting on him. What do you think?" she laughed and ask. We slapped hands with each other, and I walked Danielle to the door.

Mother Dear and Ms. Gladys went to play Bingo and I think they said they were going to Bigelows after that, so they weren't home. I ran upstairs to look in the mirror. I looked cute. The house phone was ringing. I checked the caller-ID and it was Danielle.

"Hey, what's up?" I asked?

"Bitch, that nigga is sneaky as fuck. As soon as I stepped on the porch. I saw a Mercedes Benz E-Class pull up and killed the lights. I don't know if that's him or not, but I think it is. I knew he would come early. Walk out the house and see if that's him." She screamed and was clapping her hands loudly.

"No bitch, I'm scared now." I laughed. I've never been on a real date before.

"Bitch, if you don't take your funky ass outside now. I'm going to drag your ass outside my damn self," she yelled and laughed.

"Okay, bye Danielle." I grabbed his phone, my key and headed out. As soon as I stepped on the porch, I locked up the house. I looked down the street and it was a Benz parked. Here goes nothing.

Chapter-4

♡

Griff

Crimson Rose Tristan. Her grandmother gave me all that. Shawty was bad as fuck. She's the baddest I've seen in a minute. She was mean and feisty just like I like them. She was natural in every sense. Her undertones turned red when I stepped into her personal space. Even under pressure with a little sweat in the mix, she was it. Yes, she was going to be the mother of my children. I could tell she was young, but she was old enough for a nigga like me. I couldn't stop thinking about her ass when I ran across her sorting through the fruits and veggies and shit at the Farmers Market. I was mad as fuck Keondra sent me on a dummy mission, but it was worth it because I ran into her. I couldn't stop thinking about her. I was determined to know a little bit more about her.

I swear watching her check off her grocery list was sexy as fuck. I couldn't keep my eyes off her. She had me in a trance. My dick wouldn't be still in my pants. I know I got a situation but Keondra and I are a wrap. She ain't talking about shit. I couldn't let Crimson Rose slide through my hands. Her grandmother already told me she didn't have a man. I'm ready to put my bid in. I had to move differently with Crimson. I wanted to move differently with her. It's something about shawty. I don't know what is yet, but it's something.

She lives around the way, but I've never seen her posted up in the hood. Shit, I've never seen her at the corner store or in the club. Shit, I've never seen her at the nail shop next to my barber shop where all the hoes post up at on the weekend. She has a face that you can't forget. If I saw her before I would've recognized her. What was it about her? All of that speaks volumes. I swear I've been thinking about her all day. She knew I was pulling up at nine. I'm always on time. I knew she would try to leave before I pulled up.

She didn't return any of my texts. Her phone was clean as a whistle. I emailed a few of her pictures to my iCloud. I'm pulling up on her ass right about now. It's a little after 8:00 p.m. I pulled down the street, not in front of her house. I killed the engine and the lights quick.

I noticed the front door open and she was creeping out. She was on feet and wasn't driving. Where the fuck was, she headed too? I knew she was thick but not that thick. She had on a skirt on and it was short. If she bent over, I guarantee you I could see that pussy from the back. She got me fucked up. It displayed all her curves. As soon as she reached the side walk. I hopped out my BENZ and walked up on her.

"Damn Shawty, I told you I was coming at 9:00 p.m. I'm glad I came a little early to catch up with your fine ass. I see what type of shit you on." I yelled and laughed. She jumped instantly. She kept walking. She didn't say anything to me or acknowledge me. She was walking fast as hell too. I smoke too much to be running. I ran up on her, wrapped my hands around her waist and held her in place. She was trying to break free from my embrace. I wasn't about to ease up. I had a death grip on her.

"Move." She argued and yelled. Yeah. shawty might be the one. In all my twenty-five years of living. I've never had a female turn me down. She couldn't have known who I was, and I wanted to keep it that way.

"Nah shawty, I'm not going anywhere. Lower your fuckin' voice. You knew I was coming. I'm not going to hurt you. We got a date." I whispered in her ear. I could feel her body tense up. I had her right where I wanted her. She finally relaxed. "That's more like it."

"No, we don't. I told you I had a man. Why do you keep bothering me?" She argued and pouted. I could hear her huffing and puffing. She was mad as fuck I got a hold of her ass.

"I want to get to know you, Crimson Rose. Can I get a chance? Whatever nigga hurt you, I'm sorry about that but I'm not him. Don't take that shit out on me." I argued and explained. She removed my hands from around her waist. She turned around to face me. She placed her free hand on her thick ass hips. This was the first time I was able to take in her beauty without her being defiant. She was beautiful as fuck and I'm trying my luck.

"What makes you think a man hurt me? It could be a woman? Why do you want to get to know me so bad? I'm not easy and I'm not giving up no pussy." She argued. I grabbed her free hand from off her hip. I pulled her into my arms, and I inhaled her scent. She smelled good as fuck too. I was surprised as fuck that she didn't object.

"Listen Shawty, excuse me for assuming shit. I got to ask questions, so I can get some answers. I'm not pressed for pussy. I didn't come at you and ask you for the pussy? I don't want that right now, but I do want it. I think we can get there later.

If it wasn't a man than, who was it? Are you into women because I didn't get that impression? I know you don't have a man. Mother Dear already gave me the run down on that. Why are you fighting this Crimson? I don't even do this type of shit, but for some reason I want to do this shit with you. I know you feel the vibes between us? Let's keep vibing and see where it leads us."

"What vibes are between us? You know a lot about me, but I don't know anything about you. The only thing I know about you is your street name, Griff. I'm not one to judge but you're crazy as fuck. Who takes someone's phone that they don't even know? Who pulls up at someone's house demanding a date? My life is simple, not sweet. Getting to know you is not up for debate. Stay the fuck away from my grandmother, okay?" She argued. Crimson Rose was a real piece of work. On the outside looking in I wouldn't think she would have this much mouth. I got my work cut out for me.

"What do you want to know about me? I hate my name. Griffey is my last name, so I go by Griff. Carius is my first name and Deon's my middle name. I'm twenty-five. Is there anything else you want to know about me shawty? You got me doing wild ass shit to get your attention. I pulled out a few stops today. It's all good though because here you are. When a man wants something, well, when I want something. I do what I got to do because I'm persistent as fuck, so what's up? Are we going to stand here all night and go back and forth? Can I take you out on a real date, so can we can get to know each other over some food and a few drinks?" I asked.

"I ain't got you doing shit. You could've ended your little cat and mouse game at the Farmers Market, and we wouldn't even be here. I don't drink or smoke. One date Carius and that's it, you hear me?" She sassed and rolled her eyes.

"Okay Crimson, that's what your mouth says." I chuckled. I got to do something about that attitude. I led her to my car and opened my car door up for her. She slid in the passenger seat and folded her arms across her chest. Crimson's full of shit though. She got dolled up for a nigga.

She had on a Levi's Skirt and a crop top that showed her stomach. She had pretty feet. I couldn't stop looking at the tattoos that covered her feet. I didn't even want her putting on, so another nigga could look at her. Her hair was wild and curly. She didn't have any make up on and I liked that shit. I pulled off down the street headed to Spondivits. "Put your seat belt on." She put her seat belt on and started sucking her teeth.

"I need you to come up off my phone." She sassed and held her hands out.

"It's mine now. I want you to keep mine too, so I can stay in contact with you." She turned around and faced me. She had the biggest mug on her face. I knew she was about to say some shit that I didn't like. She wants me to hurt her ass.

"Carius, I told you this was a one-time thing. I need my phone back and you can get yours back. Why do we need to keep in touch?" She asked, sassed and sucked her teeth. I hate my name, but I love the way she says it.

"Crimson let your guard down for me? I swear I'm not trying to hurt you shawty. I ain't perfect and I'm not a saint. I live a life of sin. I'm just being honest but my intentions with you are sincere. Why can't we be friends Crimson?"

"We can be friends Carius. That's it. Nothing more nothing less. I'll call you, don't call me." She argued and pouted. I swear she was trying to fight me so hard on this shit. Mother Dear already warned me it would go down like this.

"I'll take that for now." I chuckled. Crimson was trying hard as fuck to avoid me. I kept catching glances of her.

Crimson

What did I get myself into? I got to check my damn horoscope. It's August 1ST and I've had the same routine for years, but all of this is new to me. Never have I EVER ran into a Carius Griffey in the fuckin' Farmers Market. Now that I think about it, he didn't have any groceries, or did he? Why did we cross paths? Why was he so fuckin' persistent? Why couldn't he just let me be? Mother Dear jinxed my ass. I couldn't wait to go home and give her a mouth full. He confirmed my suspicions of what I already knew and what Danielle told me. He said he was in the streets in so many words. I don't know how I feel about that. I'm sure we wouldn't lead to anything.

Carius knew a lot about me, but I didn't know enough about him. He was coming on to strong for me. I didn't like that. I have never been in a relationship before, but Mother Dear taught me how to smell bullshit from a mile away. Carius or should I say, Griff, he's easy on the eyes. I can't lie. I didn't get to look at him like I wanted to in the grocery store, but tonight it was just the two of us. I was able to take him in without it being awkward.

He was handsome I can't lie. His skin was the color of a fresh jar of melted caramel with a little peanut butter. Even though he had two gold fangs he had nice teeth. He had hazel eyes and was cut nice too. I almost melted in his arms when he wrapped them around me. I could still smell his cologne on my shirt. I'm going to need him to stop invading my personal space.

"Damn shawty, why are you so quiet?" He asked. I didn't have anything to say. I was ready to get this little date over with. He was doing to much for me.

"I'm always quiet. I'm not much of a talker. I'm an observer." I sighed and rolled my eyes. I'm sure Mother Dear gave him an earful.

"So, tell me a little bit about yourself, Crimson Rose." He commanded. We were stopped at the red light and he was looking at me. His eyes were pouring into my soul. I had to blink a few times because he had me in a trance. I turned my head quickly. "Don't do that. Your mouth is too smart to be shy and intimidated by little ole me."

"Do what? What do you know about me and why?"
I asked.

"You know what you did. Every time I look at you,
you turn your head and look away. I like looking at you.
You're something to look at, never question that. I want to
know everything about you." He explained.

"Whatever, it wasn't that. I was just taking in my
surroundings. My personal life is private, and I don't know
you to open up about it." I didn't know him like that to tell
him my whole life story. We could get there but not today.

"I can respect that. Can I get to know you though?
Do you have any brother or sisters?"

"We'll see! I'm twenty-three. My birthday is on
July 13th. I work part time and attend school full time. My
major is a medical assistant. After I finish that I'm going
back to be an RN. I don't know if I have any siblings or
not. I've never met my mother or father. My mother
abandoned me when I was about two days old and never
looked back. I've been with Mother Dear ever since." I
sighed. Why did he ask me that? I swear he was opening
wounds that I don't feel like patching up tonight.

"Oh, you didn't miss out on much. Fuck'em, it's there lost. Since I missed your birthday. I got to make up for that. Your grandmother is cool as hell. I like her. Do you have any kids?" He asked. On the outside looking in that's easy to say, but what little girl doesn't want her mother around. Shit, what little girl doesn't want to be a daddy's girl. I wanted that, but I never got the chance to experience it.

"You don't have to get me anything for my birthday. Thank you. I would let you borrow Mother Dear, but I can't. No, I don't have any kids yet, but I want some later. What about you, do you have any?" I asked and laughed.

"You can't tell me what to do with my money. If I want to get you something for your birthday, I will believe that. I don't have any kids yet either. I want some, but I haven't had the chance to make any." He explained. Thank God no crazy baby mommas.

Griff and I finally made our way to Spondivits. Oh my God, why did he come here out of all places? He was cool so far. Thank God I put something cute and decent on. You never know who you might run into here. I haven't been here in a while. Danielle likes to come here all the time on a late-night tip to snag a boss. She gets lucky every time.

Griff opened the car door for me, grabbed my hand, and led me into the busy restaurant. All eyes were on us. I could tell that he was somebody important. Everybody was acknowledging him. I locked eyes with Jermesha. Even though she was my cousin we don't speak. No need for the fake shit now. She looked me up and down. Her and her little trifling ass friends. The host greeted us and led Griff and me to our section. The waiter slid the menus in front of us. I already knew what I was ordering so I didn't feel the need to look. I gave the menu back. Griff looked at me to see what was going on.

"What's wrong?" He asked.

"I already know what I want. I order the same thing every time I come here." I explained.

"I'll order for you. It's your first time coming with me. Let's try something different," he explained. Griff loved to be in control. I just let him have his way because this is a one-time thing.

"Okay," Griff ordered for the both of us. The waiter came back with two drinks. I looked at Griff like he was crazy. I had a mean scowl on my face. I told him that I don't drink.

"Chill out I got you. It's not even that strong. Loosen up. It's a fruity girl drink. Sip slow. I'm not going to let anything happen to you or do anything that you don't want me too." He argued and laughed. I threw my middle finger up at his ass.

"I'm on to you. Good thing this is the first and last time we'll be doing this," I laughed. His smile quickly turned into a frown.

"You really think that Crimson Rose? I got you here, so it doesn't end here. How much you want to put down on that? It's just the beginning! Cheers to a new beginning. I always get what I want, and I won't stop trying until I make that happen." He argued. My body tensed up when he said that. He reached across the table and grabbed my hands. "Think about that."

"It's a lot of things that I want, but if I don't get them. It doesn't make or break me. My life has been filled with disappointments. I always take the good with the bad. I always make the best of what I have," I explained.

"I respect and understand that Crimson. I know we just met, but shawty I want to be there for you, if you would allow me too? I can handle your wants and your needs even though I know you'll object. I know you've been through a lot of shit and even though I'm not the cause of that, I'm sorry for that. Give me a chance. I promise you won't regret that." He explained.

"I appreciate you, and you don't even know me. I'll give you a chance and we can take it one day at a time. The rules still apply I'll call you don't call me." I beamed.

"You want me to fuck you up Crimson? Stop playing with me shawty," he laughed.

"Of course, I don't want that." I laughed. Griff and my food finally came out. I looked at the plate and rolled my eyes. "I can't eat all of this." My plate was loaded with steak, shrimp, lobster, and oysters. Griff thought that was the funniest shit.

"I'm trying to thicken you up. Eat what you can, we can grab a to-go box or you can toss it. It doesn't matter to me." He chuckled and continued to eat his food.

"Oh, hey Crimson, I thought that was you." She stated. I didn't even acknowledge Jermesha. She never speaks to me and we live in the same house. Crazy huh. So why speak now because I'm with someone who these hoes were begging attention from.

"Come on Crimson Rose let's clear this joint. The night is still young, and I need all of my time!" He yelled. He was making his presence known. He placed his arm around my lower back. Jermesha and her friends were staring a hole in us. I don't care. They're always talking about somebody. I'm sure I would be their topic of discussion tonight. We exited out of Spondivits and made our way to Griff's car. I was waiting for him to open the door for me, but he threw me his keys.

"Drive and I'll give you the directions. It's my turn to look at you from the passenger side." He chuckled. I swear I can't stand his cocky ass. "You better know how to drive too."

"Whatever. How are you taking me out on a date, and I have to drive you? The man is supposed to drive the woman."

"I hear you shawty, so you're finally acknowledging that we're on a date? I don't have a problem driving but if you ready to be my woman just say so. It's not like you have a choice anyway." He chuckled and smirked.

"Whatever, where to," I asked and blushed?

"Follow my lead and you'll see where the road leads too." He chuckled. I swear he's to much for me. I put my seat belt on and pulled off. It was a car show out here. Females were trying to be seen. Everybody was staring at us when we pulled off. Griff was throwing his hands up at few guys in passing. Jermesha and her friends were breaking their necks to see who was driving his car. Griff rolled down the windows, so they could see us. I just shook my head. He was too much for me.

"What you do that for shawty? I wanted to ask you how you know those sluts anyway?" He asked. If he only knew how I knew them.

"The question is, how do you know them? It seems like they know you?" I asked. If he ever messed with Jermesha or anybody in her crew it was a done deal and I mean that. All conversations stop here. Jermesha and her crew get around.

"I know of them. I ain't never messed with any of them if that's what you're asking. How do you know them because I've never seen you in the hood EVER?" Of course, he wouldn't see me in the hood because, I'm not a hood rat and that's not my type of shit.

"Jermesha and I live together. She's my first cousin. Our mothers are sisters, but we're not cool. I was surprised she even spoke. I can't think of the last time she's said two words to me. Why speak now if you walk around the house and don't say anything to me? Mother Dear and I look after her children while she run the streets." I explained.

It pisses me off just speaking on it. I always got the shitty hand. No shade but her momma would always buy her shit, but never buy me anything.

They would take me to the mall just to flex in my face and grab Jermesha everything. They wouldn't even buy me fuckin' food. If the ice-cream man pulled up, they wouldn't even get me a fuckin' popsicle. What type of shit is that? I didn't even realize a tear slid down my face. I dried my eyes with my free hand making sure I still had control of the wheel.

"Pull over. What's wrong with you?" He asked. I did as I was told. Griff hopped out the car, opened the door and pulled me out. "What's wrong with you?" He asked again.

"Nothing. I'm good. I just had a moment." I sniffled. Griff wasn't buying that. He was searching my face for a lie.

"Nah shawty, you're not okay. Tears are sliding down your face. I didn't put them there so tell me what's up. We're not moving until you talk to me." He raised his voice.

"Griff, please don't do this. I've already said to much. Somethings are better left unsaid." I sighed. I'm in my feelings and I shouldn't be.

"You didn't say enough Crimson. When you're fucking' with a nigga like me it ain't no secrets baby and no hurt feelings. I want you to speak on that shit. Yeah, some shit is better left unsaid, but if you're shedding tears behind it baby you need to get that shit off your chest. Holding shit in isn't good for you. Let me in. I'm not going anywhere." He explained. I felt that. I could feel that he meant every word that he said.

I gave Griff the rundown. I could tell he was pissed off. The smile that was etched on his face quickly turned into a frown. He pulled me into his arms, and I broke down crying. A person can only take so much. He cupped my chin with his free hand forcing me to look at him. He wiped my tears with his thumbs, and I sniffled a little bit. I tried to stop the tears from falling but I couldn't. For some reason, they wouldn't stop.

"On some real shit Crimson, I can't even say I feel your pain because I never experienced any of that. Shawty, your tears are fucking with me and I'm liable to hurt a motherfucka for playing with you like that. I don't want to see you cry because of that. I can't change the past, but I can brighten up your future. I know it hurts but baby girl let that hurt go."

"I did but you're asking all of these questions making this hurt resurface," I sighed.

"I'm sorry. I'm just curious about you. I don't know what it is about you. You pique my interest. I like you Crimson, and I want to get to know you some more. I want to be the thorn to your rose. Come on, let's get off the side of this road. I still want you to drive though."

"Okay." We hopped in the car and pulled off and Griff keyed in an address on the GPS.

Griff

I'm a street nigga. I always have been, and I always will be until the death of me. I didn't choose this life it chose me. I live and die by that shit. It's not much that can make a nigga like me bend or fold, but the shit Crimson Rose told me hurt my fuckin' soul. It's some really fucked up people out here. I hate she went through that shit. Jermesha is a fuckin' hater. How are you jealous of your own fuckin cousin? She used to run with Keondra back in the day? Sluts flock together. I knew she was salty, but it is what it is. I'm sure she'll run it back to Keondra about me and Crimson, but I don't give a fuck. If a bitch touches her, they'll regret it. I put that shit on God. Crimson's life and mine are similar. She doesn't know her parents and I don't have any living parents, maybe that's why we vibe? I miss my OG's though. My mother would've liked Crimson.

"Why are you so quiet Carius," she asked. I looked at Crimson as she was whipping my shit through traffic. I forgot she was here, my had mind traveled off for a minute. She looked good driving my shit. I swear I wasn't trying to settle down again, but I'm feeling her in the worst way. I wasn't a dog ass nigga. Fucking a lot of women didn't excite me. I never wanted my name out in the streets for females to gossip about how they fucked me. Females talk and mentioning my name around the wrong nigga could lead to my demise. I wasn't trying to have that.

Even with Keondra, I didn't cheat on her. She cheated on me. I made her my wife for a reason. I only wanted to be with her. I had mad love for shawty, but she wanted to run the streets instead of making our house a home. She wanted to be the Dope man's wife. I just wanted a wife. You can lose the status of the Dope man at any given moment. During one of her many late nights of her running the streets, one of her drunken nights lead her to fuckin' a nigga. One of her so-called friends recorded it and sent it to me. She denied that shit for the longest too. So, I had to let her go.

"Why do you want to know?" I asked. Crimson was in my business and I wanted her to be. I'm feeling her, and I wanted us to be on the same page.

"Because I do, you were invading my thoughts and my personal business. So now I'm in yours," she explained. She had the biggest smile on her face.

"You were thinking about me Crimson? I'm thinking about you. Did I commit a crime? If so, let a nigga know something."

"Why are you thinking about me?" She asked.

"I'll let you know when we get to our destination." I laughed. She didn't like that. I noticed she turned her top lip up.

"Okay." We're about ten minutes away from my spot. Crimson was looking nervous. The GPS went off notifying us that we have arrived, and Crimson looked at me.

"Where are we Griff?" She asked. I wasn't about to respond. She'll find out when we get inside. I keyed the gate code in from my cell phone and it opened.

"Drive Crimson." She unbuckled her seatbelt and threw the Benz in park. She folded her arms across her chest.

"Answer my question CARIUS GRIFFEY?"

"We're at home. I had to stop by here to get a few things. I'm not trying to try anything with you shawty. When the time is right it'll happen. Come on and drive. I'm not that type of man. I got patience." Crimson put the car in drive and pulled in the garage. I opened my door and she refused to get out. I opened the driver's door and unfastened her seat belt and grabbed her hands.

"Come on I'm not telling you twice."

"Who do you think you're talking too like that?" She argued.

"Crimson Rose Tristan, that's your name right shawty?" I asked. She ignored me. "Crimson you hear me talking to you right?" I was all up in her face. She refused to look at me. I grabbed her chin and pressed my lips against hers. I could feel her body tense up.

"You hear me talking to you right? I ain't gone kiss your scared ass yet but come on." She backed up a little leaving some space in between us.

"Why are you so demanding? I know what your problem is? You're not used to anybody telling you NO.

Get used to it Griff. I'm not coming inside your house. If you need to get something inside of your house, I'll wait outside in the car. You have ten minutes." She argued. Crimson folded her arms across her chest. She wasn't scaring me at all. I picked her up and she was surprised. Her eyes got big.

"Put me down." She pouted. She can forget about that.

"I will when I get you in the house. Get used to this." I chuckled.

"I can't stand you." She pouted and blushed. I swear she has the prettiest smile.

"You can't stand me? I ain't did shit to you Crimson. All I want to do is love you, but you scared of that. The next words I want to hear from you is I love you, Carius Griffey. I'm going to work on that." I chuckled. She thought I was bull shitting, but I was dead ass serious.

"You're so full of yourself. Why do you always rhyme when you talk? Are you a poet or something? Do you rap?"

"I'm not a poet Crimson or a rapper. I just have a way with words, but I'll be a poet for you if you want me too?"

"Put me down, that's what I want you to do." She argued. I snarled my face up at her. I wasn't doing that. I've been wanting to do this to her all day. Her legs fit perfect around my waist.

"Nah I can't do that because I don't want too. I like holding you. You thought a nigga couldn't get next to you? Crimson Rose Tristan, I'm a different breed baby, believe that. I got you right where I want you! In my arms is the only place I want you." I explained.

"You talk a good game, Griff. I may be a little naive, but you'll have to come better than that. What separates you from the rest? It sounds good, but this date right here is where it ends for us." She sassed and sucked her teeth. She ran her tongue across her top lip. She was blushing. I swear she likes fucking' with me and getting my blood hot. I got hot instantly. I didn't even notice that I broke a sweat. Crimson wiped the sweat off my nose. "I didn't mean to make you sweat," she laughed.

"Oh yeah?" I asked. Crimson thought I was playing with her ass. I carried her into the kitchen and backed her into the wall. I pressed my lips up against hers. I sucked on her bottom li and she started breathing heavy. "Who's sweating now?" She wrapped her arms around my neck. "You can't use my neck for support. I didn't give you permission to do that." She looked at me with wide eyes. I knew she wanted to say some smart-ass shit.

"Whatever," she mumbled and rolled her eyes.

"I can't hear you, SPEAK UP." My tongue found its way inside her mouth. I was surprised she didn't object. The kiss we exchanged had our hearts beating the same tune, were the only sounds you could hear throughout the kitchen. Crimson broke the kiss. I looked at her and she looked at me. I wasn't about to ease up.

"It's getting late Carius. I better head home now." I nodded my head in agreement. I threw her my keys to her. I wasn't driving back to the Eastside this time of night. I had planed to, but I had too many drinks. I wasn't trying to catch a DUI or let a nigga catch me slipping.

"What's this for?" She asked.

"Drive yourself home. I'll see you tomorrow. When I call you, you better answer the phone?" I explained and walked off.

"I can't take your car Carius. You picked me up from home, so you can drive me back home." She argued. I stopped in my tracks.

"I'm tipsy and I'm tired. That's why I asked you to drive. I know you're not trying to spend the night. So, I'm giving you my keys and you can drive yourself home. If you want to spend the night you can sleep in my guest room." I explained. I was just putting it out there.

I had a slew of cars if she decided to drive home. I was going to let her keep that car because it's the car we met in. I want her ass to spend the night, so she can chill with me. I want to get to know her a little more.

"You know what, I'm on to you. I told you this date is where it ends for us. Why won't you take no for an answer? If I drive your car home, then that means I'll have to see you again. Show me your guest room. I need to be at home by 9:00 a.m.

I have to be to work at 11:00 a.m. I don't like being late." She argued. I heard her loud and clear. I can make that shit happen and cook her breakfast too before nine.

"What I do Crimson? I gave you my keys, so you can make it home. If you want to chill with your man, it's all good. Let me know something? I don't want you to leave, but I won't force you to stay. If you think this date is where it ends for us than you're crazy, and you don't look crazy to me. Keep thinking that you're about to walk away from me."

"Whatever Carius. It's too late for me to be driving back to the Eastside. I don't like being out over there when it gets dark. Let me call Mother Dear and let her know I'll be home in the morning. You still haven't shown me the guest room YET. I don't even have any night clothes. Give me a t-shirt and some shorts," she argued. Crimson called Mother Dear. I don't know what Mother Dear said to her on the phone, but she handed the phone to me. I tried to object but she forced the phone in my hand. Crimson was bullying me, she got me fucked up.

"Hey Mother, Dear, what's happening?" I asked. I put the phone on speaker. I could hear her sucking her teeth, so I knew this call wasn't about to go well.

"Don't hey me Griff. I'm on to you. I got my two eyes on you. I know how niggas roll and I'm dead on your stroll," she laughed. I got my eyes on her too if she wants to be technical. I swear this lady is a trip and I just met her ass today. With a name like Mother Dear, you would think she was a kind, soft spoken and well-mannered, but that's not the case.

"What I do Mother Dear? I've been on my best behavior. I haven't done anything. I told her she could drive home and gave her my keys. She didn't want to go home. She wanted to stay with me. I knew she liked me, she just didn't want to admit it. I told you I was her man and you thought I was playing. Do you want my address you can come and pick her up?" I asked. Crimson was grilling me with an evil glare, trying to grab the phone from me. It wasn't happening. I kept blocking her from getting the phone.

"He's lying Mother Dear," she argued and pouted. She was my woman. She just didn't know it yet. I'm patient I'll take my time with her.

"Be quiet Crimson Rose, your ass ain't slick either. I see right through you too. I'm not going anywhere this time of night, and she knows that. I've had a few drinks myself and these fools are already shooting. Dekalb County police are hot tonight. I trust you and you don't want to lose my trust or get on my bad side. Don't let anything happen to my Apple Face ass granddaughter.

Crimson Rose, if your grown ass wanted to spend the night with him, you should've said something. Don't start that lying and shit," she argued and laughed, then hung up the phone. I busted out laughing. Crimson's face was red as a rose. I knew she was mad at me. I stepped in her personal space and she didn't budge. She placed her hand on my chest telling me to back up.

"Why did you tell my grandmother that? Now she's going to be teasing me and thinking that I'm fast in the ass and I'M NOT." She argued and pouted. I cupped her chin forcing her to look at me. She rolled her eyes.

"Don't do that shawty, I'm sorry. Your grandmother knows she raised a good girl. She was just messing with you. I like you Crimson. I don't want sex from you. I know you're not fast. I'm not attracted to a fast woman. It doesn't excite me. I love diamonds in the ruff. A woman that I can polish up. Nobody should think that about you because you don't carry yourself as a fast woman." I explained. If she was fast, I wouldn't have approached her.

"Whatever Griff. Show me to my room." She pouted. I got my work cut out for me with this one. Crimson followed me upstairs to the guest room.

"Hold up, let me get you a shirt and some shorts and you can take your ass to bed." I ran in my room and grabbed Crimson a polo wife beater and a pair of boxers. She snatched them out of my hand and slammed the door. I just shook my head and laughed at her ass. She's crazy as fuck.

Chapter-5

Crimson

My mind was in a million places and my heart was disobeying me. I've had a lock and key in place forever guarding my heart, but somehow, she was trying to break free. It's too early to give him the key. Griff was invading my space. He was trying to suffocate me with his affection. I needed him to back up a little bit. For some odd reason, he managed to bring a few smiles to my face. Even a few laughs escaped my lips. Just thinking about him, my face lit up. I enjoyed his company, but I would never tell him that. As soon as I got inside the guest room, I locked the door and slid down the back of it.

I had to pick myself up quick. I went inside the bathroom and stripped naked. I cut the shower on and adjusted it to my liking. As soon as I stepped in, my mind began to roam. How the fuck did I end up at this man's home? All alone. It was just him and I and the only things between us were a few walls. His room was right across the hall. I could've driven home, but I wanted to stay here. Griff was a cool ass guy for real. I can't even lie, but I wasn't ready to start liking his ass just yet. He's charming as fuck. I guess it was just my luck?

Why did he kiss me? Who told him to do that? Our kiss was so passionate. I swear I felt my heart skip a beat. My knees got weak. Damn, why was he doing this shit to me? My legs wrapped around his hips. I wanted to bite my bottom lip. He was a real ass nigga and for him to be in the streets he was different. I was judging him at first and I shouldn't have done that. If I fell, I'm sure he would catch me. He's not the typical dope boy that I see in the hood. Why was he single? It's a question that I wanted to ask, but I don't want to over step my boundaries. Fuckin' with Griff I could tell he didn't have any boundaries.

I handled my hygiene. I took a long hot shower. I felt the water turning cold, so I stepped out and dried off. I wish I had my phone, so I could text Danielle and tell her about my night. I guess she'll have to wait until tomorrow. I slid into Griff's shorts and his wife beater.

As soon as I entered the room. I hopped in the bed and pulled the covers back. Damn this bed was comfortable. His phone went off. I looked at it and it was text from him

678-266-9247-Good night

I wasn't about to respond. I'm trying to get some sleep. The phone went off again.

678-266-9247- You can't respond and I'm a few feet away from you??

I ignored him again and put the phone on silent. I had the biggest smile on my face. He wasn't used to anybody ignoring him. He better gets used to it. It's a first time for everything. My eyes started to get heavy. I drifted off thinking about Griff until I heard him laughing out loud. I had a mean scowl on my face. I hate being woken up out of my sleep. I was sleeping good too. I don't know who was louder, him or the TV. I raised up out of the bed and opened the door and marched over to his room quick. His eyes roamed my body as soon as I entered his room.

"Can you turn this TV down and lower your voice? You're too LOUD and I'm trying to sleep." I argued. My hands were resting on my hips, waiting for an answer from him. Griff ignored me and continued to laugh at me as if I wasn't standing there. I got something for his ass. If he doesn't want to turn it down, I'll turn it down for him. I stood on my tippy toes to turn the TV down since he wanted to ignore me. I could feel him raise up out the bed. He was right on my heels. I could feel him hovering over me.

"Don't touch my TV Crimson." He argued. I could feel chills run down my spine. He was breathing down my neck. I could smell the weed with liquor on his breath.

"Back- up PLEASE. I asked you nicely," I argued.

"I thought you were sleep. I told you Goodnight and you didn't respond so I assumed you were sleep. As soon as I turn my TV up you want to haul your ass up in here, thinking you running shit. Crimson you can only run shit from this bedroom right here, not the guest room." He argued. I wasn't about to respond to him. I tried to move around but he was blocking me. He picked me up. I wish he would stop doing that.

"Put me down Griff you play too much. I'm sleepy." I argued. He tossed me on his bed. I tried to raise up.

"Lay your ass down." I wasn't even about to argue with him. He's not even my man and he's doing to much. I shouldn't even be listening to him because he thinks he's running shit and clearly that's not the case.

"Turn the fuckin' TV down so I can lay down. If you wanted me to sleep in here that's all you had to say." I argued. I grabbed the covers and buried myself underneath them. He baited me. He turned the TV up so I would come in here and say something. I took it like an idiot.

"You know I wanted you too. I knew you weren't asleep when I sent you a text. Why you didn't text me back? Don't be in my bed snoring all loud either." He explained. I rolled my eyes up under the cover as if he could see me. I felt Griff get up under the cover. He pushed up behind me and I scooted up some. We needed space between us. As big as this bed is there's no need for him to be all up on me.

"Can I hold you, Crimson Rose?" He whispered in my ear. I swear this man gave me chills. I needed to get the fuck away from him fast.

"Do I have a choice and why do you want to do that?" I asked. He wrapped his arms around me anyway.

My body tensed up immediately. His touch alone sent chills through my body.

"Not really and because I want too. When I laid eyes on you earlier, I knew I had to have you. I don't know what it is about you, but I'm drawn to you. I'm a moth to your flame. I'm trying to find out what it is I'm drawn to. I got to see where this road leads too. Are you going to let me find out? I want to protect you from the bullshit." He asked and explained.

"Why should I trust you Carius? Why should I let you in? On the outside looking in, your perfect, but why are you single? Why are you trying to make me fall for you Carius? I shouldn't even be this close to you. I shouldn't even be lying here next to you. I feel so open with you. I'm not ready to open myself up to you right now, but I am. You got a hold on me and I wish you would let it go and set me free.

What the fuck are you trying to do to me? My trust is fucked up and it shouldn't be. I don't know how to love anybody, because a motherfucka ain't never loved me. I ain't never been in a relationship before. The two people that were supposed to love me couldn't even do that. They left that up to Mother Dear." I sighed. A few tears started to escape from my eyes.

Griff lifted me up and laid me on his chest. I could barely catch my breath. He cupped my chin and forced me to look at him. My heart was beating at a fast pace. I'm so embarrassed I know he could see it written all over my face. He wrapped his arms around my waist. He kept looking me in my eyes trying to read me. I had to look away. I wish he would stop it. He cupped my face again forcing me to look at him.

"Every time I look at you Crimson, you look away. Our hearts are beating the same tune. I just need you to get on beat and stop pushing me away. I'm not out to hurt you. If given the chance I want to love you. I was in a relationship, but she cheated so I'm single. I'm not trying to make you fall for me Crimson. I'm just being honest with you. I had no intentions of running across you, but shawty, we crossed paths for a reason.

I had to get your attention some type of way. I wanted to see you again and if I didn't try, we probably wouldn't have ended up here. I'm not asking you to trust me right away. I don't want you to give me anything. I want to earn it. Crimson, you're more than worth it. You can't deny your feelings or our chemistry. You're doing this because it's something that you're supposed to do. I'm glad you feel the hold I got on you. I can't let you walk away from me because I'm determined to find out what we're meant to be.

You ain't never been in a relationship before Crimson? That's a good thing. I guess I got to work on being your first and your last. You told me you had a man, I guess that'll be me. You got a good heart Crimson but fuck your mother and father. Just because they didn't teach you how to love doesn't mean anything. Mother Dear taught you enough. Don't let what they did to you effect how you live. Release that hold they got on you so, I can love you."

"How do you know Carius Griffey that you can love me? Why are you so sure of yourself?" I asked.

"I know I can Crimson. I'm confident as fuck. Just let me in and quit trying to shut me out. Are you going to let me love you without holding back? Answer that?" He yawned. Griff and I finished talking after about another hour. We were both getting sleepy. I was trying to lay beside him, but he refused to let me lie next to him.

"Where are you going? Why are you trying to leave me?" He asked. I wasn't going anywhere. I was trying to sleep in the other room, but he wouldn't allow me to leave in peace. I wanted to think about his fine ass from across the hall. Lying close to him, it'll be hard to do.

"I'm not. I can't leave. Every time I try to roll over, you won't let me," I explained. He kissed me on my forehead before he went to sleep. I traced his eyebrows with my manicured nail. His eyebrows were bushy, but he had the perfect arch. I was wide awake, and I needed to go to sleep. I closed my eyes and laid my head on his chest. In his arms, I guess is where I'm supposed to be. His heart beat put me to sleep.

Griff

If I was dreaming a nigga for damn sure didn't want to wake up. I got to thank God and his angels from the heavens above. Somebody was looking out for your boy big time. I swear I was good on females for a while after the shit Keondra pulled. Crimson Rose was different, and I wanted to be the only man that's in her league. I meant what I said, I want to be her first and her last. It's crazy but I think shawty was made for me. Crimson has been through a lot. She has some fucked up family members. Thank God for Mother Dear. Her tears be fuckin' with a nigga soul making my chest tighten. I feel her pain.

I know I want to make some serious moves with her. I want to do right by her. I got to get this divorce finalized with Keondra first. I fell asleep with shawty on my chest. I woke up listening to her snore. I gently laid her to the side and crept out the bedroom door. It was a little after 7:00 a.m. and I wanted to cook breakfast for her. It's been a minute since I did this shit. Keondra liked to eat out. She never cooked or wanted me to cook. Crimson made it clear that she wanted to be at home by 9:00 a.m. I swear she better end up mine. Shawty got a nigga jumping through hoops for her mean ass. I grabbed some turkey bacon and regular pork bacon out the refrigerator. I grabbed a pot underneath the sink to make some grits.

Crimson was thick as fuck, so I knew Mother Dear fed her ass some grits. I grabbed the eggs out of the refrigerator and then some waffle mix out the pantry. I know my OG laughing at me. My momma always told me you'll know she's the one when you're doing shit you have no business doing. I'm in the kitchen early cooking her some breakfast. She always said you'll change your ways for her. Crimson Rose better be her.

I'm not a dog ass nigga. Juggling females was never my thing. Since Keondra and I split I haven't smashed anything. I wasn't focused on getting her back. She always accused me of cheating, but that wasn't me. That's not who I am. My father cheated and did my mother dirty for years and I vowed to never treat a woman that way. I never wanted a woman crying because of me. I had the food going. I wanted to surprise Crimson with breakfast in bed.

It's been a minute since I cooked anything. I'm praying I don't fuck shit up. My OG taught me how to cook. She never wanted me to depend on a woman to feed me. My father thought it was stupid, but my mother was on to something. The kitchen was starting to smell good. I had the bacon cooking on low, so it wouldn't burn. I flipped the last pancake over and topped it with butter and few strawberries and placed it in the warmer. The oatmeal was done. I got a spoonful to make sure it tasted right. It was good. The last thing I had to do was scrambled the eggs and top mine with cheese. I heard a few footsteps. I knew it was her. I didn't bother to look over my shoulders. I could feel her coming closer.

"I wanted to brush my teeth, but SOMEBODY never gave me a tooth brush. When I woke up you were gone. I didn't want to go through your stuff looking for a tooth brush. Can you assist me, and I'll watch your food?" She asked. Crimson was rude as fuck too. She had her hands placed on her thick hips. God my dick was getting hard looking at her thighs and ass swallow my boxers. Her titties were begging to be freed out of my wife beater. I had to adjust my dick fuckin' with her ass.

"Good Morning Crimson you could've used my tooth brush," I chuckled. I knew she was about to say something smart. I swear I got to do something about that reckless mouth.

"Good Morning Griff. I meant Carius. Yeah right, I would never do that. I don't know where your mouth has been. I don't know whose cat you've been eating," she argued and sassed.

"My mouth has been on you Crimson. If you want to know if I eat pussy just ask and I'll eat yours for breakfast if you want me too. I know your mean ass is scared but be careful with that mouth before you find yourself in trouble. Go look under my sink it's a pack of tooth brushes under there. I ain't got nothing to hide Crimson. Go brush your teeth so you can eat, and I can get you home by 9:00 a.m." I don't know why shawty like trying me for real?

"Whatever Griff." She argued. I cut her off before she could say anything else. I walked up on her ass. She was backing up until I backed her into the same wall she backed into last night. She didn't like me invading her space. She better get used to this shit. I gripped her ass and I pressed my body up against hers.

"Stop," she pouted and whined.

"Nah I want you to back that shit up that you were talking earlier. I'm not stopping shit. Say what you have to say because just a few minutes ago you had a lot to say." I argued. Crimson and I were both mouth to mouth. I could feel her body tense up and her nipples were erect. They were poking through the wife beater. I placed my arms over the kitchen wall blocking Crimson from moving. I had her boxed in. I leaned in and stole a kiss. She tried to move her face. I cupped her face and kissed her again. I was surprised she kissed me back.

"Say something. I dare you too?" I chuckled.

"Move, I didn't tell you that you had permission to kiss me. You play too much." She pouted.

"I'm a grown ass man Crimson. I don't play games. If I want something, I just go after it. Come on so you can brush your teeth after you eat. I was trying to surprise your big face ass, but you just had to wake up. You were looking for me this morning and couldn't sleep without me? You owe me another shirt too. I had a big ass wet spot on my shirt from you slobbering and shit. You better be glad I like your ass or else I would've thrown you off me."

"You could've but you wanted me right there. Last I checked I tried to move several times, but you wouldn't let me, so that's what you get." She argued. I grabbed Crimson's hand and led her to the kitchen. She took a seat at the table. I fixed our plates and slid hers in front of her then poured two glasses of orange juice. Crimson said grace.

"I hope you can cook." She laughed. I'm not even about to go back and forth with her. I pretended like I didn't hear it. I ate my food and caught a couple of glances of her while she was eating. I finished eating before her.

"Throw the dishes in the trash and I'll take the trash out." I left out of the kitchen. I heard Crimson say something. I looked over my shoulder to see what she had to say.

"I'm not Carius, thank you for breakfast it was really good. I'll clean the kitchen it's the least I can do since you cooked." She stated and smiled.

"Thank you. I'll sit your tooth brush in the guest room." I had a few moves to make myself. I don't know how shit will play out between Crimson and me, but we'll see.

Chapter-6

Crimson

My date with Griff is almost over. I hate to admit it but I'm going to miss him. I enjoyed this little time we spent together. Even the few kisses we exchanged brought a few smiles to my face just thinking about it. I can't wait to go home and tell Danielle about my date. I need my phone back too. He was a cool guy and he could cook too. His mother or father taught him something right. I like him. How can I not.

I was falling for his ass but I'm not telling him that. I cleaned the kitchen. I refused to throw away these dishes because he was too lazy to wash them. The kitchen was spotless. I wiped off the counters and headed upstairs to shower. It's almost 9:00 a.m. I'm running behind. I headed upstairs to take a quick shower. I walked passed Griff's room to get to the guest room. He had a towel wrapped around him and the water was still dripping off his skin.

I walked into the guest room and slammed the door. I swear he does the most. I jumped in the shower to handle my hygiene. Every time I thought about Griff a small smile crept up on my face. I cut the shower off and pulled the curtain back. Carius was sitting on the toilet with a smirk on his face. My heart dropped and I almost pissed on myself. I tried to cover myself quick. I was so embarrassed. He tossed me a towel. I stepped back in and closed the shower curtain. He started busting out laughing. What was so fuckin' funny? He plays too much.

"Get out now. Why are you in here? You play too much. Go in your own bathroom. Damn, I can't even shower and get dressed in peace." I argued. He ruined the moment I was having.

"I am in my bathroom. What are you shy for? I'm not leaving until you come out here. You talk a lot of shit Crimson, back it up for once." He argued and chuckled. I wrapped the towel around me as tight as I could. I snatched the curtain back. I made sure my feet were dry. I wasn't trying to bust my ass. I pushed pass Griff and he wrapped his arms around my waist.

"I'm shy because you're in here and I don't want you to see my goodies. Could you please leave? I need to put my clothes on." I asked.

"I'm not stopping you, put them on. I want to see how your ass squeezed in that skirt?"

"You're stopping me by just being in here. You're making me uncomfortable."

"Get comfortable Crimson because I'm about to pull you out of your comfort zone. I just want to see all of you. I'm not going to touch. I just want to look and see if it's all real. You're perfect shawty." I grabbed my skirt off the bed and put it on. I tried to avoid looking at Griff because he was biting his bottom lip.

"Where the fuck are your panties," he asked. I ignored him. I grabbed my shirt and threw it on. I didn't put my bra on either. He wanted to watch me, he would get feelings hurt today. It looks like I won't be the only one out of my comfort zone. I slid my feet in my sandals and grabbed my purse. I tossed my panties and bra in my purse. Griff eyed me like a hawk.

"I'm ready."

"We can leave after you put your bra and panties on."

"I'm not putting them on. You can take me home, so I can put on a fresh pair." Griff pinched the bridge of his nose. I could see a vein appear on the side of his forehead. Yeah, I had that nigga in a place where he didn't want to be.

"It's not going down like that, CRIMSON. I'm not telling you what you can and can't wear, but you're not leaving this house without a bra or panties on. You came here with both on so you're going to leave here with them on. I'm not with the games and shit." He argued.

"You wouldn't know if I had either of them on if you weren't determined to watch me put my clothes on. CAN you step out for a minute so I can put my stuff on, and you can take me HOME?" I argued.

"Put it on in front of me so I can make sure you got it on, so I can take you home."

"I don't need you fuckin' watching me. I'm grown, and I don't need parental vision. Excuse yourself or I'll excuse myself." I argued. Griff left the room. Thank you, Jesus. I put my bra on and slid my panties on.

Lord knows I didn't want to go home with either one of them on because Mother Dear would've sworn, I gave up my pussy on the first night. I opened the door and Griff was outside waiting on me.

"I'm ready and I need my phone back." He placed my phone in my hands.

The whole car ride was silent. Griff was in his feelings and I wasn't in my mine. I had my phone and as far as I was concerned our date was over. I had no plans on seeing him again. I sent Danielle a text. She was asking about my date. It's only so much that I could say through text. We had to be at work at 11:00 a.m. so I'm sure we'll talk about it on our way to work. Griff pulled up at my house and before he could even throw the car in park good, I was hopping out. He was getting out behind me.

"Where are you going?" I asked him. We haven't said two words two each other and I was perfectly fine with that. He started it and I didn't have a problem finishing it.

"I'm coming in to say hi and good morning to Mother Dear. Is that okay with you?" He asked.

"No, you're not coming in. I'll tell her you said hi. Bye Griff and thanks for the ride" I explained. Before I could even step foot on the porch good, Mother Dear was opening the front door. That was the last thing I fuckin' needed. I could tell she already had her a fresh cup of coffee with a shot of Hennessy. I just shook my head because I already knew how this conversation would go.

"Look what the wind blew in. Crimson Rose Tristan finally made it home in one piece. I've been waiting for you. Griff, she didn't give you a hard time, did she?" She asked. I swear Mother Dear play too much. As soon as I looked over my shoulder to see what he was about to say, he had the biggest smile on his face and Danielle was pulling up with her nosey ass. She hopped out the car quick. Danielle was smiling from ear to ear. I swear I can't stand her sometimes.

"Hey Crimson, it's nice to see you this morning. Who do we have here? Let me introduce myself I'm Danielle Crimson's best friend. I guess you're the man that kept answering her phone yesterday?" She asked. Griff and Danielle shook hands.

"It's nice to meet you D. Elle, right? I'm Griff. Mother Dear, of course she did. It's cool though I'll be seeing her soon. Y'all be easy out here." He stated. Griff walked to his car coolly and pulled off. Mother Dear couldn't wait until he pulled off to ignite fire into my ass. As soon as I walked in the house she was on my heels. She gave me an evil look that I tried hard to avoid. I didn't want to talk about it. She already embarrassed me last night.

"Crimson Rose Tristan, I hope you didn't run that man off already?" She asked. I hope I did run him off. I don't like what he does to me. I feel so open and free with him.

"I'm sure I did Mother Dear but oh well. It was just one date. I need to get ready for work. Give me a minute Danielle so I can change clothes."

"Crimson Rose Tristan, this conversation isn't over. I'll talk to you when you get home." I went upstairs to my room and Danielle followed right behind me like I knew she would. I couldn't even close the door good.

"Spill it, bitch! Did you fuck him? Ain't nobody spending the night without fuckin'. I saw the way he looked at you. He's trying to be more than what you're trying to give him." Danielle swore she was Ms. fuckin' Cleo.

"No bitch, I didn't fuck him. You know me better than that. I laid on his chest, we exchanged a few kisses that's it. He cooked me breakfast and I told him one date and that's it." I beamed. Griff was a romantic too. I could lay on his chest all night.

"So that's all that happened? You are leaving shit out Crimson, come on now. I tell you everything," she argued. I gave Danielle the rundown of our date play for play. Why wouldn't she let me be great and reminisce in peace.

"Bitch, he might be the one. I ain't never really heard nothing bad about him. He seems like he's a good guy. Crimson, you should give him a chance to see where it leads. I'm not saying let your guard down but be open to dating him. I love the way he looks at you. So, do you like him and be honest about that?" She asked.

"I do like him. He's a cool ass nigga. Come on before we're late to work Danielle. If he calls me again, I'll see where it leads too." Just as I was putting my shirt on a text came through. I looked at my phone and it was an unknown number.

404-886-2322- I'm sorry about earlier. I want to see you again tonight. Can I see you again Crimson? What time do you get off tonight?

I was blushing. He wanted to see me again. Danielle snatched my phone out of my hand. Maybe it's something between us. Only time would tell. I wasn't ready to respond just yet.

"What happened last night? You're leaving shit out. Since when do you start keeping secrets? Bitch, are you going to see him again? I thought it was just one date. Judging by that smile, it's a lie. It looks like tonight is date number two. Text that nigga back and tell him yes. Bitch, you're going to need your own shit. Mother Dear ain't gonna have you running in and out of her shit late at night. It's time we get our own spot."

"Girl I'm not leaving Mother Dear here by herself with these vultures. I'd be damn." I argued. I haven't even thought about moving out. I was connected at the hip with my grandmother.

"Yes, the fuck you are. Get your own shit Crimson. I don't want you coming in my house doing the walk of shame like Jermesha's ass. I got this shit over here, trust me. Get your ass out and live your fuckin' life. You have my blessing. Trust me, fuckin' with a man like Griff you won't be here for too much longer. He's a persistent ass young nigga. I like him and his swag.

He got you right where he wants you. You want his ass too and you can't even hide it. I see it written all of your face," she argued and explained. Mother Dear was nosey as fuck. She's been outside of the door listening the whole time.

"Dang Mother Dear, that's pretty low to be eavesdropping at my door. Why do I have to get out and these vultures get a free pass?" I asked.

"I'm not putting you out Crimson. This will always be your home no matter what. I'm not enabling you. You're going places. These motherfuckas ain't got shit going for themselves. When I leave this world, they'll be lost without me because they're always depending on me.

You don't need me for anything. I want you to have independence. I want you to be open to loving that man that just dropped you off. Don't shut him out. I know a few things. I've been around the block before, but I see something in Griff that I saw in your grandfather. Take heed to what I'm saying. In my 65 years of living, I've never steered you wrong. Listen to me when I talk, and you'll go a long way." She explained. Here she goes preaching. I'm not ready to move out.

"Okay, Mother Dear I'll see you later." I sighed and pouted.

"Don't do that Crimson Rose Tristan. Everything will be alright. Griff isn't out to hurt you. It's not even about pussy with him. He wants to know you. He's been through some shit too. I can see it, but his mother raised him right. It ain't too many niggas coming to meet your grandmother and walking you to your door after a date. They'll pull off as soon as you get out the car. Pay attention to the small shit." She argued. I let Mother Dear's words sink in my head. I wasn't ready to leave the nest just yet, but it was time. I guess I'll start looking for me a place. Danielle and I left work. I sent Griff a text back.

678-266-9247 - Apology accepted. Yeah, you can see me again. I get off at 7:00.

I locked his number in my phone finally.

Carius - You finally texted me back. I'll see you at 8. Pack an overnight bag or text me your size and I'll grab you a few things.

678-266-9247 - What am I packing a bag for? If you just want to see me again?

Carius - I want you to spend the night again? I want to hold you without you being defiant. Can I do that Crimson Rose?

678-266-9247 - I don't know. Let me think about it. You don't think it's too soon for us to be staying the night with each other?

Griff must not have liked my response because he didn't text back. Oh well. I'm asking questions. I needed a valid response. We just met yesterday, and he wants me to stay the night with him? I don't think so. I would love too, but we're moving too fast.

Chapter-7

Griff

Crimson really plays hard to get. I'm not tripping because I don't mind putting in work because I feel like she's worth it. I didn't even respond to her last text message about moving too fast because life moves, and I just roll with the punches. You can't put a time limit on feelings. You know when someone is the one. I feel it based on our brief encounter yesterday. It was my mission to see her again today. It was a little after 8:00 p.m. I pulled up at Mother Dears. I wasn't even about to call Crimson because I didn't need any excuses. She knew I was pulling up. I knocked on Mother Dear's door and I could tell she was cooking something. I could smell it as soon as I hit the porch. Mother Dear opened the door.

"What's going on, Griff? What brings you by besides you are sniffing up behind Crimson Rose," she asked and laughed. I just shook my head. This lady is off the chain.

"I came by to see you and Crimson Rose. Are you going to invite me in and fix me a plate of whatever you're cooking?" I asked.

"Yes come in. Crimson is feeding her face. She can fix you a plate because you're her man and not mine."

"Okay." Mother Dear led the way to the kitchen and Crimson was sitting at the table eating. She looked up at me and cracked a faint smile.

"What's up Carius, what are you doing here," she asked?

"You know why I'm here. I told you I would be through here at 8:00 p.m. Fix me a   plate."

"Okay you never replied to my text, so I didn't think you were coming? What do you want? You don't even know if this food is good or not," she asked and laughed?

"Stop assuming and just ask. You didn't bother to text me back either to see why I didn't respond, but we'll talk about that later. You got your bag packed?" She bit her bottom lip and nodded her head no.

"Fix my plate and handle that or we can stop by Walmart and Target to cop you a few things." Crimson fixed my plate. Mother Dear cooked ribs, baked beans with ground beef, potato salad, corn on the cob, salad, and a strawberry short cake. Crimson petty as hell. This food was good as fuck. I'm full and can't even move. Crimson sat a glass of Kool aid in front of me. Mother Dear walked into the kitchen and stood there looking at me.

"Normally I don't feed people because once you start feeding them you can't keep them away, but I like you Griff, so I not going to shun you away. Crimson, on the other hand, you got to work on her," she laughed.

"Tell me something I don't know Mother Dear. She's hard on me." I laughed. Crimson finally strutted in the kitchen with her bag. Mother Dear was looking at me and smiling.

"Crimson Rose, where are you going with that bag Ms. Lady," she asked?

"Carius and I have a date. I don't know how long we'll be gone, but I don't want to come into your house at any time of the night. So, I'm staying at his house." She sighed.

"Are y'all fuckin'," she asked. Crimson's face turned red. I could tell she wasn't expecting that. I had to step in and let Mother Dear know it wasn't going down like that.

"Mother Dear, excuse my language but we're not having sex. I'm not trying to get to know Crimson because I want sex from her. I want to get to know HER but, in the future, if and when, we cross that line you'll know."

"Damn Crimson, I guess he told me." We cleaned Mother's Dear kitchen up and headed out. I grabbed Crimson's bag out of her hand and tossed in the back seat and tossed her the keys.

"What is this for," she asked. She knew what the keys were for. I wanted her to drive.

"I'm full and I don't feel like driving."

"Did it ever occur to you that I might be full too? I just got off work myself. Don't be using me to drive all the time either." She argued. "Where too Carius? I don't know where we're going?" She asked.

"I'm not using you Crimson. I'm full and you weren't trying to share your dinner with me. That's shady. I want to share it all with you. We're going home. I had plans to take you to dinner, but Mother Dear had me covered with that." I chuckled and I keyed my address in the GPS.

"Don't be popping up at my grandmother's house. I don't want her to think that I'm screwing you because I'm not. I have plans tomorrow so you can't see me okay." She argued.

"Your grandmother likes the kid, Crimson. You heard her. It's not about sex with me. I'm sorry she put you on the spot, but your face was priceless. I can't see you tomorrow. Why not? What's your plans so I can fit myself in?" I asked.

"None of your business Griff. This is our last date. Am I making myself clear?" She argued. Crimson ain't talking about shit. I'm not even listening I'm deaf to the bullshit she's spitting.

"Crimson your mouth says a lot shawty but listen to your heart. She's not steering you wrong. I'm listening to mine and I shouldn't, but I like this little thing we got going on. You and I both know this isn't where it ends for us. It's just the beginning baby."

"How do you know what my heart says? You're confident as fuck Griff? My heart can steer me wrong. That's why I'm doing the opposite because I'm not trying to be out here looking crazy and foolish fuckin' with you. What little thing do we have going on because I'm confused? Feel me in. What is your heart telling you Carius?" She asked. I swear she's so hard headed.

"Do you care Crimson, because if not I can keep my feelings to myself?"

"I care or else Carius I wouldn't have asked."

"I know you been through some shit. I'm not trying to take you through any additional shit. I wanna love you, that's it. Your heart beats me for shawty, recognize that. You heard the tune last night. I'm patient and willing to march to your beat whenever you're ready.

Crimson, I don't know what you see when you look at me, but shawty I'm not a dog ass nigga. I'm not a cheater. Yeah, I'm in these streets heavy and females throw their pussy at me on the regular.

My father dogged my mother out for years. I never wanted to treat a woman how my father treated my mother. I only got eyes for one. I don't have the time nor energy to juggle multiple women. You can't put a time limit on love.

I'm not saying that I'm in love with you, but I probably could get there if you're willing to meet me half way. I'm feeling you and I'm not putting myself on restrictions because of you. You can keep denying and trying to fight this shit if you want too but let me know how that works out for you. Don't let me get away, let that marinate." I said what I had to say. I'm official and I don't have to put on. It is what it is with me. She'll just have to find out and see.

"I'm scared, Carius. All of this is new to me. I've come across a few guys, but I've never run into a man like you. I tried to run you off, but it didn't work with you. I like you a lot and I'm not even about to front about it. I can't deny it so what are we going to do?" She asked.

"I know you're scared, but I'm not out to hurt you. We can take it one day at a time and see where it leads to, but I know I want you. So whatever plans you thought you had scheduled for tomorrow plug me in, because it's me in you for the weekend. Wherever you want to go, I'll be the host. Just let me know." Man, about time we're on the same page. Crimson had me thinking I was crazy. I knew she was feeling the kid. I had to put hands in front of my mouth so she wouldn't catch my smile. I kept catching glances at her while she was driving.

"Stop looking at me! I'll see if I can arrange that. Remove your hand from your mouth. What the fuck are you hiding?" She asked.

"Ain't nobody looking at you yet. Keep that same energy when we get to the house."

"Oh, I plan on it. I'm sleeping in the guest room too. I don't need you in my face incase my boyfriend calls," she sassed and laughed.

"Oh yeah? Call that pussy ass motherfucka up so I can tell him may the best man win. You already know you mine anyway. Stop fuckin' playing with me.

I don't want you to see this side of me." I argued and laughed. Crimson was blushing. I swear she has a beautiful smile. We finally made it to the house.

I couldn't get at Crimson like I wanted too because Mother Dear was close and all in a niggas business. She had on some gray spandex shorts with the matching sports bra. Her hair was braided in three braids to the back.

Crimson was sexy as fuck and she knew it. She didn't even have to try. She bent over and reached for her bag out the back seat. I had to stand behind her and grip that ass from the back. Shawty was stout back there. I knew she felt me grab a handful. As soon as she felt me back there, she looked over her shoulders with a small scowl on her face. I couldn't help myself. It's just the savage in me. I had to go for what I know.

"Back up Carius, you're too close. Give me some space. Act like you got some sense." She argued. I lost my sense the moment she got in the car.

"I ain't got no sense. I lost it looking at all that ass from the back. I had to grip it. Is it fake Crimson, how much you pay for it?" I laughed. I meant that shit.

"Ain't nothing fake about me. This ass is home grown. Money couldn't buy this. It's the cornbread and the cabbage and 100% peer beef. USDA shit you feel me?"

"Crimson Rose Tristan, your mouth is slick as fuck. What's crazy is when I'm in your personal space your tone changes and you can't back nothing up? You got too much ass for that. You're on mute but as soon as I give you some room, you're running your mouth talking real fly and jazzy." Crimson and I finally made our way into the house and I'm right on her heels. I grabbed her bag and dropped it on the kitchen floor.

"What you do that for Carius?" She asked.

"Because I wanted to. Does it matter? I want to carry you upstairs to my room. I want to feel those thick ass thighs around my waist. Is that cool with you?" I asked.

"I can walk," she laughed. I know she can, but I've seen enough of that ass walking in front of me.

"I don't want you too." I stepped in her personal space, closing the gap between us.

"Why are trying to make me fall for you? I'm too big for you to be picking me up."

"I'm not trying Crimson. This is me. This is who I am. If you're falling, then it means I'm doing something right. You're perfect and not too big for me. I can lift all that ass."

I carried Crimson upstairs to my room. We couldn't keep our eyes off each other.

"You know you don't have to carry me," she stated smiling. I bit her bottom lip and slid my tongue in her mouth.

"Stop before I bite your tongue," she laughed.

"Don't tell me what to do." As soon as we entered my room. I tossed her on the bed and hovered over her, she was about to say something smart.

"Carius, I told you I was sleeping in the guest room," she pouted.

"It's getting remolded. You got to sleep in my room like you did last night. I can't hold you in the other room.

Stop trying me Crimson, for real. Make yourself comfortable while I go get your bag."

"I'm not trying you Carius. I'm not shacking up with you." She argued.

"Hold up let me get your bag and we can finish this conversation. Do you want anything from the kitchen?" I asked.

"A bottled water and one of those green apples that you're letting go to waste. Thank you." I headed downstairs to get Crimson's stuff. What the fuck did she mean by shacking up with me? She's been sitting around Mother Dear for too long. I grabbed her bag, two bottles of water, two apples, and a knife and plate. I made my way back upstairs and she was laid up under the covers looking for something to watch on TV. I handed her the water and the apple. I patted the spot next to me for her to come and join me. "What's up, Carius? What do you want to talk about? I thought we were about to watch TV? What I do?" She asked. Crimson was shooting question after question.

"I want to talk about the comment you made about shacking up? I felt offended. I'm not that type of man. So, I want to shed some light on shacking up. I was in a relationship with my ex for four years. I wanted to marry shawty because I didn't want to shack with her.

I thought what we had was solid. I guess I was the only one that was solid in the relationship. She was it for me, but shawty cheated on me. I like you Crimson, but my intentions aren't to shack with you. If we get serious, I could see myself building something with you.

On the real Crimson, if how I move is too much for you let me know and I'll fall back." I meant that shit. I'm not about to be putting myself out here for her. Just thinking about the shit is pissing me off. I shouldn't be doing this shit. My father always told me my heart will get me in the trouble. I got up and went down stairs in the living room. I couldn't be near her right now. I heard some footsteps coming down the stairs. She stood in front of me and cupped my face. I gave her my full attention. I wanted to hear what she had to say.

"I'm sorry Carius for assuming and prejudging you. You're a good guy. I'm on the outside looking in. She was crazy for cheating you. You know part of my story. It's the main reason why I have trust issues. Good things don't happen to girls like me. I don't want to fall for you and end up getting hurt by you. I'm moving with caution Carius, but for some reason, I'm not scared to love you or be open and submissive to you. I question myself why me and that's what I'm afraid of. I've never felt like this before. I can't control it even if I wanted too." She explained.

"Come here." I freed my legs open. So, Crimson could come in between them. I pulled Crimson on my lap. I wrapped my arms around her waist. My tongue traced the crook of her neck. A soft moan escaped her lips.

"I feel it too Crimson. I couldn't hold back even if I wanted too. I know I'm supposed to protect you. That's all I want to do. For some odd reason, I trust you. Some shit you can't change shawty. Some shit is meant to be. You can't control your destiny. Crimson, this life we're living is already written. It's up to us how we live it. I can't dwell on what shawty did to me. I met you for a reason. I wasn't looking for you. Shit, I was good on females. My only focus was this paper I'm forever chasing." I explained. I wasn't looking for Crimson. I ran into the store to get Keondra some shit for a cold and I forgot everything once I laid eyes on her. I guess she was my beautiful distraction.

"I hear you Carius but what changed though? If you just got out of something don't you think you should chill for a minute? I'm not a rebound. If so, we can end this thing right now. Are you coming upstairs to watch TV? It's freezing in here. I need to put my pajamas on." She asked. Crimson is always assuming shit.

"Are you listening Crimson? You're not a rebound shawty. If you were, trust me you wouldn't have made it this far. I wouldn't have come down here if you weren't tripping. Come on." I grabbed Crimson's hand leading her to the bedroom.

"I wasn't tripping. I don't want to walk. I want you to carry me." She pouted.

"Is that what you think Crimson Rose? It's not going down like that? I'm going to need you to stop fuckin' playing with me. Come on, I'm tired fuckin' with you. You're stressing me out." I argued. I was ready to lay it down.

"You started something. You see what I mean I shouldn't have got used to it, because you're taking it away." She pouted.

"Don't do that Shawty because you can't get your way," I argued. She tried to flip the shit on me. "Stop beating around the bush and tell me what you want."

"I'm telling you I want you to carry me. If I walk back up these stairs, I'm going in the guest room and ain't shit you can do about it. I don't care about you turning the TV up. I brought my headphones and ear plugs." She argued and sassed. I swear I'm not about to do this petty shit with her. She's tripping for no reason, at first, she didn't want me to pick her up, but now she's demanding it. She can walk.

"I'm not carrying you. You can walk remember? Let's go." I asked and tapped her on her legs. Crimson stood in place not giving a fuck what I had to say.

"Whatever Griff." She argued. I noticed when she's mad, she'll call me Griff instead of Carius. Crimson stood up and pushed past me. Her shoulders brushed mine. She tried to walk off from me. I was right on her heels. She hauled ass up those stairs.

She grabbed her bag out of my room. She tried to exit and go to the guest room. I was blocking her from leaving. I yanked the bag out of her hand and closed the door. I stepped in her space. I knew she would back up but this time she didn't bust a move. We shouldn't even be doing this.

"Move out my way Griff." She argued. She was sexy as fuck when she was mad. She had no clue this shit was turning me on in the worse way. I wasn't going anywhere, and neither was she.

"Why are you mad? If I don't move, what the fuck are you going to do about it?" I asked. Crimson has been trying for two days now. We're not even together but we act as if we are.

"I'm not mad, but you don't want to fuckin' try me." She stated. She had her hands on her thick hips. She had a mug on her face. I wasn't threatened. If she thought she was sleeping in the guest room, she has life fucked up.

"I do want to try you. I'm trying to see what your tough ass is about to do?" I laughed. Crimson placed her hands on my chest attempting to move me out the way. I picked her up and tossed her on the bed. She tried to jump up off the bed. I climbed on top of her. She was mad as hell, but I don't give a fuck.

"Move Griff. I don't feel like playing with you." She argued. She rolled her eyes as if she was mad at a nigga. Her chest was bouncing up and down. I bit her bottom lip.

"I'm not moving and you're not leaving this room. We're doing all of this because I didn't carry you upstairs? I wanted to but I didn't because you've been trying the fuck out of me. You're not even my woman yet, but you act like it. Crimson Rose Tristan, I just want to spoil you and adore you shawty. I'm not trying to be at odds with you. It's too early for us to be at odds with each other because we can't fuck and make up. You feel me?" I asked. I felt Crimson's body tense up.

"Whatever Griff raise up off me. Actions speak louder than words. I heard what you had to say, and I listened. I'm tired. I worked eight hours today. I just want to go to sleep." She argued and pouted.

"You can go to sleep. I'm not stopping you. I'm about to take a shower. You better be in here after I get out."

"Bye Griff get off me you stink," she laughed and snarled her face up.

"Crimson when you're mad at me you call me Griff. Why do you do that shit though? It's a little too early for you to be mad at me and shit. Come wash me up since I stink? Take a shower with me? I'm trying to get you in routine." I explained and chuckled. I knew Crimson wasn't going, but I like to fuck with her.

"When you want to be an ass, I call you Griff. When you want to be serious it's Carius. I give you what you give me. Bye Griff go take a shower. I won't be here when you get out. You know what, I'm taking your keys and I'm driving myself home. I'll see you around. I'll leave Mother Dear with your keys. Don't call me either." She argued. Crimson had me fucked up.

"Why do you keep trying to leave me? It's not that easy getting rid of me." I asked and explained. I bit Crimson on her neck. She was squirming trying to break free from my embrace. I applied a little more pressure and eased up. I started kissing her on the side of her neck and she moaned.

"Stop Griff please," she moaned. "Stop." She moaned.

"What I need to stop for? It doesn't sound like you want me to stop. You said you were leaving right? I'm giving you something to miss on your way home." I argued. I continued doing what the fuck I was doing. I felt Crimson's body shake. I had her right where I wanted her. I raised up and tossed her the keys.

"I'll see you around shawty, be safe out here. You need me to walk you to the garage?" I asked. I grabbed her bag off the floor and handed it to her. She snatched it out of my hand. It's late I'm tired as fuck and I'm not about to do this shit with her.

"I got a ride. I'm good. He'll be here in about ten minutes." She argued and sassed. She gave me a devilish smirk. Crimson tried to walk off from me. I ran up on her ass. She really got me fucked up. I'm not with the games and shit.

"You got a nigga that can come and pick you up from my house?" I asked.

"What Griff, I thought you were taking a shower? You gave me my bag so I'm leaving." She argued.

"I asked you a motherfuckin' question? You got a nigga that can come and pick you up from here Crimson?" I asked and argued. She wanted to see the real Griff. The ruthless ass nigga that I've been keeping at arm's length. I don't even want her to see this side of me. Crimson refused to answer me. I grabbed the strap on her sports bra with so much force she had no choice but to look at me. She looked over her shoulder to see what I wanted. "Answer my fuckin question?"

"My uncle Tommy is coming to pick me up. Are you satisfied?" She argued and snatched her arm away from me. I held Crimson in place so she wouldn't move. She was still trying to walk out the front door. I wasn't having that.

"Hell no, I'm not satisfied," I argued.

"Let me go, Griff. You asked for an answer and I gave it to you. You wanted me to leave so I'm gone. I don't have to be anywhere I'm not welcomed. Could you please let me go?" She argued.

"Crimson, I'm sorry. I don't even want to be doing this with you. You're spoiled as fuck. All of this just because I didn't carry you upstairs to my room?

I don't want you to leave because I wanted you to stay the night with me. I'm not a selfish ass nigga, but damn shawty meet me half way? We're about to throw this thing away before we even get a chance to see what we could be because we're having a small misunderstanding. Call your uncle and tell him you're good, I got you." I picked Crimson up and carried her upstairs. She refused to look at me. She had a big ass smirk on her face. "Are you happy now?"

"I'm good Carius." I was staring a hole in her, but she refused to open her eyes and acknowledge me. I placed her gently on the bed.

"I'm about to take a shower. You'll be here when I get out?"

"Yes, I'm going to take a shower in the guest bed room."

"Thank you. You can take one with me if you want?" I was surprised that she agreed to it. I walked in the bathroom first and she followed behind me. I cut the shower on. I got my work cut out for me. I swear I wish my mother was around. She said this day would come and to be honest, I wasn't ready for it.

I'm going to see her tomorrow at her gravesite. I stepped in the shower. I had a lot of shit on my mind. Crimson Rose got me tripping hard. I couldn't even focus on the site behind me and brushing up against me. If she would've been anybody else, I would've let her walk out that door and not give a fuck about her leaving, but for some odd reason, I couldn't do that.

My mind was telling me to say fuck her, but my heart was about to bust out my chest because every step she took toward that door I felt like this would be my last time seeing her. She has a hold on me, and I can't shake her. I washed my face and covered my body with soap. I stroked my dick. I felt Crimson breasts touch my back. I looked over my shoulder to see what was up.

"I'm sorry." I nodded my head in agreement and turned back around. I felt the cool air hit my back when she stepped out. I cut the shower off and stepped out right behind her. She had a towel in her hand. I grabbed the towel from her and dried her body off from head to toe. Crimson's eyes roamed my body. I could feel it, but I didn't want to discuss it. Her night clothes were lying on the sink. She had sexy tight fitted night shirt she threw over her head and walked out the bathroom. I had to adjust my dick before I stepped out. As soon as I stepped out after brushing my teeth, Crimson was underneath the covers acting as if she was asleep. I climbed in right behind her and cut the TV off. I picked her up and laid her on my chest. My hands roamed her body and I grabbed a hand full of her ass.

"Wake up, I know you're not asleep that fast," I whispered in her ear. My tongue traced the inside of her ear. I could feel her body tense up. She needed to get used to this.

"I'm up, my eyes are just closed. I see you can't keep your hands to yourself," she whispered?

"I can't. You know I'm feeling you? I care about you Crimson Rose and it's crazy. I was just thinking to myself. I wish my mother was here so I could share some insight with her about you. I can't shake you even if I wanted too. I don't ask for much. I'm not hard to please. I just want love, loyalty, and respect. I want you to myself. I don't want to share you with anybody else. You're mine Crimson, don't forget that." Crimson raised up and looked at me.

"I'm feeling you too Carius. I'm sorry about earlier. I was just fuckin' with you. I care about you a lot. You seem like a nice guy so far but only time would tell. I want love, loyalty, and respect too."

"Do you want me to yourself?" I asked. Crimson looked at me and smiled.

"I do Carius." I flipped Crimson on her backside and climbed in between her legs. I wanted to dive in head first, but it was too early to take it there. When she's ready she'll let me know. I decided to kiss her instead.

Chapter - 8

Crimson

If I fall, somebody better catch me. If I'm dreaming somebody better pinch me. My life has changed drastically in a matter of weeks. Griff and I haven't put a title on what we have. We're just taking it one day at a time. I like him a lot. I'm falling hard for him. All I want is HIM. Danielle and I moved out two weeks ago. We got us a spot ducked off in Lithonia, not too far from Stonecrest Mall. It's a cute little cozy town house. We decorated it to our liking. It's just the two of us.

Our rent is $975.00 a month. We split all the bills in half. Mother Dear kicked my ass out quick. I asked her to pick me up from work the other day because I wanted to lay in her bed and chill. I missed her so much. Chile, she drove me home to my spot instead of her house. I bust out laughing. As soon as we pulled up, Griff was in the parking lot waiting on me. I'm hardly ever home because Griff insists that I stay with him at night.

I'm so accustomed to lying with him it's crazy. I crave him. I couldn't even get comfortable in my spot because I'm always with him. I feel bad because I'm always leaving Danielle hanging. We haven't crossed that line yet. I want too so bad, but it's too soon. We just met four weeks ago. It's my off day and Griff has been on my mind heavy. I couldn't wait to see him later. Danielle came into my room and laid across my bed.

"Don't try to hide that smile bitch. Let's do something before your man pulls up and kidnap you. I'm surprised you're still here. Have you let Griff bust that pussy wide open yet? I know it's something sexual going on Crimson. Bitch, you at that nigga house every fuckin' night? You should've moved in with his ass. I went to pay the rent this morning and guess what the apartment manager said? Our rent was paid up until the lease was up." She beamed. I know Griff paid our rent. I don't need him taking care of me.

"Girl, Griff did that. He's been asking me since we moved in how much our rent was. I refused to tell him because I knew what he was up too. I'm not moving in with him. I barely have known him for a month. Yes, I'm home today. I told him last night I needed to get accustomed to sleeping by myself at night and he was hot about that. I don't care. I'll see him later. No, Danielle I haven't given him the pussy yet, but I want too.

All we do is kiss, but the other night when I was laying on him. I was adjusting my shorts and my hand touched his dick. It was long, thick and hard. He grabbed my hand and made me hold it. I almost fainted. How do you know when it's time?" I asked. Just thinking about that night, it did something to me. I wanted that man in the worst way. I wanted him to fuck some good sense into me. If I was a dumb, bitch I wanted him to make me smart. It's so hard to fight the temptation.

"Griff is a real one. He cares about you Crimson. It's written all over his face. What man do you know is paying our lease for a chick he just met? I can't name one. I appreciate that. It's more money in our pockets. You know its time if you're ready to do it. If you're thinking about it Crimson than you're ready. You've been saving yourself for a long time. So, maybe he's worthy to be the first one to break you off. I hate to say it and I don't want to jinx you but if you give that nigga the pussy, you're going to fuck around and make me a Godmother to a child. Does he know that you're a virgin?" She asked.

"Danielle, why would you say that? I'm not a fan of birth control, but I want to protect myself. No, he doesn't know I'm a virgin. We don't talk about sex, because he doesn't want that from me. He's made himself clear about that. I'm ready to take it there. I got to fan myself. One night we were in the shower and my soap fell. He was behind me when I bent over to pick it up. He put his hands on my waist, Danielle. I felt the tip of his dick touch the opening of my pussy. I was scared. I just knew it was about to go down. I WASN'T READY. My heart dropped and he bust out laughing. I was so embarrassed bitch. He tried ME. I was so mad at his ass for that. He said he was getting ready." I screamed with excitement. I swear he does the most.

"Crimson Rose Tristan, bitch, you done got too motherfuckin grown. You're real motherfuckin comfortable with Griff bitch. Girl, I could feel the heat and the passion between y'all. He's ready. BEEN READY to break you off something proper! Poor baby. What are you going to do, besides teasing him? You knew what the fuck you were doing Crimson." She laughed. I was teasing him, but I want him to ask me and if he did, I would gladly comply.

"It's not funny. Danielle, I dropped the soap. I'm always careful. Griff doesn't have any kids, but he wants some. I'm not ready for any yet, but it's too many side effects with birth control. He's going to have to strap up and pull out."

"Okay Crimson, you think you know it all? Girl, that nigga isn't about to strap up with you. How much do you want to bet? Pretty soon I'll be having this town house all to myself. You're always welcome to come here, but I'm not taking you off this lease." She laughed. Danielle had nothing to worry about. I wasn't moving in with Griff no time soon. Speaking of Griff, he was already calling my phone this morning.

"Answer the phone bitch and put it on speaker. I want to hear the conversation." She laughed. I cut my eyes at Danielle.

"Danielle, you're too damn nosey, bye. I need a little privacy." I laughed and answered the phone. Every time I hear his voice, I got weak. It's so deep, sexy and hood.

"Hello." My face was buried into the pillow. Danielle pulled it from my face quick. I can't stand her. I just want to have my moment in peace.

"What's up baby, I miss you. What time can I see you? I'm mad I couldn't kiss you when I rolled over this morning. Your side of the bed was empty. You know I'm not used to that. What do I have to do so we can change that?" He asked. I had the biggest smile on face. I had to take the phone off speaker. Danielle snatched my phone and put it back on speaker. I popped her on her arm.

"I miss you too Griff. I just saw you yesterday, cut it out. I do want to see you later though. Danielle and I have a few plans later. I went to pay rent this morning and the apartment manager said my lease was paid up. You wouldn't know anything about that would you?" I asked and Griff got quiet as hell. "Carius, who told you to do that? Don't get quiet now."

"Boys do what they can Crimson, and men do what they want. I'm a man and I handle your finances. You knew I did it. You didn't even have to ask that. I paid it up for Danielle because you won't even be staying there in a few months. Maybe weeks, who knows. I couldn't leave shawty hanging with that responsibility." He explained. I swear he always looking out.

"Carius, nobody told you to do that. You can't be paying people's bills up. What you mean I won't be living here in a few months or maybe a few weeks?" I asked. Danielle smacked me in the back of my head." Ouch." I whined.

"Crimson Rose, you're smart as fuck. You can read between the lines or do I need to break it down for you. You know what it is with us." He chuckled. I needed him to break it down for him.

"What is it with us Griff," I asked. I swear he makes me so weak. I melt in his arms when I'm with him. I love the way he touches me. I love it, even more, when he caresses me at night when I'm lying on his chest.

"Crimson Rose Tristan, or should I say Griffey. That shit sounds good, don't it? You know you're mine! You know we're together, so stop fronting like we ain't." He explained. I blushed hearing him say that. I hated when he did that shit. He swears he's my man and he hasn't even asked me out. Danielle was slapping me on my leg and whispering, "Go, Bitch." I had to pop her ass.

"I hear you Carius, and I'm listening. It sounds good but you haven't officially asked me out yet. What makes you so sure that I'll say yes?" I giggled.

"Crimson Rose, shawty, you think shit is a game? Do you think I'm a funny ass nigga? You know I care about you. I can't hide that even if I wanted too. I know you're going to say yes. Saying no isn't an option. Open up the front door right now, so I can ask you," he commanded.

My heart dropped. Danielle ran out of the room so fast. It sounded like a heard of horses. She stuck her tongue out and hauled ass. So much for a bitch being nosey. I swallowed my spit and got my voice together.

"I'm not home Carius," I whispered. My heart dropped instantly. Who told him to pop up at my house this early? He's too sneaky for me. I swear he's full of surprises.

"Crimson Rose Tristan, open the fuckin door now. You ain't never been good at lying." He argued. I can't stand him. I opened the door and he had the biggest ass smile on his face. Damn, he looked good. He pulled me into his arms and picked me up. I wrapped my legs around his waist. He bit the creases of my neck. He carried me to my room. He smelled so good. He tossed me on the bed and climbed in between my legs and bit my bottom lip. My eyes rolled in the back of my head.

"Why are you lying to me? I fucked you up, didn't I? What's up Danielle? I was already in route." He laughed.

"Hey Griff," she yelled sounding hood as fuck. Danielle was so ghetto.

"Why didn't you tell me that you were on your way over here? You're sneaky." I asked.

"I wanted to see you. I didn't tell you because I knew you had an excuse. You were bullshitting last night. I had to see you this morning before I made some moves. Crimson Rose Tristan, would you be my lady?" He asked. He was staring hard in the eyes. I tried to look away and he grabbed my face. I could feel his words.

"I wasn't bullshitting you. We stayed on the phone for two hours until I fell asleep on you. Yes, Carius Deon Griffey, I MIGHT be your lady." I giggled. I tried to play it off, but I couldn't. I should've stayed with him last night because I missed him like crazy. I tossed and turned all night and I didn't have too. I wanted him to miss me, but I was missing him like crazy.

"You can stop playing with me. It ain't no might it's either yes or no." He argued. I love when he lays down the law. Let me stop playing with this man because I wanted him just as bad as he wants me. I wanted him to ask me to be with him.

"Yes Carius, I'll be your lady. Why are you trying to make me fall in love with you?" He shoved his tongue down my throat. Thank God I brushed my teeth this morning. I could still smell the fresh mint on his breath. He broke the kiss and grabbed something out of his pocket. It was a jewelry box. He pulled out a necklace and it had

Griff on it. It was flooded with diamonds. He pulled out a diamond tester. Testing each diamond to confirm it was real.

"Do you love me, because if so, that means I'm doing my job right. Raise up so I can put this on your neck and you better not take it off." He argued. He knows I'm falling for him, how can I not. I do love him and it's crazy.

"I'm falling for you Carius. Is that good enough for you? I wish you would stop putting spells on me. I swear somebody wants to be my daddy so bad." I mumbled.

"I don't want to be your daddy. I wanted to be your man. I accomplished that, but I'll gladly be the father of a few of your kids. When you're ready they can call me daddy." He laughed. I punched him in his shoulders.

"Whatever Carius. I have an appointment today to get on some form of birth control." I explained. I wanted to see what he thought about it. I could already tell where this conversation was going already. His nose flared up instantly. He wiped the brim of his nose with his hand.

"Birth control? What the fuck you need that shit for? It's designed to fuck up your body not help it. We were put on this earth to reproduce. Whatever happens, happens. I'll take care of my kids no matter what. They'll forever be straight. I'm telling you now when I dive in that pussy I'm not pulling out. Cancel that appointment. Why are you going anyway? You're not having sex. Who are you fuckin' Crimson?" He asked.

"Calm down I'm not fuckin' nobody yet. I don't believe in birth control either. If we get to that point, I don't want to get pregnant my first-time having sex. I don't want you to think I'm trying to trap you" Griff put his hand over my mouth and cut me off before I could say anything else.

"What you mean your first time? I know you ain't trying to trap me. You can kill that shit right now. I know you're not fuckin' with me for what I have because you don't ask me for anything. I want you in the worst way, but baby if it happens it happens. I told you our life was already written. We just got to live it, and I'll take care of my kids and grandkids."

"I hear you, Griff. I'm a virgin. I never had sex before. I'm saving myself." I mumbled and sighed. I put my head down. Griff lifted my head up and kissed me on my lips.

"I hope you're listening. Don't put your head down. It's nothing to be ashamed of. I got you and I want to be your first and last. I can't wait to teach you a few things. I'm about to ease up out here. You and Danielle can do whatever plans the two of you have. I want to see you later. I'm not picking you up. You can drive yourself." He explained and tossed me a set of keys and kissed me on my forehead. Griff tried to run up out of my room. I grabbed his shirt before he could even get out the door. He was up to something and I was about to find out what it was.

"What is this for and why are you running off? If you drove over here, how are you getting home?" I asked. He had the biggest smile on his face.

"My partner Shad followed me over here. He's outside waiting on me. Hit the key fob and you'll see what's out there. I'll see you later baby, be easy." He pulled me in for a hug and kissed me on my lips. I swear he's so sexy to me. It's shit like this that has me tripping so hard.

"Bye Carius." He chucked the deuces up at me. I just shook my head thinking about his actions. I swear he does the most.

"Danielle, you can come out now." I laughed. I knew she was somewhere listening.

"Crimson, bitch, as soon as that nigga shut the door, I was standing by the door listening. Please stop playing with that man and lock his ass down. He shut that shit all the way down about the birth control. He doesn't give a fuck. He wants you to have his baby. Shit, he's ready for his babies to have babies." She laughed. We slapped hands with each other.

"Danielle, why are you so damn nosey? You could've waited on me to tell you what happened." I argued.

"No bitch, I couldn't wait. I was done with you when you tried to act as if we weren't at home. That nigga was already in route. I almost pissed on myself when he said open the door. Bitch, you be leaving shit out. Y'all so gawd damn cute together. I love it. You deserve it Crimson. I swear to God you do. I know I'm next bitch. I'm claiming it. How can I not be? I know Griff got partners that got money and bitch you're going to hook me up.

He spoils you like crazy. Look at your necklace? You got the keys to a BENZ, bitch. I'm ready to ride the fuck out. Our lease is paid up too. Shit! Bitch let's go to the mall and shop. He's a fuckin' keeper." She laughed. Danielle was so damn crazy. I love her to death. I wouldn't trade her for anything in this world.

"Danielle I'm falling for him. I swear he's everything. He's my prince charming in a hood fairytale. I miss him already. He's trying to make me fall in love with him. I pray this isn't a façade, shit. I'll kill his ass if he left me feeling like this." I beamed and I was serious.

"Bitch I'm falling for his ass too. We ain't got to pay no rent. I can't wait until you move out, so I can decorate your room as my woman cave. Get his ass to put a credit on the utilities. He's falling for you too and he hasn't even sampled the pussy. Bitch, which farmers market did you go to? Shit, I need to go there too if you are pulling niggas like Griff." She explained.

I couldn't wait to take it there with him. Danielle and I finished getting dressed. It was nice outside. I didn't even get cute. We were just going to the mall and I wasn't trying to impress anybody. I already had a man and I couldn't wait to see him later. Danielle locked the door and we headed out. I hit the alarm on the key fob, and it was a BENZ that I've never seen before.

"Bitch, that's not the same BENZ that Griff pulled up in at Mother Dear's house? This is a Big Boy Benz." I nodded my head in agreement. I hopped in the car. It smelled brand new. Danielle snatched the door open. I looked to my right to see what was up.

"Crimson, get the fuck out the car now, right fuckin' now." She yelled and screamed.

"What's wrong," I ask. She was making me nervous.

"Bitch, this is a fuckin' Maybach Benz. Brand fuckin' new with a drive out tag. Damn, Griff ain't playing no fuckin' games when it comes to you. Do you know how much this fuckin' car cost?" She yelled. I don't keep up with trends or none of that extra shit.

"No, I don't Danielle. Should I care?" I asked.

"Yes, bitch! It's $170,000 just for the basic model and this motherfucka ain't basic." She beamed. I wasn't comfortable driving this car if it cost this much. It's too expensive.

"Let me call Griff and see what's up?" He answered on the first ring.

"What's up baby, what you doing? You miss a nigga already," He asked?

"Of course, I miss you, but that's not why I called. Whose car is this?" I asked. I could hear him huffing and puffing in the back ground. I knew he was being sneaky when he ran up out of here. I couldn't keep this car. I would have a target on my back.

"Who got the keys Crimson? Check the registration in the glove compartment. It'll tell you whose car it is." He argued and explained. Danielle handed me the registration and shook her head. It had my name on it. There was an envelope attached also. I opened it and it was filled with one hundred-dollar bills. I just shook my head.

"Griff, why did you get me this expensive ass car? You didn't have to do that. Ain't nobody told you to buy me a car. I can't accept this from you. I'm calling AAA and I'm getting this car towed to your house. Stop spending your money so reckless. You need to invest your money in some stocks and bonds, not materialistic shit that can depreciate." I argued. It was a nice gift, but I didn't need a car this expensive.

"Crimson Rose Tristan, you said you were my lady when I pull up. I want a motherfucka to know that, so that's why I brought you a Maybach BENZ. I'm not taking it back. It's your fuckin' car and you're going to drive it until I feel like buying you something else." He argued. I looked at the phone. I don't know who he thought he was talking too.

"Whatever Griff." I wasn't even about to go back and forth with him about this. It was pointless.

"What the fuck is that supposed to mean CRIMSON? The money that's in the envelope, put it in the bank and the black card that's stuffed in between bills, use it for emergencies only. Go grocery shopping. I want some of that barbecue that Mother Dear cooked. I'll see you later." He explained. Griff ended the call. Danielle looked me at, and I looked at her. I knew she couldn't hold water.

"Spit it out," I argued and rolled my eyes.

"Don't do that because your man checked you. Girl, Griff told you what it was. Let that nigga spoil you if he wants too. The car is in your name. You heard what the fuck he said. I want a plate of that barbecue too. Bitch go cook for your man, but let's go shopping first. Let me count this money up. I need a few of these bills," she laughed. Leave it to Danielle to cheer me up.

I swear Griff put a sour taste in my mouth. I knew he was up to some shit. This conversation is far from over. I was headed to the bank to make a deposit. Danielle counted the money up. It was $21,000.00 in cash.

Danielle and I had a long day. We shopped until we couldn't shop anymore. I dropped her off at home and grabbed a few things because I wasn't coming back home tonight. I headed over to Griff's house. I haven't heard from him all day. I was slick mad at his ass because he didn't consult with me about buying me a car. We never had that conversation. As soon as I hit the gate, I realized I needed the code. I was about to text him for the code, but the gate automatically raised up. It was a little after 4:00 p.m. I stopped by the Farmers Market to get some chicken wings and beef ribs. I didn't like cooking late. Mother Dear always had dinner ready by 5:00 p.m. no later than 7:00 p.m. I grabbed everything that we would need for our dinner tonight. I don't know why he wanted me to cook for him.

I didn't know if he liked potato salad or coleslaw, so I was making a small thing of the two of them. What made him want me to cook him some barbecue? He's been talking about it since he ate it. I unloaded the trunk with the groceries that I bought and started preparing dinner. I covered the chicken and beef with spices and marinade.

I let it sit for thirty minutes before I put it in the oven. I made the coleslaw and potato salad. I cut my onions and peppers up for the baked beans and seasoned the ground beef to add in my baked beans. I added a few cups of brown sugar and barbecue sauce. I put the baked beans on low so it could simmer. The food would be ready in about three hours. I could shower and take a quick nap. My phone rang and it was Griff. I started not to answer.

"Hello," I yawned. I tried to sound like I was asleep.

"What's up baby, did I wake you up? I haven't heard from you all day. I was just checking in. I was headed to the house. What time are you coming through," he asked?

"I was taking a nap, but you're good. I've been a little busy. I went to the Farmers Market earlier. I was hoping that I would run into you, but I didn't. I'm already at the house waiting on you." I yawned.

"Why didn't you let know you were there already, I would've been made it home," he asked. I had to start cooking and I knew Griff would've been all up on me.

"I knew you were coming, but I wanted dinner to be ready by the time you made it home." I beamed. This is my first-time cooking for Griff, so it had to be perfect. Mother Dear taught me well. I wasn't the least bit worried.

"Oh yeah, I'll be there in about forty-five minutes. Traffic is crazy, do you need me to stop and get anything before I come home?" He asked.

"Nope, I just need you to get here. I got everything. Hurry up so I can feed you. I want to get back home before it gets too late." I sighed. I like fuckin' with Griff. I knew he was about to trip.

"You are at home. I got to eat dinner by myself? Stop playing with me Crimson. I'll see you in a minute." Griff hung up the phone. I'm sure a forty-minute drive will be about twenty minutes fuckin' with him. I cuddled up on the sofa. We had another hour to go on the food. What am I doing? I swear I've been questioning myself about that for the past few days. Everything feels so right. I'm just going with the flow.

Chapter-9

Griff

Crimson put the biggest smile on my face. I couldn't wait to make it back home to her. I know things are moving a little too fast with us, but I think she's the one. I feel like she is. Nothing is telling me to hold back. I had to handle the divorce with Keondra first. That's why I ran the fuck up out of there. I had to meet my attorney. Keondra didn't want much. I wasn't going to leave her assed out, but I wasn't breaking her off either. We didn't have a prenup. Whatever she came with is what she was leaving with. She could keep our house and her car. I was giving her $200,000.00. She better make that shit last.

She's been blowing up my phone like crazy. I put her ass on the block list. I wasn't thinking about her. Whatever nigga she's fuckin' she can continue too. Shit happens for a reason. She couldn't be faithful, so we didn't need to be together. She never wanted to be a wife. Keondra was too busy running the streets and spending my money like it wasn't no tomorrow. It's a big difference between Keondra and Crimson. The Maybach. It was catch to it. I was baiting her to see if she was really with a nigga for his money or not. Crimson passed the test. She didn't want that car. She jumped down my throat about spending so recklessly that spoke volumes.

Rashad nodded his head in agreement. It tripped me out when she said she was getting it towed to the crib. Yes, she was a keeper and I for damn sure was keeping her. Keondra ain't never cooked dinner for a nigga. I gave her the fuckin' world and she didn't deserve that shit. The most I ever got from her was a hamburger and maybe some fries. She felt as if she didn't have to cook. She had a good life and I'm glad she cheated because she didn't deserve it.

I finally made it home. As soon as I entered the garage and stepped out. I could smell the food aroma. I could get used to this. I grab the duffel bag out of my trunk. I had to place these bills in my safe. I finished doing that and I went to find Ms. Tristan. I didn't have to look too far because she was laid out on the sofa asleep. I picked her up and carried her upstairs to my room.

"Griff, why did you pick me up? The food is almost done, and I have to fix your plate." She yawned.

"Have you eaten yet?" I asked.

"Nope."

"I'll fix our plates and bring dinner to you. It smells good. Thank you."

"Okay, you welcome," she smiled. "Wait, Griff, I made potato salad and coleslaw because I didn't know which one you wanted?" She stated and yawned.

"I want them both, which ones do you want."

"Both," She was tired. She didn't even open her eyes up, but she's going home before it gets late. She can forget about it. The food smelled good. I pulled the meat out the oven. She cooked barbecue ribs and chicken, baked beans, with ground meat, coleslaw, and potato salad. Crimson threw down.

I tasted a piece of the rib to see if it tasted as good as Mother Dear's and it did. Damn, I had to eat another piece. Fuck it, I'm hungry as hell. Let me stop now because I'm never going to make it upstairs. I fixed our plates and grabbed the food trays. I had to come back for the lemonade and paper towels. Crimson didn't even notice me set everything up. I'll come back later to put the food up and clean the kitchen.

"Wake up Crimson," I yelled. I tapped her on legs, and she refused to wake up. I hovered over and pressed my lips up against hers. I started kissing her and she kissed me back. I pulled back from her and she grabbed the back of my head forcing her tongue down my throat.

"Why you stop?" She whined and yawned.

"Wake up so you can eat."

"I'm tired." She yawned.

"Come on and eat, or do you want me to feed you," I ask. Crimson thought I was playing but I was dead ass serious. I would feed her with or without her permission.

"I can feed myself Griff, but I'm not ready to eat yet. What makes you think it's cool for you to mess me with me while I'm asleep?" She argued. I do what I want, and I wanted to wake her up.

"I want you to eat with me. You prepared this food and I don't want to eat by myself. I appreciate you Crimson. Come on and eat and I'll put you back to sleep.

You can forget about going home it's not happening tonight." I explained. Crimson was wiping her eyes with the brim of her hand.

"You're welcome Carius. It wasn't a problem. It's the least I could do since I've met you, you've been nothing but good to me. I'll eat with you, give me a minute. Oh yeah because the kitchen is on you tonight. Why do you be trying to kidnap me and shit?" She asked. She knew why she just wanted me to confirm it.

"I don't mind cleaning the kitchen. I'm not kidnapping you. I just want to spend some time with you. I want you here. I don't want to lay by myself tonight. I love when you're lying next to me. I missed you last night. I'm not trying to miss you tonight. I want to hold you all night." I was staring Crimson in her eyes pleading with her not to leave.

"You better be glad I like you just a little bit. Why are you trying to make me fall in love with you?" She asked. It's the second time she's asked me this today.

"I want you to love me Crimson. I want you to fall in love with me. It ain't no fun falling in love by yourself. We'll get there. Let's eat." Crimson looked at me and rolled her eyes. Crimson and I ate our food and it was good. I didn't even think that she would be able to cook this good, but she surprised me. Crimson kept stealing glances at me while she ate. We finished eating our food and Crimson passed me a paper towel and the glass of lemonade. She walked out of the bedroom and gave me a devilish smirk.

"Where are you going?" I yelled with my mouth full.

"Home," she yelled. I sat my lemonade on the dresser and ran up behind her. She was heading down the steps when I stopped her midway.

"Where are you going? I told you I wanted you to stay."

"I'm going to get my phone, Griff. I'm not going anywhere but to the kitchen to put this food up and to grab me another piece of chicken. Is that cool with you?" She asked.

"Yeah that's cool, but I know what the fuck I heard." I went upstairs to grab my glass to join Crimson in the kitchen. I swear she was hard headed as fuck I told her I had the kitchen. She was washing the dishes anyway.

She had her headphones in her ear. I walked up behind her and wrapped my arms around her waist. She looked over her shoulder and looked up at me. I leaned in to give her a kiss.

"I told you I had the kitchen. I didn't need you to assist me."

"I know but it's just a habit of mine. I can't help myself. You already woke me up, so I didn't want to be waiting forever on you to come to bed. I'm just making it a little easier for you." She explained. I grabbed Crimson's hands and dried them off and backed her into the counter.

"I appreciate that. I got it though. I asked you to cook so I had the kitchen. Team work makes the dream work."

"Okay, Carius. It feels like you're trying to get rid of me. Hurry up. You don't have that much to do. I'm waiting on you." She sighed and smiled. Crimson eased her way out the kitchen. I smacked her on her ass on the way out.

"Stop! That hurts. You play too much. Hurry up and finish the kitchen. You don't have that much to do." She argued. Crimson knocked out the hard part. I had one pot left to wash. I handled that and cleaned the countertops off. Crimson was clean because there wasn't any food left on the counters. I needed to take a shower before I could suffocate her. I still smelled like the Trap and I didn't want Crimson smelling like this.

I finally made my way upstairs. Crimson wasn't in the bed. I heard the shower running. I decided to join her. As soon as I stepped in, she was stepping out. The water dripping from Crimson's body was a sexy sight to see. My eyes roamed her body from her head to her toes. She grabbed a towel and attempted to dry off. I snatched it from her and handled that.

"I can dry myself off. You might miss a spot," she argued.

"I know you can, but I want too. I can guarantee you I won't miss shit. How much you want to bet," I asked?

"Whatever," she mumbled.

"I can't hear you Crimson, say that shit a little louder."

"Stop being a bully." I took my time drying her off. She had chill bumps appearing on her body because of my touch. Her nipples had become erect. I finished drying her off and I smacked her on her ass.

"Aye, you need to stop being scared of my touch and get used to this shit Crimson." I chuckled. She popped me on the back of my head. "Watch your hands."

"Ain't nobody scared of you or your touch. Trust me if I was, I wouldn't have let you get this far. I'm comfortable with you. It's the cold ass air that's giving me the chills." She argued and sassed. My eyes were trained on her ass and her hips as she exited the bathroom.

"Don't put no clothes on either," I yelled. I cut the shower on and adjusted the water temperature. I stepped in the shower head first. The water temperature was too hot. It cascaded down my body. I had a lot on my mind, but Crimson was the only thing getting attention. Her being a virgin really changes the game. I wanted to take my time with her, but now I'll really have to take my time with her. She had to be meant for me because I was going to be her first and last. I've been thinking about that shit all day.

I couldn't even cook up the dope right because that shit was on my mind. Shad had to put in extra work. I was about to fuck up the churches money and I had mouths to feed for September. I handled my hygiene, stepped out of the shower and dried off quickly. I had something sexy as fuck waiting on me. Shit with Crimson feels so real and different. It's not forced. It just flows. As soon as I made it to the bedroom, she was tucked underneath the covers.

"Why are you staring at me like that," she asked?

"Because I can, and you better not have any clothes on either."

"And If I do what are you going to do about it," she asked?

"You'll see smart ass." She busted out laughing. I climbed in the bed and I pulled her right next to me. She was naked as the day she was born. Her lying next to me wasn't good enough. I wanted her lying right on top of me. I lifted her up and laid her on my chest. My hands roamed her body. I wanted this but only when she's ready.

"Crimson." She raised her head up and looked at me. She placed her elbows on my chest.

"Carius." She laughed.

"What's so funny?"

"You."

"What I do?"

"What don't you do?"

"Why ask a question with a question? I ain't trying to wrap about that. I got some serious shit I want to say. I'm feeling you. I like this thing that we have going on. Crimson you're not a fling for me. I like coming home to you. I want to get used to you being here when I come home soon. I live a life of sin and I risk pen chances on the daily, but I'm willing to separate the two because I need you and I really want to be with you.

I like the way you think. You mind fucked the shit out me earlier. I spend a lot, but I stack way more. Don't take offense to what I'm saying. The Maybach. It was bait. I just wanted to see where your head was at. I do want to buy you a car and before you say no, I'm buying it anyway." I had Crimson's attention. She cupped my chin trying to figure me out. Her manicured nail traced my eyebrows. What you see is what you get with me. I ain't never felt like this before. Keondra and I never did shit like this. I used to beat her home.

Her excuse was she thought I was still out trapping. That ain't got shit to do with you. She never gave a fuck if I ate or not. I never came home to a home cooked meal. None of that shit. My momma told me to pay attention, but I didn't listen. I learned the hard way, but I met Crimson so I ain't tripping. I had to go through that to get to where I'm going.

"You baited me? Griff, I don't want you for your money. That shit doesn't excite me. I'm not impressed by that. I meant what I said about the car too. I like you too. Shit, I think I'm falling in love with you. I care about you a lot and minus all the extra shit we could still probably roc, because we connect. I could get used to this too. Promise me you'll stay true? I pray this isn't a façade." She explained. I flipped Crimson on her backside and cupped her chin. This shit we got going on is real and I wanted her to know that.

"I promise it's not a façade Crimson. It's the real thing. I promise to stay true. You got a nigga falling hard for you. I love the feeling that I get when I'm with you. I don't ever want to lose you." I explained. Crimson and I went to sleep. For the first in a long time, I was comfortable and content with her. I didn't have any second thoughts about her.

Chapter-10

Jermesha

I wish I could meet a boss ass nigga to take care of me and my kids. The only niggas I fucked with had changed. Hell, even my kids' fathers had changed. They wouldn't take care of me, just their kids only. What type of shit is that? Three different baby daddies and it was the same shit with each one of them. My kids were well taken cared of but not me. I had to steal everything I had. My baby daddies were so fuckin' petty. They wouldn't give me cash to buy anything. They bought everything and took the tags off and I didn't have any receipts. They knew off the top I was taking that shit back and getting the money. It was nice outside today. Not to hot or cold. More of a reason why I needed to be in the streets.

I couldn't even bust a move if I wanted too. Mother Dear has been tripping hard and she refuses to watch my kids. Crimson moved out and I hated it because I could always leave them here with her and she'll look out for them. My mother was on the same type of shit I was on.

She refuses to be a grandmother to her grandchildren. Hell, she wasn't even a mother to me. I got dressed early hoping that I could sneak off and leave Mother Dear here with my kids. As soon as I tried to tip toe out the house she was sitting on the porch with Ms. Gladys and caught my ass. I was so fuckin' embarrassed.

"It's too pretty to be in this fuckin' house." I spat. Tasha, Mia, and I were sitting outside on the porch kicking it. My kids were running around in the yard playing. I wanted to do something, but I didn't have any money. The first was in a few days. I had a welfare check coming that I couldn't wait to blow. I guess I had no choice but to suck it up and chill in the house because Labor Day Weekend was approaching and I'm in these streets with plans to bag an out of town boss. My kid's fathers always get them for the Holiday's and that's it. I didn't have to worry about a babysitter. It was a big boy Benz pulling up in front of the house. I licked my lips because I found my prey. I applied a little lip gloss to make my lips pop.

"Damn Mesha, who is that in the Maybach Benz that's just pulled up? Is that one of your new boo's," My girl Mia asked. He wasn't my boo yet, but he could potentially be next. I had one shot and I was for damn sure about to make it count. I started to walk passed the car just for the hell of it. I knew I had something he wanted.

"Maybe we're about to see." I beamed. I slapped hands with Mia and Tasha. Whoever this was I was about to pull them and get all up in their pockets. I need a wad full of cash. I might do some strange shit for some change. I stood up and dug my shorts out my ass and fixed my breasts in my tank top.

It was a bitch that stepped outside the car. Ugh, just my luck. I looked at Tasha and Mia and we both cut our eyes at each other. So much for a fuckin' come up. I had plans to fuck the shit out of whoever was pulling up in that. Maybe Mother Dear was buying some new life insurance. I know it wasn't DFACS doing a home visit. I don't even fuck with bitches that would report me. The closer the bitch got the more heated I got. I could tell who it was by the big ass smile on her face. Ugh, I can't stand Crimson. I hated her and that's a strong fuckin' word to use.

I used to make her life a living hell growing up, just because I couldn't stand her.

"Mesha bitch is that Crimson? Whose nigga did she fuckin' bag. You need to take notes. She's pushing a fuckin' Maybach Benz and it's a 2012 hoe." My girl Tasha beamed. My kids ran up to Crimson and gave her a hug. They loved her more than they loved me. Shit, they considered her as their mother. She took them to school every fuckin' day. She was the one to take them to get their shots. Everything a mother is supposed to do. She knew more about my kids than I did.

"We love and we miss you Crimson. We want you to come back home." They beamed. It made me sick to my stomach just to hear that much excitement in their voices for someone else other than their mother.

"Hey, Crimson, I see you girl." As soon as she hit the porch Mia and Tasha were acting like groupies and speaking and shit. Crimson ignored them. If you didn't fuck with her, she didn't fuck with you. She was cute I could never deny that good genes ran in our family, but the chain that sat on her neck with GRIFF spoke fuckin' volumes.

Oh, she's fuckin' with him heavy. I couldn't wait to tell Keondra. How was it possible that she could pull a nigga like Griff? She's not his fuckin' type at all.

"Bitches think they're all that because they're fuckin' the dope man. She's still dusty to me. Always have been and always will be." I laughed. Tasha and Mia slapped hands with me. I knew Crimson wouldn't say shit. She knew I would fuck her up. I heard her laugh too.

"See it's a difference between YOU and me. I ain't got to fuck nann nigga to get what the fuck I want. My talk game is relentless. Something you know nothing about. Learn how to talk before you come at me reckless. YOU got to fuck a nigga to get what you want. That's you hoe and don't ever forget that. Dusty never have I ever been that. Bitch, you know that. You're the same bitch that was wearing my dirty panties in case you forgot. He hasn't even sniffed or licked the pussy yet. When he does, you'll be the first bitch to know. When you speak on me, SPEAK FACTS BITCH." She argued. I stood up to my feet. How dare she tell a motherfucka I was wearing her dirty drawls. I was ready to beat her motherfuckin' ass.

I don't know who she thought she was, but she can get it today. I would snatch her fuckin' bald. Griff got her feeling herself. I'm the bitch that will bring her back to reality.

"Jermesha, what the fuck do you want to do bitch? I'm sick of you! Show out in front of your friends if you want too. I'll beat your ass in front of your kids. Try me. I'm begging you too. I don't fuck with you and you don't fuck with me. That's cool, but you ain't gone disrespect me period because the joke will be on you," she argued.

"Crimson, you want to show your ass now let's go lil bitch," I argued. I threw Tasha my phone. I kicked my flip flops off. I'm going to beat her ass today. I cocked my fist back. Crimson pushed me in my head with her fist. She caught me off guard. I stumbled and hit the rail on the porch. As soon as I tried to hit her back. Mother Dear and Uncle Tony ran outside. "Bitch, I'm going to kill you."

"I got your bitch Mesha, I'll treat you like one." She argued. She wanted to talk shit now because Mother Dear was saving her ass.

"What the fuck are y'all two yapping about on my fuckin porch? Crimson Rose, get your ass in the fuckin' house right now. Mesha, your friends got to fuckin' go right now. I know you weren't about to fight in front of your kids? Don't make a fuckin' scene at my fuckin' house. Get your own shit and you can clown there," Mother Dear argued.

"Mother Dear, she started with me I was minding my own business. She wanted to throw slick shots at me in front of her friends. I don't fuck with her and she doesn't fuck with me. It's been understood for years and I'm okay with that," she argued. I already know Mother Dear was about to take Crimson's side and uncle Tony too. I wish my momma was here to have my fuckin' back.

"Crimson and Mesha I don't give a fuck about none of that. Blood is thicker than water. I raised y'all two together. What's the fuckin issue? Y'all can agree to disagree but it ain't about to be no blows thrown on my fuckin' porch unless I'm the one passing out ass whooping's. Y'all can dead that shit right fuckin' now."

"Crimson, thinks she's better than people Mother Dear and it's your fault. It ain't my fault her mammy or daddy didn't want her.

She's messing with a man that has a little bit of money so now she wants to pop slick at the mouth." I laughed. Little did Crimson know she's a side chick and my bitch Keondra is Griff's main bitch. I got something for her ass. I can't touch her, but Keondra can. I got a few phone calls to make.

"You know what Mother Dear, I don't even know why I gave her any energy because she's mad. Mad for what Jermesha? My momma ain't shit just like your momma. Your daddy ain't shit just like my daddy.

So, we're even. The only difference is your mother stayed around to free load off Mother Dear and she still didn't do shit for you. The only time she did anything for you is when she wanted to shit on me. It's all good though. Mother Dear always made sure I was straight. So, if I got it, she got it, make no fuckin' mistake about that. I don't know my mother but nor do I give a FUCK. She said fuck me, so it's always FUCK HER. It's always FUCK YOU. You're just like your momma. You ain't shit and you never will be shit.

I'm not gone even waste my time arguing with a bitch that's beneath me, family or not. With or without him I got money. He can go today, and I'll be good. I don't depend on no nigga to feed me. I can feed my motherfuckin' self.

You know why because I go to work every day and I go to school full-time. So, I ain't never gone be broke, because I bust my ass to make sure I won't be.

I ain't got to sell my pussy to the highest bidder. I'm nobody's fuck. Oh, and I ain't never sucked a dick in front of my grandmother's house to pay my cell phone bill. I ain't never fucked a nigga in front of my grandmother's house and he busted a nut on my face and threw me out of the car. Yeah, I saw all of that. BITCH, you disgust me. When you call yourself digging a ditch for me hoe, dig three for your motherfuckin' self.

You and I aren't the same hoe. Don't get that shit confused. I BROKE the cycle bitch. YOU ARE STILL IN THE CYCLE DUMB ASS HOE," she argued. I tried to reach across Mother Dear and smack fire from her ass.

How dare she embarrass me in front of my fuckin' friends. Crimson Rose got me fucked up, she can count her last fuckin' days. Mother Dear ended up smacking me in my face. My kids started crying.

"Mesha, I told you ain't no licks being passed over here unless I'm passing them. I meant that shit. Crimson Rose, watch your gawd damn mouth. You ain't got to cuss to get your fuckin' point across. I'll beat both of y'all ass'. Try me and fuckin see. Pass another gawd damn lick. You threw your shots. Mesha, Crimson threw hers so shut the fuck up. I better not EVER catch you bussing it open in front of my house. If a nigga can't take you to a room to fuck, then he's not worthy of fucking. Get you a job Mesha to take care of you and your kids, because I want you out of my fuckin house.

Stop hoeing around. That shit gets old. You ain't doing nothing but putting extra miles on that pussy. It's only so much a douche and Kegel exercises can do. It's time for you to get off your ass and do something. Sucking dick for $30.00 or $40.00 ain't worth it. What the fuck can you do with that?" She asked. Crimson was laughing and smiling. I can't stand her.

"Mother Dear, why are you always taking up for her? You think she's perfect. She's not. She ain't a saint. She's giving it up just like everybody else. The only difference between her and I is that I'm real about my shit. If you think for one minute, she ain't fuckin' that nigga you're sadly mistaken. She ain't no better than me. She's sneaky as fuck. You mean to tell me she's driving a Maybach Benz and she's wearing this man's chain that she barely knows and she ain't fuckin' him? Guess what Crimson, you're a jump off because that niggas whose chain you're wearing has a main bitch and you ain't it." I argued and laughed. I had to give it to her one good time and rain on her fuckin' parade. Crimson started busting out laughing only making me even madder.

"Jermesha, I don't take up for neither one of y'all so don't start that shit. I treat you both the same. Always have and I always will. If Crimson is giving it up why do you care so much? Why do you have so much hate in your heart for your own fuckin' cousin? At least she has a car to fuckin' drive. Hell, you're still using your feet to get where the fuck you need to go. I met Griff and he's a good guy. I can vouch for that.

He isn't with Crimson for what's in between her legs. When was the last time you had a man that wanted you for you and not the pussy that you offering? You need to get your shit together Jermesha and I fuckin' mean it. If you're going to continue to stay here with your kids, you need a fuckin' job. I didn't raise you to be a hoe.

You need to pay rent and give me your fuckin' food stamp card because you're not selling shit next month. It's not my job to feed your kids, it's yours. Do I make myself clear? Whatever issues y'all have with each that shit ends right fuckin' here."

"Yes, ma'am." I sighed.

"I'm talking to you too Crimson." Mother Dear argued.

"Yes ma'am." Damn, if Mother Dear met Griff, they're fucking with each other heavy. I got to call Keondra asap. Mother Dear and my kids left with Crimson. Uncle Tony was looking at me in the door and he just shook his head.

"What are you looking at dead beat?" I asked. I couldn't stand Uncle Tony too.

"I'm looking at you dead beat. You're trouble just like your fuckin' momma. Jealousy doesn't look good on you. Get that hate out of your heart. Crimson ain't never did anything to you." I wasn't even about to argue with Uncle Tony. I'm sick of him. I can't believe Mother Dear hurt my feelings like that. I don't appreciate that at all. I know I need to do better if I could just find the right man. I grabbed my phone to call my mammy to see what she was up too. She answered on the third ring.

"What Jermesha," she yelled and ask. I put on the water works.

"Momma where you at? I need you." I cried.

"Jermesha, what's wrong with you," she asked. I had her attention now.

"Everything. Mother Dear and Crimson jumped me, and Uncle Tony helped them. Momma they beat my ass in front of my kids." I cried.

"Jermesha are you serious? Momma knows better than to do that shit. I know one thing you better beat Crimson's ass like I used to do her momma. I'm on my way. She got you fucked up. I'm going to watch you beat her ass." My mother hung up the phone. I would catch Crimson later without Mother Dear.

Keondra

I've been receiving a shit load of phone calls from a strange number for the past few days. I wanted to know who was calling my phone and not leaving a message. I gave my number to a few niggas in passing, but they weren't talking about shit. I was running through niggas left and right when I had the right nigga. I fucked up royally with Griff and I regret that shit every day. I couldn't talk on my phone for free. I needed a nigga with the same stance as him. I don't chat with niggas without any cash on demand. I don't know who it could be, but I refused to answer because I don't answer the phone for numbers that I don't know. I was curious to see who was calling my phone. It had to be somebody important because they kept calling. I sent a text message to the number to see if I could get a response.

404-688-3214 - What up? Who dis?

770-269-2219 - Keondra? It's me Jermesha call me it's an emergency bitch

I don't even fuck with Jermesha like that, so I'm curious to see why she's calling my phone? I decided to call her back to see what she wanted. We haven't spoken in months since her Tasha and Mia let somebody record me fuckin' Dre. How the fuck is y'all my girls and y'all let that shit go down? I fed those bitches when they couldn't feed themselves. It's crazy because Dre and I were fuckin' around for months, but somehow the tape made it to Griff.

I don't know who it was, but they ruined my fuckin' marriage. So, no I don't fuck with any of my old crew. I cut them, bitches, off. I felt they didn't mean me any good. Jermesha answered on the third ring. I was about to hang up. I wasn't trying to play phone tag with her. We've done enough of that.

"Keondra, bitch, I got something to tell you. Can you talk?" She asked. I knew something was up by the tone of her voice. I heard her clapping her hands in the background. I've never heard her sound so fuckin' serious.

"Yes, go ahead. What's wrong Mesha, is everything okay?" I asked. What did Jermesha have to tell me?

We haven't talked in months because of the bull shit that happened a few months ago and nobody told the truth about leaking my business. Real bitches do real things. When I got with Griff and he started breaking me off. I made sure all my girls were straight. Griff had it. Whenever he bussed down and gave me a few racks to blow, I made sure my girls were straight too.

"What's up with you and Griff? It's some shit going on, but I wasn't about to hit you with it until I had solid proof. I know we haven't spoken in a few months, but you're still my girl no matter what. I got your back forever and if some shit doesn't seem right, I'm going to tell you," she explained. Yeah right. Cut the bullshit and get straight to the point. You won't tell me who leaked the tape and it was from a bitch with a cheap ass phone. I know it was one of them.

My heart dropped instantly when she said Griff's name. I just knew he was fuckin' with somebody because all of my calls go unanswered and I can't get in touch with him at all. I wasn't about to lose my husband to no bitch period. I know I fucked up, but if I couldn't have him nobody could, and I meant that shit.

What happened to for better or for worse? Griff always claimed he never cheated on me, but I didn't believe him. Everybody wanted my husband. As soon as we broke up, I'm hearing about him. It wasn't going down like that at all.

"Griff and I are still together. We're still going through some shit, but it's still us against the world." I beamed and lied. I wouldn't dare tell Jermesha that Griff and I weren't together. Jermesha was a hoe and we did some dirt together. Griff would be free game for her. I wasn't ready to face my reality. I never thought the day would come when I would lose Griff. If I could help it that day wasn't coming at all.

"Bitch, I thought so. So, let me get straight to it. A few weeks ago, Tasha and I were at Spondivits on some late-night creep shit. We came up on a few wads of cash. Griff walked in with Crimson. I knew something was odd with that because she's not even his type but fuck all that. She was whipping his Benz afterwards.

To make matters worse she moved out of my grandmother's house and TODAY when she pulled up over here. She was whipping something different, a 2012 BENZ

MAYBACH with dealer tag. Girl she had a fuckin' chain on with his name on it.

I know for a fact he's breaking her off? My grandmother vouched that she had met him. Keondra what the fuck is going on?" My heart was beating fast. Griff got life fucked up if thinks he's about to move on and flaunt another bitch in my face. It's not going down like that at all.

"Crimson? Griff is fuckin' with your dusty ass cousin. Bitch, you a motherfuckin lie and it ain't April Fools hoe. Get the fuck off my phone with this clown ass shit Jermesha. What the fuck would Griff need with a goofy ass bitch like her? Jermesha, if you hooked your cousin up with my nigga, I swear to God I'm going to beat your ass," I argued and asked. I don't trust Jermesha.

"Keondra, bitch, you know me better than that? If I hooked her up with him, why would I tell you? I wish I was lying. Bitch, I saw him at Spondivits with her and the nigga didn't even speak. He looked at us like we were motherfuckin' crazy. Bitch, he was on some this is my woman type shit.

He knew I was gone run my mouth. I'm curious where did he meet her at? I had to call to put you up on game." She argued. She didn't have to tell me because we haven't spoken in a few months. Her loyalty should've been with her cousin, but it was with me.

"I appreciate that. I'm about to bust Griff in his shit, keep me posted. I know Crimson is your cousin, but Jermesha, on gawd that bitch gone see me soon behind HIM. Soon as in today. I don't play about him." I argued. I've never had to fight or check a bitch behind Griff but today it was going down. He's still my husband regardless of what the fuck we're going through.

"You know I got you because you're my girl. Fuck Crimson. Blood or not, my loyalty lies with you. You know I got the drop on her. Just let me know when you want to make a move and I'll give you whatever you want. She's not hard to find and she ain't no fighter. Check that bitch behind your man." She argued. I'm going to do more than check a bitch behind him. If Crimson and Griff think they can be together without any repercussions, they're sadly mistaken.

His momma tried to interfere with us and for that reason alone I sent her to her maker. The worst thing Griff can do is wake up the beast in me. It ain't no breaking up. It's until death do us apart. If I killed his momma behind him, I won't hesitate to kill a bitch or kill him.

"I appreciate that. What are you doing later? I'll have to treat you to lunch and Mani and Pedi. It's my treat since you put me up on game." I beamed. Jermesha just don't know what the fuck she has started. I was in the dumps earlier but now I'm own my good bull shit.

"Girl nothing, I don't have any plans. I'm down. Just let me know what time I need to be ready?" She asked. Just like a broke bitch, no plans. I could use Jermesha. She'll be responsible for her cousin's downfall and death.

"I'll be through there by 4:00 p.m." I finished talking to Jermesha. I knew Griff was up to some shit that's why I haven't heard from him. I even stopped by the Trap a few days ago. Griff nor Rashad was there. Dre and Slap were both there. I almost shitted bricks when I saw Dre there. I just knew he was about to beat my ass. I thought he wasn't working with Griff anymore. I was so fuckin' nervous.

I shouldn't have fucked Dre. The crazy thing about it was that on the video, Dre's face was never shown just mine.

Griff didn't know who I was fuckin'. He knew I fucked somebody because my face was shown, and he heard my moans. I was so fuckin' humiliated. Speaking of Dre, he was calling my phone right now. I liked Dre at first, but I didn't know he worked for Griff. If I would've known that I would've never given him the pussy. Dre was tight with his cash, he was bussing down with cash for real. I was still spending Griff's money.

"Hello," I cooed.

"What's up with that pussy? I haven't heard from you in a few days. Let me find out you're trying to slide back in with Griff. I swear I'm going to hurt your ass Keondra," he argued. I looked at my phone. I knew he was tripping for real. You are not my man. I fucked him one too many times.

"Dre, did you forget that I was still married to him? Why would I leave Griff for you? You can't even provide for me. Every time I ask you for something it's no. So why would I fuck you for free? Unless you got some money to put in my pockets, I don't have any conversation for you." I argued. I hung up in his face. I wasn't about to argue with him.

Chapter-11

Crimson

I couldn't wait to get home to tell Danielle about my day. I couldn't even enjoy my lunch date with Mother Dear and Jermesha kids because that shit was heavy on my mind. I can't believe my own fuckin' cousin has so much fuckin' hate for me. I haven't talked to Griff all day. I missed him like crazy. Griff was right about her all along. Jermesha was salty as fuck. We ain't never been cool but we've never come to blows either. I knew she was jealous of me, but today it really showed. She wanted to fight me in front of her friends.

I ain't been nothing but good to her and all she has ever done was give me her ass to kiss. I wasn't about to let her keep disrespecting me either. I'm sick of it. I've been silent long enough. She ain't got to like me but she's going to respect me. She had the nerve to throw cheap shots at me about my mother and father. I'm used to it, but that shit doesn't bother me anymore. I'm not the same little girl that would cry about her mother never returning home.

"Crimson Rose Tristan, I'm so surprised at you."
She argued and shook her head in disbelief. "You know
better than to stoop down to Jermesha's fuckin' level. I'm
really surprised at you," she argued. I knew this
conversation was far from over. I tried my best to ignore
her. "I know you hear me fuckin' talking to you? Since
when did you start to ignore me when we're having a
conversation?" She argued. I didn't want to talk about it
anymore.

"Mother Dear I'm not ignoring you. I'm tired and I
don't want to talk about Jermesha in front of her kids. I
know I'm wrong, but it's only so much I can fuckin' take.
Excuse my language but why do I always have to be the
bigger person? I've let her get away with it for years. I'm
sick of it. I don't bother anybody, but she was coming for
me hard." I explained. Mother Dear turned up the music.

"They're asleep so now is the perfect time to talk
about it. I know how messy she can be Crimson, but never
stoop to anybody's level, if they're not on your level. I've
always told you that. Baby if it ain't directed it ain't
respected.

Jermesha is just like her mother and I know you don't want to hear it, but you're just like your mother in a lot of ways too. History has a way of repeating itself. People hate you because they ain't you. Next time just laugh that shit off. What's up with you and Griff, Crimson?

You have a glow to your face that says you've been fucked? I like this Maybach Benz you're driving. Honey this is the reason why Jermesha is mad?" She asked and laughed. Mother Dear is the queen of shade and she just drained all the life out of my face. Why did she have to go there?

"Griff and I are good and no we haven't taken it there yet. Mother Dear why do you always assume the worst? Why is she mad at me? She's had plenty of good men. She just fucked them over?" I guess the saying is true, you don't miss a good thing until it's gone. It ain't my fault she wanted to be a hoe and juggle multiple men.

"Good but you better be careful Crimson because you're in heat and it's written all over your face. I had a dream about fish a few nights ago and it wasn't the plates I order from Maxine's. I made sure Jermesha got her tubes tied but you, on the other hand you're able to reproduce."

She explained. I gave Mother Dear the side eye. Here she goes jinxing me again. Damn, I'm scared to have sex now. She's having dreams and shit about fish. Griff ain't gone never get this pussy. I don't want a baby.

"Trust me, I'm going to be careful. I'm scared to take it there because I don't want to get pregnant. It's safe to say I'll be waiting." I explained.

"Crimson there's nothing wrong with having kids. You're a grown ass woman and you'll be a wonderful mother so stop doing that." She explained. Mother Dear and I finished talking. I pulled up to her house and walked the kids in. Jermesha was nowhere in sight. I kissed Mother Dear on her cheek and headed back to my spot. I had so much shit on my mind. The moment things start to change for me a whole lot of other bullshit appears.

I finally made it home and Danielle was sitting on the couch playing with her phone. I tossed my keys on the counter. I grabbed a seat right next to Danielle and laid my head on her shoulder. She looked at me with wide eyes.

"What's wrong with you, bitch?" She asked. I already knew she was about to go in.

"Everything. I almost had to beat Jermesha ass. She was trying to show out in front of Tasha and Mia. She accused me of fuckin' Griff because I'm driving his car and rocking his chain. She said I was his side bitch and he had a main chick." I argued. Danielle stood up from the couch and slid her feet in her shoes. I knew it was about to go down.

"Girl fuck her. That bitch is jealous as fuck. You should've beat her ass. Ugh, I can't stand her trifling ass. If you were fuckin' Griff, why is she so worried about it? She probably wanted him. She couldn't pull a nigga like him on her worst day. He deserves the pussy if you ask me. I can't wait until you decide to give it to him." She argued. Danielle was team Griff all day.

"It's crazy. She's really feeling some type of way, but I had to let her have it. I couldn't let that bitch slide today."

"You should've been checked her. I told you to check that hoe a long time ago and you wouldn't have to check that hoe again. Cousin or not. Don't ever let that bitch play you. As much as you do for her kids, she has her fuckin' nerve." She argued. "I feel like driving over there right now to beat her ass."

"Trust me I know," I sighed. I needed a nap. I haven't heard from Griff all day. I grabbed my phone out my purse to call him. I had four missed calls from him. Somehow my phone ended up on silent. I called him back to see what he was up too.

"What's up Ms. Lady, I've been calling you for the past hour. What's up with you?" He asked. I swear just hearing from him makes my fucked-up day a better day.

"I know my phone was on silent. I don't know how that happened. I'm about to take a shower and go to sleep." I yawned.

"No don't do that. My cousin is having her birthday party tonight. I want you and Danielle to fall through," he stated. Griff knows I don't party, but for him, I'll make an appearance.

"Okay. So, where's the birthday party? What's the dress code? I'll ask Danielle if she wants to come."

"It's at Central Station. It's an all-white affair. I copped you something at the mall earlier. I need you to match my fly. You can come to the house to get dressed." He explained. A true boss.

"Okay. I'll see you in a few." Griff and I hung up the phone with each other. I bit my bottom lip just thinking about him. Tonight might be the night.

"Danielle, Griff's cousin is having a party at Central Station he wants us to come. Are you down? It's an all-white affair." I beamed.

"Hell, yeah I'm down let me get dressed, so I can see if I can snag me a boss." Danielle and I slapped hands with each other. I already knew she was about to show out. Ugh, he should've told me this earlier I would've done my hair. I guess I'll have to get dolled up. Who told him to pick out some clothes for me? I wish Griff would've given me the head up earlier about this party. My hair was a mess and it needed to be tamed.

I jumped in the shower and washed my hair while I was inside. I needed a deep conditioner bad. I handled my hygiene and deep conditioned my scalp. I stepped out the shower and dried off.

I blow dried my hair out. I hated applying heat to my hair but oh well. I flat ironed my hair bone straight. It turned out good. Danielle beat my face with a nude lip and a little gold eye shadow to make my eyes pop. I stood back to admire Danielle's attire. My best friend was KILLING IT like I knew she would. She had on some cut up white jeans that were fitted. They accentuated her curves with the matching white vest. Her breasts sat up, so she didn't need a bra. Danielle's hair was styled into a Mo-hawk with blonde tips. White Christian Louboutin adorned her feet with silver rhinestones.

"Danielle, you look so pretty." I beamed.

"Thank you! You know when I step out, I step the fuck out. I'm looking for prey. I can only imagine what Griff got you," she beamed and smiled. "If he was smart, he'll get you a thong and a bra and make it easy access to that pussy." I gave Danielle a smug look. Her mouth is too reckless for me. We locked up our place and headed to Griffs. I couldn't wait to see him.

Chapter-12

Griff

Tonight was my cousin Maria's Birthday Bash and it was going down at Central Station. I should've told Crimson earlier, but she wasn't answering the phone. I meant what I said the other night. I didn't want to lay by myself if we were together. I got an alert to my phone the gate went up. It was Crimson because Rashad already made it. As soon as I heard the garage go up. My face lit up instantly I couldn't wait to see my baby. Rashad and Crimson haven't met yet. This would be their first-time meeting. As soon as I heard the door knob turn, I got excited. I had to meet Crimson half way. I missed her ass something serious today. I pulled Crimson in for a hug. She wrapped her arms around my neck.

"You smell good and I missed you. What's up Danielle?"

"Hey Griff, what's up!" I picked Crimson up and carried her upstairs to our bedroom so she could get dressed. I had to introduce Danielle and Rashad to each other. I didn't want them around each other, and it'll be awkward. We entered the living room. Rashad was sitting on the couch messing with his phone.

"Aye Rashad, this is Crimson's best friend Danielle. Danielle, this is my right-hand man Rashad." I explained. Rashad looked up and Danielle looked at him with so much hate and venom. I got to ask him what was that about?

"Griff, we don't need an introduction," she argued. "Okay." Crimson looked at Danielle and their eyes had a conversation between themselves.

"Danielle, are you straight?" I asked.

"I'm good Griff. I just wish I would've gotten the heads up, but it's cool. One clown could never stop my show," she laughed. Rashad didn't even say anything. Crimson and I made our way upstairs. I couldn't keep my hands off her. I had to keep my ears open in case anything popped off. I tossed Crimson on the bed and pulled her clothes off and hovered over her. She was beautiful as fuck.

"Stop Griff. You're going to mess up my hair and make-up." She pouted. She didn't need it anyway.

"I don't care. I can get it fixed." I argued. Crimson tried to raise up. I wouldn't get up.

"You know you're not going home tonight right," I asked.

"I know, but Griff what about Danielle?" she asked.

"She can stay here. The house is big enough or we can take her home if she doesn't want to stay here." I grabbed Crimson's hand and led her to the closet. Versace was my favorite designer. I had to grab her something to match my fly. I told Maria we were coming through. She knew of Crimson through Mother Dear, but she didn't know her personally.

"Griff, you didn't have to buy me this dress. You don't even know my size," she argued. Little did she know I spoke with Mother Dear earlier and she gave me her size.

"I know more than you'll ever know. Let's get dressed so we can get out of here. What's up with Danielle and Rashad?"

"Oh Griff, it's a long story. He's your right-hand man and you don't know? Ask him. Its three sides to every story. His, hers and the truth. I wish you would've given me the heads up. I never met him until today, but they got history that isn't pretty." She explained. Crimson was getting dressed on her side of the bathroom.

She slid into her Versace dress and swallowed it. She knelt to slide her heels on, and I had to adjust my dick. I brought her a bracelet to match her necklace. I finished putting my clothes on and was waiting on Crimson to finish up. She turned around to face me.

"Hey handsome, I'm ready. What about you?" she asked. Crimson had the biggest smile on her face.

"I'm ready beautiful." I grabbed Crimson's hand and secured the bracelet around her wrist and fastened it.

"What's this for Griff?" she asked.

"It's the bracelet that matches your necklace."

"Thank you." I nodded my head acknowledging what she said. I grabbed her hand and we headed down stairs.

Rashad was sitting on one end of the couch and Danielle was on the other end with her head stuck in her phone. I could feel the tension between the two of them. I got to see what the fuck Rashad did. I've been telling my nigga for years to quit handling females like hoes because that shit will bite him in the ass in the end.

"Come on let's roll." My driver was already outside waiting on us. Crimson and Danielle walked ahead of me and Rashad. I had to stop him and see what was up.

"What the fuck happened between you and Danielle? Why you didn't tell me you knew shawty's best friend? I'm trying to hook you up with her, but you already done fucked up any future chances." I argued. Rashad looked at me and laughed.

"Griff chill out for real. I fucked up and can't change that. How the fuck do you think I feel? You put me on the spot, and I didn't need any light shining on me. I did care about shawty despite how she may feel, but sometimes I got to jugg a female with no explanation. You know how that shit goes. I don't be trying to get attached. I should've known something was up when we pulled up on that street man. It's a small world.

I never thought I would run into her again. I had no plans on it." Rashad and I finished our conversation and headed out to the truck with Crimson and Danielle.

In all my twenty-five years of living, I've never heard Rashad admit that he cared about anyone. I'm looking at my nigga sideways now. It's more to the story than he cared to indulge on. I need the full story. This conversation is far from over. I know seeing Danielle tonight fucked him up. I would've never placed them in the room with each other if it was bad blood between the two of them. I owe Danielle an apology. I'm not a fuck nigga and I would've never made her feel uncomfortable because I didn't know. I wanted her to come with Crimson because she didn't know my people. I wanted her to be comfortable so why not bring Danielle, so she could move around freely.

Rashad and I opened the back door to the Escalade, and it got quiet all of a sudden. I knew Crimson and Danielle were talking about us. Rashad and I took our seats behind them.

"Are y'all done talking about us?" I asked. Danielle and Crimson busted out laughing. Danielle spoke up.

"Griff, Crimson was talking about you. I wasn't talking about anybody. Rashad ain't shit to talk about." She laughed. Rashad looked at me and shook his head. Crimson turned around in her seat and faced Danielle.

"Really Danielle, that's how you're giving it up," she asked and laughed. Danielle busted out laughing.

"Yep." Danielle smiled.

"Oh yeah Crimson, what I do? You don't ever have to talk behind my back. I want you to speak on how you feel." I explained. Crimson didn't say anything. I popped the top on a bottle of Ace of Spades. I knew Crimson didn't drink but I wanted her to at least take a sip. I handed Danielle and Crimson both a champagne flute. Crimson turned around to face me. I could tell she was about to say something smart. I cut her off instantly. I covered her lips with my mouth.

"Look I know you don't drink, but I want you to at least take a sip for me."

"Okay," she pouted. Danielle started clapping her hands. I heard her clear her throat. I knew she was about to say something.

"That's what the fuck I'm talking about Griff put her in her place." Danielle laughed.

"I want to make a toast. Cheers to a new beginning Crimson Rose Tristan."

"I'll definitely make a toast to that Griff." Danielle stated. She was petty as fuck. She refused to give Rashad a toast. Damn, she's giving it to my nigga raw. I like Danielle. She's cool as fuck. She would've been good for him. The ride to the club was cool and we were vibing. It wasn't as bad as I thought it would be. Crimson and Danielle were doing their own thing. I could tell Rashad was a little hot by Danielle's actions but that was on him.

We finally made it to Central Station. It was thick. My driver pulled us up front and let us out. I grabbed Crimson's hand and we walked straight through the VIP line. Maria had a VIP section and ours was right beside hers. I didn't mind chilling with my cousin on her birthday, but I needed my own space. Crimson was following close behind me.

We made it to Maria's VIP Section. I dapped up a few of my cousins and introduced them to Crimson. They hit it off good. Crimson wasn't hood rich like Keondra. She was well reserved. I loved that about her. She wanted something out of life, and I was going to die giving it to her. My Aunt BeBe nodded her head in approval of Crimson. Aunt Kaye, she was my father's sister. Maria, Crimson and Danielle gave each other hugs as if they've known each other for years. I didn't know Maria knew Crimson. I pulled Crimson away from them and wrapped my arms around her waist. She looked up at me and smiled.

"Why you didn't tell me Maria was your cousin?" She asked and laughed.

"I don't know. When I ordered Mother Dear's food a few weeks ago, she knew who she was. I didn't know you knew her. It's a small world baby. I ain't never seen you up through there though. I would've been done pulled up on you. You would've been mine years ago. You probably would have a few of my babies by now." I explained. Crimson smiled at me I leaned in and gave her a kiss. I didn't give a fuck where we were.

She was mine and I wanted every nigga and bitch to know that. When they see her in the streets, they automatically knew she was off limits.

"She went to school with us. She was always cool with me and Danielle. We played Volley Ball together in Middle and High School." She beamed.

"That's what's up. Volley Ball huh?" I asked.

"Yep." I grabbed Crimson's hand and led her to our VIP Section. On our way out Keondra, Jermesha, Tasha and Mia were approaching Maria's VIP section. Keondra locked eyes with me. I didn't even acknowledge her. I dared her to say something or step out of place. She knew not to show her ass because I would put her in her fuckin' place. She fucked up, not me. Crimson wouldn't even be in the picture if she didn't cheat.

Until this day she still denies it. Come on now I know how you look and I'm real familiar with your moans. I just want to know who the pussy ass nigga was she was fuckin behind my back. I knew she would die seeing me with Crimson, but I wasn't even doing this shit out of spite. She better get used to this because Crimson wasn't going anywhere.

"Keondra you ain't gone say shit," Jermesha yelled. I cleared that shit up quick.

"What is she going to say? She knows what it is." I argued. Jermesha, Mia, and Tasha cocked their heads back looking at Keondra for an explanation. "You heard what the fuck I said, and Keondra doesn't want me to repeat my fuckin' self," I argued. They can move around with all this clown ass shit. I'm not the nigga for it. Crimson's body jerked. She gave her cousin an evil glare. I could tell she got heated quickly. I could tell it was about to be some shit. I heard Danielle yell. I looked over my shoulder to see what she had to say.

"I wish a bitch would. I will DONKEY KONG all four of you hoes. Y'all bitches know how I give it up." She argued. I grabbed Crimson and wrapped my arms around her waist. I didn't want her entertaining any of them. I looked back at Rashad giving him a stern look to get Danielle.

"Don't fuckin' touch me. I'm good nigga. Griff don't do that, please don't. His rights have been revoked months ago. Find another nigga that can grab me. ANYBODY but HIM." She argued. Danielle was wild as fuck. She was trying my nigga for sure. She was getting the best of him too. It was written all on his face. We finally made it to our VIP section. I pulled Crimson on to my lap. I had to see what was up with her. She had her arms folded across her chest. I whispered in her ear.

"What's wrong with you? You're too beautiful to have a frown on your face." I asked then stated.

"Nothing, I'm just sick of Jermesha trying me and everybody expects me to be the bigger person," she sighed and pouted.

"What I tell you about that Crimson? Fuck Jermesha. I told you she was jealous of you. You're a Queen shawty. Don't ever come off your throne to address a rat. Cousin or not, if she touches you rock her ass to sleep and I mean that shit literally. I don't give a fuck."

I care about Crimson a lot and normally I don't get into females' business but Jermesha wasn't Keondra's friend. She tried to offer me the pussy on numerous occasions, but I never took the bait. She can't do shit for me.

"I hear you, Griff." She sighed.

"I hope your listening," I whispered and bit her earlobe. Keondra stood outside of my VIP looking in trying to get my attention. I had security on the outside. She wasn't allowed to come near me. The only thing she could do at this point was to sign the divorce papers. I wanted to move on like her and spoil the fuck out of Ms. Tristan, that's it. I don't have any conversation for her.

Keondra wasn't about to ruin my night at all. I don't give two fucks about the crocodile tears. I could see that shit from afar. That shit didn't move me at all. She cheated. That's some shit she must deal with. It's Maria's birthday and I had too much to be thankful for. I found a woman that's on my level mentally and she wants me for me and not what I have. Crimson didn't run the streets and I was infatuated by that.

She went to school and had a job. She didn't need me to provide for her. **Futures Ain't No Way Round It** came on. Crimson and Danielle got up and started dancing. Crimson had too much ass for me not stand behind her and catch it. I wasn't about to watch her bounce that ass from afar. All eyes were on us as soon as we entered the building.

A bitch gone be a bitch

A hoe gone be a hoe

A killer gone be a killer

That's sum thin' you need to know

Ain't no way around it, ain't no way around it

Rashad passed me the bottle of the Ace of Spade. I took a big gulp and passed it back to him. I wasn't trying to get too fucked up, because I had my baby with me. I was all up on Crimson. She was the only thing in this room that had my attention. My partner D-man tapped me on my shoulder. He whispered some bullshit in my ears. D-Man was my muscle.

I knew I felt a pair of eyes on me earlier. I didn't play that shit no mind. He pointed in the opposite direction. It was Keondra. She was crying and shit. I swear I'm not beat for her shit. I whispered in Crimson's ear and told her I was going to the bathroom.

I dipped off through the cut. I didn't want Crimson to see me arguing with Keondra. As soon as I exited my VIP and headed to the bathroom. I knew she would follow me, and she did. As soon as I opened the bathroom door. I felt a pair of tiny hands on my arm. I looked over my shoulder to see what was up. I gave her a mean ass scowl.

"Griff," she cried. I hated to see Keondra cry but she's not my problem anymore.

"What's up with you? Why are you crying and don't lie and say that shit is because of me because it ain't?" I argued. Keondra was making a scene and I didn't need that shit at all. Motherfuckas are looking at me crazy like I'm a dog ass nigga and that's not me.

"Why are you cheating on me with her? Does she know about me," she asked and cried?

"Keondra, you and I aren't together, and you know that. I'm not cheating on you. Yes, she knows about you. She knows you're my ex and you cheated. What more does she need to know? Crimson and I are together. I need you to move around. Our divorce will be final next week. It ain't no more you and me." I explained.

"Are we really over Griff?" She asked and cried. Keondra knew damn well it was over between us. I backed her into the wall because she was drawing too much fuckin' attention to me. I had to hurry up and get this shit over it. I couldn't disrespect Crimson by even entertaining this shit.

"Keondra, don't do that. We were over the moment you decided to give yourself to another man and let him record you fuckin' him. You stepped out on our marriage Keondra. You gave that nigga some shit that was supposed to belong to me. If you weren't happy you should've let me know, but you wanted to sneak around and fuck another nigga behind my back. How do you think I felt? You didn't give two fucks about me? I gave you everything. I gave you my last name and the keys to the range. Until this day you're still lying and denying the shit. I'm happy Keondra and I can't thank you enough for fuckin' up.

I'm not even trying to make you jealous Keondra, but Crimson is everything you ain't. I thank God every day for her. I love waking up to her. My mother tried to warn me about you, but I wasn't trying to hear that shit. I went against my mother because I loved you. I learned a lot of lessons fuckin' with you, but I just received the biggest blessing because of you." I argued and explained. I had to break it down to her.

"You don't mean that Griff. So, you mean to tell me you're willing to throw away what we have and built for a bitch you just met?" She argued and cried.

"Keondra stop all of that fuckin' crying. You threw us away when you fucked another nigga. Did you forget? I'm not about to do this with you. I got to go. I gave you too much time already." I moved passed Keondra. She was grabbing on my shirt and I brushed her off me.

"Don't leave Griff," she yelled and cried. I refused to turn around and even acknowledge her. She has embarrassed me enough. I made my way back to my VIP section. I was missing Crimson like crazy. I didn't see her or Danielle in sight. Rashad, D-Man, Dre were posted up smoking. I approached them to see what was up.

"Where's Crimson?" I asked. Rashad pointed to Maria's VIP section and started laughing at me.

"Damn Griff, shawty got you gone. Let her breath a little bit." He laughed.

"Fuck you, nigga! I got your medicine. Danielle my nigga. Don't make me have shawty clown you." I laughed. Rashad's smile instantly turned into a frown. He knew he fucked up good with her. I headed over to Maria's VIP and pulled Crimson into my arms. I whispered in her ear.

"I thought you dipped on me? I was about to go crazy." Crimson looked up at me.

"I should've. You were gone to the bathroom for a long ass time. I figured you had some business to handle and I don't smile up in niggas faces, so we moved around." She explained.

"Yeah, I did, I'm sorry about that. On the real Crimson, if you would've left me, I would've found you. I can't let you roam around without me. Let me know when you're ready to clear it and we can take it in."

Keondra

I can't believe Griff played me like that. He was so fuckin' disrespectful bringing her to Maria's party to meet his fuckin' family and our divorce isn't finalized. I was hoping and praying the things Jermesha told me wasn't true, but they were. It hurts so much seeing him with her. It made me sick to my stomach. It was supposed to be me on his arms and not her. It's a little too soon for him to have her out in the open. We've only been separated for four months. I love him. I know I fucked up, but I am sorry.

Why couldn't he forgive me? It wasn't supposed to go down like this at all. He embarrassed the fuck out of me. I couldn't stop the tears from falling. Each word I spoke I felt my heart cave in. Reality has finally set in. Griff wasn't forgiving me. Auntie Kaye was giving me evil glares. She looked at me with disgust. I knew Griff told them about me cheating on him. Our business was in the streets heavy. Everybody knew he left me and Crimson being on his arm confirmed all the rumors that were buzzing.

Everybody was looking at me crazy. I'm fighting for my marriage in front of all these people and he couldn't even console me. I had to swallow my throw up when he said she was his blessing. More like his fuckin' downfall. If Griff thinks he can be with Crimson without me saying shit, he's sadly mistaken. I will be that niggas downfall. I know everything about him.

I will call the FEDS right now and make sure that nigga gets a life fuckin' sentence. I wish I wouldn't have brought Jermesha, Tasha, and Mia here. I should've left them hoes right on Jermesha's granny's porch. I went to the bathroom to dry my face and fix my makeup. I had to get myself together quick. My eyes are puffy and red. Thank God I had some eye drops. The bathroom door opened, and it was Tasha, Maria, and Jermesha. I rolled my eyes I couldn't stand the sight of them.

"Keondra, where have you fuckin' been? We've been looking all over for you? What's going on with you and Griff? Why didn't you say anything when you saw them? I wanted you to beat Crimson's ass." She argued and asked. I couldn't believe Jermesha.

If she would turn on her own family, I knew she wouldn't hesitate to turn on me. She didn't ask if I was okay. She wanted to be nosey. Jermesha talks too fuckin' much. I would've never given her the truth.

"Griff and I are on a break right now. He can have his little fun with Crimson, it's cool. I know I fucked up, but I'm still in his pockets. Trust me he's not throwing away four years for an easy fuck." I argued. I had to pump myself up.

"I know that's right bitch." Jermesha and Mia said in unison. We slapped hands with each other. I don't know what they thought this was. I wasn't going out like a weak ass bitch. I checked the mirror one last time to make sure I was on point. I couldn't give them the real. I don't trust them for some reason. I know they set me up. I just had to prove it. I don't fuck with anybody like that. They were the only ones that knew I had a little friend.

"Come on, I'm about to buy out the bar on Griff and send Crimson a drink." I laughed.

"Let the games begin. That's what the fuck I'm talking about Keondra, show Crimson how a real bitch balls out," Jermesha argued. We walked out of the bathroom and headed to the bar. It was a lot of niggas in attendance with some money. It was about to go down in a few hours for Shower Hour. I couldn't wait to see what niggas in here who were about to really make it rain. I saw a few niggas from the Westside that was racked up.

One in particular that caught my eye. Baine Mahone. He raped me with his eyes. The stare itself was lustful and intense. I ran my tongue across my lips. I wanted to taste him. He threw his hand up telling me to come here. We always flirt with each other when we see each other, but we never act on it. I wanted to be a freak for him. One night with him wouldn't be enough for me.

"You know where to find me," I yelled and kept walking. I could feel him looking when I kept walking. I put an extra little pep in my step. He wanted to act on this thing we got going on, now would be the time.

"Keondra, if you don't give that nigga Baine some play, bitch I fuckin' will. He's been trying to get at you for the longest," Mia beamed. I laughed it off and kept walking to the bar. We finally made it to the bar. It was crowed, so I pushed a few bitches out my way. I needed a few drinks. I couldn't keep my eyes off Griff's VIP room. He was happy and I hated it.

"What are y'all drinking?" I asked. They gave me their orders. Bitches ain't never got no money, but always want to party and bullshit. I ordered Crimson a bloody Mary and sent it to her. I should've sent Griff a bottle too. The bartender came back with my card.

"We need another form of payment the card issuer said do not honor." She cut the card up in front of me. Oh, that shit really pissed me off. Griff was with the shit for real, thank God I had some cash on me. I gave the bartender cash to pay for our drinks. I loved Griff don't get me wrong, but I stole money from his ass for years. I don't even regret doing it now since he's being a bitch about, shit.

Every week I went is his shoe box and grabbed $10,000.00 out. The bartender came out with our drinks we were sipping on. I watched her deliver Crimson her drink. The bartender pointed at me. I raised my glass up. Crimson has a smug look on her face and raised her glass at me. Little did she know the game was on and I'm raising the stakes. I'm playing for keeps behind Griff.

She'll see and he will too. He wasn't even trying to work shit out. I felt somebody walk up behind me and slide their hands between my legs. He was finger fuckin' the shit out of me. Thank God I didn't have any panties on. His cologne invaded my nostrils. I was scared to turn around. I prayed it was him when he whispered in my ear.

"I know where to find you huh? That pussy ready for a nigga huh," I came all on his hands.

Chapter-13

Danielle

Never in a million years would I think I would run into Rashad again. I swear it's a small world. I always thought about what I would say if were to see him again. What are the chances Griff and Rashad are best friends? Fuck my life. My heart dropped when I saw him, and we locked eyes with each other. His eyes poured into my soul, but he didn't have a hold on me anymore. The feeling of heart break pierced through my heart again. I fuckin' hate him and that's a strong word to use. I didn't even mean to show my ass in front of Griff, but Rashad knew what it was between us. It's all good though. You live and you learn. I couldn't even shed any more tears over a nigga that wasn't worth it. I'm all cried out.

"Danielle, are you ready? We're about to get out of here," she explained.

"Yes, I'm ready." I beamed. One of my cuddy buddies was in the club so I wasn't riding back home with them. It was just my luck Crimson and Griff were ready to go, and Baine made his way to the VIP section to come and get me. He approached me and grabbed my hand.

"Hey Ms. Lady, are you ready to get up out of here," he asked? I nodded my head in agreement.

"Let me tell my girl I'm about to head out of here." I walked over to Crimson and Griff.

"Hey Crimson, I'm about to ride out with Baine I'll see you tomorrow okay." I smiled.

"Alright be easy and text me when you make it to your destination hot ass," she stated.

"I will." I tip toed back over to Baine because my feet were killing me in these shoes. I couldn't wait to take them off. I heard someone yell my name. It sounded familiar. I heard them yell my name again.

"Danielle, I know you hear me fuckin' talking to you." He yelled. I looked over my shoulder to see who it was. It was Rashad. I rolled my eyes. I hear you talking to yourself.

"Nigga please," I mumbled. I didn't want Baine to hear me. I started walking fast I almost fell. I don't know what that nigga was up too. I wasn't trying to find out either. He hasn't said shit to me all night. As soon as you see me leaving with a nigga that's not you. You want to show out. Miss me with that bullshit for real.

"Danielle you're walking slow as hell. Come on and get on my back. I know you want a nigga to carry you? I need to mob out of here quick. I parked in the back." Baine knelt so he could put me on his back. All eyes were on us when we were headed out. Jermesha and her little friends were mugging me on the way out, especially Keondra. I stared her down with a smirk on my face. I wish a bitch would. I owe her anyway for sending Crimson a drink.

"Whatever," I mumbled. Baine is a cool as nigga from the Westside. He's sexy as fuck with dark chocolate skin and his dreads hung down his back. His eyes were the color of Hennessy. His swag was on a thousand. He was a True Religion junky. We've been kicking it for a few months. I like him but I haven't given him the pussy yet. He does his thing and I do mine. I can't see me giving myself to someone if we're not committed. I know all niggas ain't Rashad, but I had to be sure. I was surprised when he hit me up and said he saw me in the club, and he asked me to meet him at the bar. He was whispering all kinds of good shit in my ear. We both had feelings for each other but refused to act on it.

He was heavy in the streets, so a female wasn't a part of the equation or coming first. I wasn't rocking with that. I couldn't give a nigga my all anymore if he was willing to only give me half of him. I wasn't looking for a relationship. Neither one of wanted to commit to anyone. We finally made it Baines car. He was a flashy ass nigga. He had a Black 2 door Maserati parked in the back. He knew I hated riding in this car because he drives too damn fast. He let me down off his back after he felt me up a few times. Every time he touches me, I get the chills. My hands landed on his chest and we were in a stare down.

"Watch yourself." I sassed.

"And if I don't," he asked?

"Ain't no free feels over here." Baine closed the space in between us. We were mouth, to mouth with each other. I could smell the liquor and weed on his breath. He pressed my body up against his car. My heart was beating fast as hell. He was so fuckin' aggressive.

"I'll back up off you because you and I both know you're not ready for a nigga like me. I'll take you down through there Danielle." He explained and bit my bottom lip. I know he will and that's what I'm afraid of. I don't even know why I agreed to come with him. I wanted to give myself to him, but I know it'll complicate things. The last thing I need is to complicate us.

"Yeah, whatever." I mumbled. Baine eased up off me. Finally, I was able to catch my breath. He opened the passenger side door for me. He made sure I was locked in safely. He jogged to the driver's side and we pulled off. I noticed he kept stealing glances at me. I was blushing.

"Why are you looking at me like that?" I asked. Baine and I were cool and there were no secrets between us. We could talk about whatever with each other. I wanted to know what was up with him. He was acting different. I wasn't used to this coming from him because we agreed to stay friends.

"You really want to know Danielle Cooper?" He asked. Anytime he called me by my government I knew he was serious. I turned around to face him to see what was up. Baine was acting differently.

"I do." He looked at me mysteriously. He grabbed my hand and squeezed it.

"What the fuck were you doing with Griff and his niggas? You fuckin' with one of them or something?" He asked. I looked at Baine like he was crazy. What would make him think that? If I was fuckin' with one of them, why should it matter? We're just friends and last I checked I haven't crossed those boundaries.

"If you got something that you want to ask me just say it; don't beat around the bush?" I asked. He snarled his face up and was swerving through the parking lot. He had the windows down where everybody could see us.

"Danielle, I peeped you before you peeped me tonight. I saw Griff was with your girl, but that nigga Rashad had his eyes were on you all night. I watched that nigga watch you. I heard him call your name when we were leaving. So, what's up with that? I never knew you fucked with him?" He asked. Okay, what the fuck is going on here? How was he able to observe all of that and why?

"Baine, what are we doing? I don't question you about your chicks. I saw you up in Keondra's ear, but I didn't say shit, because I know what it is with us. Why are you watching me? We're just friends. I don't fuck with Rashad or anybody in Griff's crew. I was just chilling with my home girl because she doesn't know them." I explained. I wasn't lying. I don't fuck with Rashad and that was the truth. Now that I know Griff and Rashad are cool. I can forget about Griff hooking me up with one of his boys. That's out the question.

"I always watch you Danielle and that'll never change. I want you to keep it real with me and be honest because I'm always honest with you. I see shit for what it is. If you ain't never fucked the nigga cool, but he kept his eyes on you like you had something that belonged to him. What the fuck do you have that has that nigga tripping so fuckin' hard? We ain't together but we might get there. I need to know what the deal is," he asked and argued? Man, here he goes what the fuck is up with him? I might as well go ahead and tell him. He knew something he just wanted me to confirm it. I feel like he's over stepping his boundaries as a friend.

"I used to fuck with Rashad months ago. Is there anything else you want to know?" I asked. What more does he want from me?

"Did you fuck him? Why didn't I know that? You two were on a double date? Does that nigga have hope; because it looks like he's trying to get back in? I thought we knew everything about each other, but you've been leaving shit out." He argued.

"Yes, I've fucked him. He's my first why do you want to know all of that. Baine don't do that. If you called me here to go back and forth about some shit that's not important you can take me home. If I was on a double date with him; do you think I would've left with you? Rashad and I are a touchy subject that I don't care to speak on. No, he doesn't have hope.

Why are you so concerned if relationships aren't your thing remember? I can't believe I'm even explaining myself to you." I argued. He's killing my vibe for real.

"I just wanted some answers. You fuckin' with Rashad is some shit I needed to know. You were leaving with me regardless Danielle. You know how that shit goes with us? Ain't shit changed. Relationships ain't my thing, but if they were than you know I would be with you. We've had that conversation already." He explained. I'm sick of this shit with him. Why talk about relationships if there's no hope in them? Baine doesn't know what he wants.

"Baine I'm not a convenience. What makes you think when you're ready to be in a relationship I'll still be around? That's the problem with men these days. Chasing money ain't everything. You'll fuck around a miss a good thing focusing on that bag. I'm not waiting for you. You can have twenty million saved by the time you're ready to settle down and I'll be long gone with a man who's ready to be with me." I argued. I meant that shit. I'm not doing this with him either.

"I hear you Danielle, be patient with me." I wasn't about to respond to him. Fuck out of here with that shit. "Danielle do you hear me," he asked? I'm not deaf so why wouldn't I be able to hear him?

"I hear you loud and clear Baine, but did you hear me? I'm not waiting for you to decide when you're ready to be with me. How is that shit fair to me?" I argued. I'm sick of these confused as niggas. Oh my God, why me?

"Danielle, I hear you and shawty I'm listening. I'm keeping it real I won't have you out here looking crazy. I ain't never came at you like this, I'm serious. I want to be with you." He explained. I wasn't even about to respond because I'm not trying to have this conversation. I could feel him staring at me.

Chapter-14

Rashad

Damn, I wasn't expecting to run into Danielle out of all fuckin' people. It was good seeing her, but I hated it was on those terms. I should've known something was up when Griff pulled up on her block a few weeks ago. It makes sense now. She always talked about her best friend Crimson. Her grandmother kept looking at me. I tried hard to avoid her gaze. I knew she didn't recognize me because we never met. I was scared to hop out because I didn't want to risk running into her ass because of our history. I did Danielle wrong and I had no plans to face her. I couldn't face her because I fucked up. I didn't want to break things off with her, but I had to leave because I fucked around and got my ex Ebony pregnant on some late-night creep shit. I loved Danielle I just made a mistake.

Ebony knew I was fucking with Danielle because one night I was leaving Danielle's and Ebony pulled up right behind me and tried to run me off the road. She ended up driving her Lexus into a ditch. I had to come, and pick up her. Danielle was bad as fuck. I couldn't deny that shit even if I wanted too. I couldn't keep my eyes off her. She's picked up a few pounds since I last seen her. I know how I left was fucked up, but I had a few situations and shit was getting hectic. I've been juggling multiple women for years.

I cut Ebony off to be with Danielle too, but she was making it hard as fuck for a nigga to leave. Ebony was threatening to have 12 run up in our spot. Griff and I switched shit up, but after she has my baby its lights out for her ass. I couldn't keep a bitch around that's a threat to my lively hood. Griff tapped me on my shoulder.

"Let's roll. Are you good?" he asked.

"Hell no, I'm not good. Danielle just pulled some disrespectful ass shit. Did you see that shit, my nigga? If she rode with us, she should've left with us. We don't fuck with those niggas from the Westside." I argued. Griff was looking at me crazy.

"Rashad you're tripping for real. I ain't never had a problem with Baine or Ike. Danielle got you tripping you need to handle that." He argued.

"I ain't tripping Griff. It's not even about Danielle. It's about my fuckin' respect. A nigga gone respect me. Yes, we haven't gone to war with those niggas in a few years. We made a truce, but this VIP section is our territory and he stepped in my territory, so I got a problem with that. The fact remains the same, don't swerve in my fuckin' lane period. We haven't had any issues, but we can make some." I argued. Griff nodded his head in agreement. Crimson wrapped her arm around Griff's waist and looked up at us.

"Is everything okay Griff," she asked. She was looking at me instead of Griff. I'm sure she overheard our conversation, but I didn't give a fuck. I want her to run it back to Danielle.

"Yeah, we're good." He explained. Griff gave me a look advising me not to say anything else, but I wanted to ask Crimson a few questions about Danielle anyway.

"Crimson, what's up with Danielle and Baine?" I ask. Crimson was my new sister in law. She had to get used to me anyway.

"Rashad don't do that, ask Danielle about her shit. You didn't say one word to her all night. Not even I'M

SORRY and you owe her that," she argued. Griff looked at me and shook his head. I threw my hands up. I can see now I wasn't about to get anywhere with Crimson. What the fuck was up with her and Baine? Something was up. She left the club with him. I could tell they were comfortable with each other just by his approach alone.

My eyes were trained on him as soon as he approached our VIP section. We locked eyes with each other. He knew he was treading lightly by even coming over here. I saw him in her face at the bar too. She better dead that shit or I'll guarantee you I will. We walked to the front of the club and our driver was up front waiting on us. Baine was flying through the parking lot with his windows down. I could see Danielle smiling up front. She got me fucked up.

I got something for Danielle's ass. I couldn't let that shit slide. The driver dropped me off at home. She had no clue I knew where she laid her head at. I was zooming through traffic to see what the fuck was up with her and Baine.

Griff slid me his key that Crimson knew nothing about. I swear that nigga is pussy whipped already and he hasn't even sampled the pussy. Shawty got his ass gone for real. We've been best friends for twelve years and I ain't never seen him like this. Crimson is a good look for him.

I appreciated that because it ain't no telling how long a nigga would be out here waiting on her to come home. It's crazy because Danielle always crossed my mind, but I had too much pride to even reach out to see what she was up too. I did need to apologize because I was sorry, and I did owe her an explanation. Seeing her with Baine, that shit had me feeling some type of way. It's like my chest caved in and the shots of patron didn't help.

I smoked a few blunts back to back and I could still feel the pain. It's the worst feeling in the world. It's the same feeling I got when my grandmother died. I finally made it to Danielle and Crimson's spot. It took me about forty-five minutes to make it over here. What are the chances as soon as I was pulling in Baine was pulling out? I raised my window down so he could see me. He gave me an icy glare and I gave him one too. Baine and I would have some problems.

He knew why I was here. He pulled off and did a doughnut. It is what it is. I don't give a fuck about that nigga being mad, he can stay mad. I would hate to break the truce all because he wants to fuck around with Danielle because she's off limits. I don't have a problem reminding him why she's off limits. It's a good thing that Danielle's here because I wouldn't have to use this key. I parked in the visitor's section and hopped out my whip. I knew Danielle was about to trip. She's been going in since we laid eyes on each other. I finally made it to her townhouse. I couldn't let her see me out here because I know she wouldn't open the door. I knocked on the door and stood to the side so she couldn't see me.

"Who is it," she yelled. I could already tell it was about to be a long night. I could hear the anger in her voice. I knocked on the door again, ignoring what the fuck she was saying.

"Just open the fuckin' door and see who it is," I yelled and asked?

"Stop playing at my fuckin' door. Baine, I swear you better take your ass on," she argued and yelled. She really pissed me off saying that niggas name. I knocked on the door again like I was the fuckin' police. I wasn't hiding behind shit when she swung the door open.

I made my way inside and closed the door behind me. I took a seat on the couch and my eyes roamed all over Danielle. I wanted her in the worst way. I knew she was surprised to see me.

"It looks like you were expecting some one?" I asked and laughed. Danielle was fuckin' with me all night and I didn't say shit. I let her get her cheap shots out, but this morning it was my turn.

"Rashad, why are you here? How do you even know where I fuckin' live? You can leave I don't have shit to say to you." She argued and pointed to the door. My eyes were trained on Danielle. She avoided eye contact with me. I wasn't leaving. Danielle had her arms folded across her chest. I walked up on her and closed the gap between us. I wasn't leaving without an understanding between us. She took a step back and stepped up again. "Move Rashad."

"You know why I'm here Danielle. It's because of you. I know you're mad at me. I'm sorry. I swear to God I am. I know the shit I did was fucked up and I'm sorry for that. I just want to apologize." I explained. I had to right my wrongs with her. She refused to look me in my face.

"I don't know why you're here. You don't fuck with me and I don't fuck with you. I'm okay with that. I'm good on your apologies Rashad. It's cool you can save it for a bitch who cares because I could give two fucks. It's too late. When I needed you, you were nowhere to be found. Save it." She argued.

"You care Danielle. The moment we laid eyes on each other, it was written on your face that you cared. Your choice of words confirmed you still care. I'm sorry and I want to apologize. I'm not asking you to forgive me, but I want you to listen to me." I explained. Danielle can give me the tough girl act all she wants but I'm not buying it.

"Rashad, you don't get, it do you? I said what I had to say because I wanted to get that shit off my chest. I couldn't be in the same room with you and not let know how I feel. You're too late. I wanted an excuse from you for months, but I never got it. I didn't even get a response from you earlier but now you want to talk? I called you and left you numerous messages that you never responded too. It's funny I would call you blocked, and you would answer. I don't want to hear shit that you have to say. I'm good and I mean that shit.

You took advantage of me but it's cool though because you live and learn. The difference between you and me. I learned from my mistakes and you're my biggest mistake. I always wondered what I would say to you if I ever saw you again. I don't owe you a conversation because you never gave me one." She argued and explained.

"Danielle, we weren't a mistake. I care about you rather you believe it or not. I made a mistake and no matter how I went about it, we would still be right here. It was easier to walk away from you because if I told you the truth it would've hurt worse. It's hard to tell someone you love you fucked up. One fuck up is liable to ruin your whole life." I explained.

"Okay Rashad you fucked up, but I don't care about your fuck up. It doesn't matter. You still took the coward's way out. You weren't man enough then so why be man enough now? It took me being in your presence for you to say something to me? You couldn't even address me hours ago, but you want to now? Why because you were calling out for me and I ignored your ass? Get the fuck out of here." She argued. I heard a knock at Danielle's door. Who was coming to her house this time of night?

"Who the fuck is that?" I asked.

"Does it matter because you're leaving?" She argued and asked. Danielle went to open the door and it was Baine grilling the fuck out of me. I could tell it was about to be a problem. He made his way into Danielle's spot and posted up by the island.

"Danielle, what the fuck is going on here? I told you I had to make a run right quick and I was coming back. What's your business here Rashad because you're in my fuckin' territory? Danielle grab your shit and let's go. We're together, I'm curious as to why you're here? It's real disrespectful," he asked and explained? Baine sat his Glock on the island in Danielle's kitchen. Yeah, it was about to go down. Baine wasn't the only nigga holding. I pulled out my Mac 11 from my waistline and I had a Glock 45 tucked behind my back. It's whatever with me. I swear if Danielle leaves with that nigga it's going down.

"Oh yeah, Baine I'm in your territory? Last I checked Danielle and I was together so when did that shit change? You're in my territory, you pulled your strap out what the fuck you want to do Baine? The moment you decided to draw down on me all the truce shit ends right now." I argued. He knew how I gave it up. If he wanted smoke, I'll be glad to light his ass up.

"You know what? The two of you both can leave. I'm single and neither one of you were invited here. Whatever bullshit y'all got going on, I don't want any parts of it. If y'all want to shoot it out y'all can right outside of my house. This is where I lay my head at and I pay the cost to be the motherfuckin' boss," she argued and pointed to the door. "I want y'all out now." Baine was the first one to leave out. He was facing me on his way out. I wasn't leaving I don't give a fuck what she's talking about.

"Bye Rashad," she argued. She grabbed my shirt and drug me to the door and slammed it in my face. I stood by the door for a minute. I could feel Danielle staring at me through the peep hole.

Chapter-15

Griff

Crimson and I made it home about an hour ago. I'm supposed to be laid up with her and lying between her legs right about now, but I had to step out the room to see what the fuck was up with Rashad. I don't know why he's calling my phone this time of night. He called my phone late as hell. I got Crimson looking at me sideways and shit. I know it had to be serious because he would never hit my line if it wasn't. Rashad gave me the rundown of what happened. He couldn't leave well enough alone. Danielle got him tripping.

"Fuck that truce Griff, Baine pulled down on me at Danielle's. A nigga can't pull down on me without getting clapped. The only reason he's still alive is because she put us out and he pulled off before me, but wherever I see that nigga at, is where I'll bury him at. I put that shit on my OG," he argued and explained.

"Hold up Rashad, how the fuck did you end up at Danielle's? Zeek dropped you off at home, you're leaving shit out," I argued. Rashad gave me the run-down of how he ended up over there. I shook my head listening to him. I'm riding with Rashad right or wrong. "I did slide you the keys to their spot, but you saw Baine leave with Danielle at the club. Come on now, you knew something was up between the two of them."

"Griff, I don't give a fuck about none of that shit. Whatever she got going on with Baine she better end that shit. On the real Griff, I think that nigga wanted to go war with us. I've been seeing him a lot in our neck of the woods. It is what it is. It ain't got shit to do with Danielle."

"Come on Rashad, you can keep it real with me? Why didn't I know shit about Danielle? Do you care about her? Your actions are telling me you do and whatever the fuck you did to her some shit isn't adding up with that? You need to apologize because you hurt her. I could hear and feel it. I don't give a fuck about going to war with them niggas, but not behind a female.

I know some niggas who know some niggas and I heard they were trying to setup shop off Gresham Road which is our fuckin' territory and I'm not having that shit. A nigga can't eat where we count up at period." I argued.

"Griff, mane, you did know about her. I just never told you her name. You don't believe in my life style, so I'm on the hush about how I do shit and why. I don't like being judged by everybody. I ain't meant to be a saint like yourself. I know you would've judged a nigga. How the fuck was I supposed to tell her that I got Ebony pregnant and we were together? No matter what I did, we would still have the same outcome. Yeah, I care about her, but I got to fall back because she's not feeling me. I tried to make amends, but I got nowhere. It is what it is. I can't change the past. I can only mold the future. I said I was sorry, and she wasn't trying to hear that." He argued.

"Rashad you were supposed to tell her the truth, no matter what. At the end of the day, you kept it real about what you did. At least if you would've been honest, she would've had the right to choose if she wanted to leave or stay. You didn't give her that option at all. I understand why you did it, but damn that was fucked up. At least you didn't string her along."

"I know-," he stated. I had to cut Rashad off it was something else that had my attention instead of talking to Rashad. "Aye Rashad. I'll get up with you later."

"Bet." I ended the call with Rashad and focused my attention on something brown, thick, red and sexy. Crimson walked in my office with my t-shirt on while she stood in the door. Her hands were rested on her thick ass hips. Her nipples were erect. Damn, I wanted her in the worst way. I motioned with my hands for her to come sit on my lap and join me. She walked over and took a seat on my lap. As soon as she sat down her t-shirt raised up. My attention was focused on her ass. It was round and plump begging for me to squeeze it. I noticed she didn't have any panties on. I started massaging her breasts and kissing the creases of her neck. A few moans escaped her lips and she tilted her head back and rested it on my chest.

"I'm sleepy Griff and I'm trying to wait up on you, but I can't hang," she pouted and yawned. I knew Crimson was tired. Shit, I was too. I wasn't expecting Rashad to hit me with that. I got to holla at Baine to see what the fuck was up.

The last thing he wanted was to go to war with a nigga like me. I want everybody to eat, but what you won't do is eat where I lay my head at. You can't do business in my territory without consulting with me signing off on it.

Its levels to this shit. I could easily setup shop on the Westside but that ain't my thang, but it can be. I got a team of niggas that's ready to expand they're just waiting on me to give them okay. If Baine and Ike want to go there, I'll put those niggas out of business. I'm not a selfish ass nigga but I can be.

"I was on my way back, but Rashad got into some shit he needed to tell me about. I'm sorry for taking so long. I was missing you I couldn't even focus like I wanted to because I know you're waiting. That's rude of me to leave you alone while I'm on your time. You know I would rather be laid up next to you then listening to him, right? I can't believe you came looking for me. How did you find me? I meant to show you this a few days ago. When I'm not laid up under you, I'm in here handling business." I explained.

"Is everything okay?" She asked. I never been a gossiping ass nigga. I'm sure Crimson would talk to Danielle tomorrow and she'll tell her everything she needs to know. I don't want any problems between us because of Danielle and Rashad so I'm staying out of it.

"Yeah, everything is cool."

"It's nice in here. Why wouldn't I come looking for you, when you left our bed to come down here? I didn't want to be rude and fall asleep while you were gone. I could've but I decided against it. It took me a minute, but I was listening to your voice and it led me here." She explained and smiled. Crimson was always thinking about me. I appreciated that. It shows she cares. She was coming around, but we still have a ways to go.

"Our bed? You're finally acknowledging that it's our bed?" I asked. I wanted Crimson to move in with me. I know it was to soon, but I wanted her here every day with me.

"You know what I meant. Is that the only thing you heard," she asked and beamed? The words slipped from her mouth, not mine.

"I heard everything you said, but the only thing that stuck was your reference to our bed. I would've woken you up to, trust me."

I had plans to eat that pussy all night. My hands had a mind of their own. I couldn't keep my hands off her. My hand gripped her thighs and my thumb rubbed the folds of her pussy. Crimson grabbed my hand so I would stop. I wasn't though.

"Stop," she moaned and pouted. I couldn't stop if I wanted too. She needed to get used to this. I removed my hands anyway because I always wanted her to be comfortable and I'm always respectful. I rubbed my hands across the bridge of my nose damn that pussy smells good.

"I'm sorry I can't help myself. Why do I need to stop? It's mine and I can't wait to mark my territory." I explained. I know Crimson's a virgin, but she must get comfortable with me. I'm not going anywhere but sooner or later I will be taking it there. I just want to get her ready.

"Because we're not ready for that yet and touching leads to other things." She pouted and mumbled. I need her to speak up because she's too old to not speak about how she feels.

"You're not ready, but I'm ready whenever you are. I promise I'll take my time with you. I'm patient but what if I wanted to taste it? CAN I?" I asked. I shouldn't have asked because I planned on doing it anyway. I didn't want Crimson to think what she says didn't matter, because it does.

"I might be open to that," she whispered.

"What are you afraid of? I know you'll like it. I'm going to make sure of that. I just want to please you that's it Crimson." I asked and explained.

"I'm not afraid," she mumbled. We're about to see.

"Okay." I picked Crimson up and carried her upstairs to my room. Our eyes were trained on each other. We finally made it to the bedroom. I tossed Crimson on the bed and removed her t-shirt from her body and tossed it on the floor. I could tell her body got tense by her facial expression. I threw her legs over my shoulder. Her ass was rested on my forearms. My face was eye level with her pussy. Crimson raised up to see what I was doing. She'll find out sooner than later.

"Relax." I chuckled. She gave me a faint smile.

"How can I and I don't know what you're up too?" she asked.

"Trust me Crimson. I got you. I promise I do. Just lay back and relax." She did as she was told. Crimson's body was sculptured perfectly. I wanted to take my time with her. I massaged her perfect feet. I sucked each toe one by one. I could hear the moans escape from her mouth.

I knew I was doing something right. My tongue traced both of her thighs. She was squirming and I haven't even put my mouth on it yet, so I went in for the kill. I tongue fucked Crimson wet, and now she was trying to run away from me. She kept backing up, but I put a grip on her legs where she couldn't move. She didn't have a choice but to take it. She was trying her hardest to break free from my embrace. I wasn't letting her get away that easily. She tasted exactly how I imagined she would.

"Crimson can I finish what I was doing or are you going to continue to be defiant?" She refused to answer me. I went in for the kill again. The only sounds you could hear throughout the room were me sucking on her pussy and the soft moans she was trying to muffle escape. Her juices were drenching my face. Her body shook a few times, her legs were shaking. I wanted to laugh but I knew she was sensitive as fuck.

"Can you please stop? I don't want to get whatever this is on your face," she moaned.

"No, I want. It's cum and I want you to let that shit go and cum on my face." I argued.

"No, I'm not doing it." She pouted. Crimson was hard headed as fuck. I don't mind showing her who the boss is. I tongued fuck Crimson real fast and sloppy. My spit and her juices were running down the crack of her ass. My sheets were fucked up. Each time my tongue would touch her spot, her body would tense up quick giving me more fuel to go in. I didn't give her time to catch her breath. I just went in. My two front teeth locked down on the inside of her pussy, my tongue applied extra pressure. Whatever she was holding onto immediately came out. Her body shook long and hard. I felt her grip my shoulders. I raised up to look at her. Her face was buried in my pillow. I just shook my head because her body was spent.

"Crimson are you okay? I need you to ease up off my shoulders." I laughed. I felt her loosen her grip. I snatched the pillow from her face. She had her hands covering her face so I wouldn't see her. "Crimson, come on baby, was I that bad? You can't even face me?" Crimson removed her hands from her face.

"No Carius, it was amazing. What are you trying to do to me? You took advantage of me and I can't even face you right now." She explained and smiled. She knew what the fuck I was trying to do. I've been doing it since I met her.

"I told you I wanted to please you. I just opened the flood gates. Raise up so I can put some new sheets on my bed since you fucked them up." I laughed. Crimson punched me in my shoulder. I pointed to the mess she created.

"Whatever." She whispered. I went in the bathroom to grab a towel so I can clean Crimson up. I pushed her down on the bed and wiped her pussy clean. She still refused to look at me while I was doing it. I went into the bathroom to wash my face. Crimson walked up behind me. I looked at her through the mirror and smiled at her.

"Stop smiling at me. Where are the sheets so I can fix the bed?" she asked.

"In the closet in the hall way." Crimson ran out of the bathroom. I busted out laughing. I took my time in that bathroom washing my face. Crimson's pussy smelled just like water. I kept sniffing my nose to make sure I wasn't tripping. I brushed my teeth and headed back out to the bedroom. Crimson was putting the fitted sheet on the bed. I walked up behind her and wrapped my arms around her waist. I leaned in and started attacking her neck.

"Stop Griff, please," she moaned and pouted. "I'm trying to make the bed up." I backed up off Crimson so she could finish making the bed. As soon as she finished, she climbed in the bed and scooted toward the edge where I couldn't touch her. I scooted up right behind her and wrapped my arms around her waist.

"What I do wrong Crimson? Why are you trying to give me space you know I hate that shit?" I whispered in her ear. She turned around to face me. She ran her hands across my face.

"You've done nothing wrong Carius, just everything right. You just caught me off guard. I need a minute to catch my breath." She explained and bit her bottom lip turning me on in the worst way.

"If I've done nothing wrong, why do you want to have your back facing me while we're asleep? You know I can't sleep if you're not lying on my chest? I didn't mean to catch you off guard, but damn I had to see how that pussy taste. I know you're not ready to have sex that's why I haven't pressured you. When you're ready I want you to tell me. I want to make your first time special."

"I know and I'm sorry Carius. We're moving so fast I'm just trying to keep up. It's like I'm dreaming and if so, I don't want to wake up. I think I'm ready Carius. That's what I'm afraid of. My body yearns for you. It responds to you in ways that I wouldn't even imagine. I couldn't control it if I wanted too. I'm scared because I'm inexperienced. I want to please you and cater to all of your needs." She explained.

"Crimson Rose Tristan. I always want you to be honest with me and speak about how you feel. I don't want to be in a relationship by myself. It's not a dream we're living in. It's our reality. It gets greater later I can promise you that. You're worried about the wrong things. You're pleasing me by just being in your presence. I'm good. When the time is right, I'll coach you. Let me lead and you can follow. If you feel like your ready tomorrow let me know and I'll make some plans for us."

"I will." Crimson climbed on my chest and placed a few kisses on my lips. My dick was getting hard, ready to murder something. I wish she would've told me earlier she was ready, but I'll wait.

"Crimson you better stop before your kisses get you in trouble." I grabbed her hand and placed it on dick. "You see what you started, get off me." I laughed.

"I'm not Carius. It ain't my fault you say all the right things," she smiled and bit my bottom lips. Our tongues had a mind of their own. I had to pull back because if we kept it up, I'm liable to bust that pussy wide open.

"Take your ass to bed, before I stretch you open."

"Good night Carius."

"Good night Crimson."

Chapter-16

Danielle

Fuck my life and I mean that shit literally. Last night was a good night. I couldn't complain at all because we had a motherfuckin' ball. It's safe to say I was filling myself. Everything changed the moment I left the club. I couldn't even sleep last night because I was still trying to process everything that happened. I can't believe all of this shit happened to me. I tossed and turned all night. My night didn't end how I wanted it to.

I just knew Baine and I was about to post up at his condo in the city and chill. I haven't seen him in a few weeks but normally when we link up that's what we do. Boy was I wrong. Shit changed as soon as we pulled off and hopped on I-20E. We got into it before we could even get comfortable. A bitch called his phone and it connected to Bluetooth and he disconnected it as soon as she spoke up. The bitch called back again, and I removed his hands because I wanted to hear what the fuck she had to say. She said she was waiting on him at the Condo. I went in on his ass and I made him take me home. The moment he got a whiff of Rashad calling my name, he was begging for a relationship because he thought I was fuckin' with Rashad.

I couldn't even trip how I wanted to because we aren't together, and I know what it is between us. I won't fuck him because I know he's fuckin' a few different chicks. I'm tripping off Rashad and Baine. I need Crimson to bring her ass home because we'll have to discuss this shit. Baine called me all night to see if Rashad was here. I wouldn't even answer. As far as I'm concerned, the bitch that was already waiting on you, tend to her. I was in the kitchen making me a fresh cup of coffee. I heard someone messing with the locks. I knew it was Crimson. She walked in with the biggest smile on her face. I grabbed another coffee mug out the cabinet and filled her cup to the brim.

"Good morning Danielle. I hope you made me a cup? Baby, when I say I have some tea to spill, I do." She sassed and smiled. Crimson has finally got fucked about time.

"It seems like we both had an eventful night. Bitch, I've been waiting on you all morning to spill my tea. I didn't want to call you in the middle of the night, but it was tempting."

"Are you serious? Danielle I couldn't wait to get home so we could talk. Thank God we don't have to be at work until 1:00 p.m. As soon as you left with Baine, Rashad asked me what was up with the two of you? I looked at that nigga like he was crazy. Girl, I NIKE checked his ass and gave it to him raw. I went in because he has you fucked up," she explained.

"Girl, I don't even want to talk about Rashad and Baine, but it went down last night," I argued. I explained to Crimson everything that happened last night, and her mouth dropped.

"Danielle it makes perfect sense now. Griff and I were laid up in the bed and Rashad called his phone in the middle of the night. Griff stepped out for a minute to see what was up. He was gone for a minute. He was gone for so long I had to go find him.

Griff didn't tell me shit. Rashad was up to no good. He's very bold as fuck to pop up over here after all this time. Did he apologize?" She asked.

"Yes Crimson, he's very bold. I wasn't even trying to hear that shit. In so many words he said he cheated, and I was one and MOTHERFUCKIN' DONE. It's nothing that he can do or say to me that'll change how I feel about him. I don't appreciate Griff telling him where we lay our head. I know that's his friend but he's over stepping my boundaries."

"Griff didn't tell him he remembered. When Griff came over that day with the BENZ when we found out he paid the lease up. Rashad followed him over here. I asked him how he was getting home, and he said, Shad. Awe he still cares about Danielle! Don't you find it odd for the two of them to be best friends? I swear I almost shitted bricks when you popped off." She laughed.

"Crimson, fuck Rashad and I mean that. I'm good on excuses. I'm not thinking about him, so much for Griff hooking me up with one of his homeboys. Don't ask me to come to no more fuckin' events with you.

What was up with Jermesha and her friends? I just knew I was about to walk a bitch like a dog. I haven't beat a bitch ass in a long time.

When Baine and I were on our way out, those bitches were grilling me. I laughed at those hoes because they're silly. I do find it VERY odd my EX and your man are best friends. What are the chances of that? It doesn't matter now because Rashad and I ain't nothing."

"Girl, you didn't tell me that Rashad was that fine? Do you still love him? You down played that shit, Danielle. Fuck Rashad, why can't you hang out with me and Griff because of him? You know you're my BESTFRIEND who else would I bring besides you?" She beamed.

"Whatever bitch don't use me. He ain't all that. Of course, I love him but fuck him. He's not worthy of my love. You're a little cheerful. Griff must have blessed you with some dick?" I ask. Crimson was smiling, so I know she fucked him. "Spill it bitch tell me about your night. I'm all ears."

"Danielle, why do you always assume the worst of me? I still have my innocence today, but it went down last night. Girl he ate my pussy like he was trying to prove something. My legs almost gave out on a bitch. I was trying to run from him. He had a death grip on my legs. I came all on his face. I was so embarrassed." She explained.

"I knew you did something. It's written all on your face. You can't even hide it if you wanted too. Crimson, bitch, you got Griff going crazy. Girl Griff is letting you know that he's that nigga. I knew shit was real when we were in the club last night. Bitch, that nigga was choosing, and he didn't give a fuck who was watching. He was letting it be known that you were his. He put his mouth on it without even sampling the pussy. Bitch, you need to come on down off that pussy for real. I'm like Future now, that nigga DESERVES IT. I need a dick report ASAP." I beamed and laughed.

"I am trust me, but the thing is I have to tell him in advance because he wants to make my first time special." She beamed. My best friend was falling in love and she doesn't even know it. Griff is that nigga I'm so happy for her.

"Griff is a real one. Lock him down. I'm so happy for you. You deserve it. Y'all look good together." I beamed.

"Thank you.

Crimson

Danielle and I had a long conversation and it was needed. Ugh, I can't believe Rashad did all that shit. It's just like a nigga to act an ass when they see you with someone else. I could feel the tension between him and Danielle last night. It was so thick. The two of them both had things they needed to say to each other. I wanted real closure for Danielle. My life is finally starting to make sense. We had a few hours or so before we had to be at work. I wasn't tired but I wanted to at least to enjoy the comforts of my home. I'm never here. I don't think I've laid in this bed for seven days straight.

I love Griff and I'm falling so hard for him. He's perfect. He's everything I ever needed and wanted in a man. I swear he's placed a permanent smile on my face. I can't stop thinking about last night. I swear he took my body to heights I thought we would never reach. He was so attentive to me. Every time he held me, I melted in his arms. I couldn't even day dream about his ass because he's already calling me. I just saw him not even two hours ago.

"Hello." I beamed and smiled. Just thoughts of him brings a smile to my face.

"What's up baby, I miss you? What you got going on over there," he asked? I bit my bottom lip just hearing his voice. His voice alone soothes me.

"I miss you too Carius. I just saw you an hour ago. I'm day dreaming, is that okay with you?" I wanted to day dream about him in peace. I guess he felt I was thinking about him and he decided to call me.

"It's cool, but what are you day dreaming about? I can make all of your dreams come true, you just got to tell me what to do?" He explained. I swear he says all the right things.

"Griff, you're nosey as fuck. I can't even day dream about you in peace." I beamed. God, I love this man. I can't wait to tell him.

"Crimson baby, you don't have to day dream about a nigga like me. Whenever you want to see me, I'm coming. I make shit happen remember that. What time do you want me to pull up tonight?

I got to get you a car ASAP and don't say no, because I'm buying you one anyway." He explained and demanded. I swear he thinks he's running things but he's not. I don't need a car if he's always picking me up. I like being chauffeured around.

"Tonight?" I asked. I threw my phone on mute instantly so he wouldn't hear me laugh. Griff was so serious and adamant about me staying with him every night.

"Yeah, tonight Crimson! You know I'm not sleeping by myself. You know what it is with us." He argued. I swear we haven't even been together for six months and he acting as if we have.

"Griff, I get off at 7:00 p.m. I'll be home by 8:00 p.m. How come you won't let me stay at home for one night?" I asked and sighed. I swear he won't let me breathe by myself. "I can't even cook a meal."

"Okay cool I'll see you at 9:00 p.m. One night away from you is too long. You might be trying to get away from me. You can cook here, what do you have in mind? I'll go by the store and pick it up?" He asked.

"Do you eat seafood? I want some lobster tails, crab legs, oysters, corn on the cob, red potatoes and some andouille sausages."

"You know I eat seafood. I ate you last night. I'll have Maria to grab that for us and you can cook it tonight. Can you add a steak with it and some garlic bread," he asked?

"Can you be serious for a minute? Sure, I'll cook you a steak. Griff can I ask you a question?" I sassed.

"Sure, what's on your mind baby? What I do?"

"You've done nothing wrong and everything right, I can assure you of that. I know this has nothing to do with us, but why did you tell Rashad where Danielle and I lay our heads?" I asked. It took a minute for Griff to answer. I know he was trying to get his words together. "Did you hear me?" I asked him.

"Crimson, it wasn't like that at all. I owe Danielle an apology. I had no clue he was going over there last night. I knew he wanted to talk to her alone without us.

I didn't say anything to you about it last night because our problems aren't theirs. I don't want to be in the middle of it."

"Okay." I didn't have anything else to say. I'm taking his word for it.

"Crimson, what's wrong? What I do?" He asked. I could hear the concern in his voice.

"Nothing is wrong I was just thinking about us and our plans for tonight. Griff I'm ready." I smiled. I wanted him in the worst way and last night only intensified it. He knew what he was doing.

"Ready for what?" He asked. He knew what I was talking about. He just wanted me to confirm it for him.

"I'm ready to take it there Griff. I want you to take my body to new heights." I explained.

"Oh yeah Crimson, are you sure about that," he asked? He told me to tell him when I was. I'm telling him now. Why is he so surprised?

"I'm positive."

"Okay I can do something about that. I'll see you at 8:00 p.m. instead of 9:00 p.m." Griff and I finished talking. I'm looking forward to tonight. I needed some new lingerie even though it wouldn't be staying on me long. I wanted to look sexy for my man.

"Danielle, we need to run to the mall really quick. I need some lingerie. I made plans to lay on back for Griff tonight," I yelled. Danielle flew in my room.

"Say what Bitch! You made plans to get that pussy busted wide open? Come on let's go. Shit what the fuck you need lingerie for freak? Griff will fuck you in a shirt with holes in it. It's not like, the lingerie is staying on you anyway," she laughed.

"Hush, damn, I want to look cute for my man. I want him to take his time with me and to rip my bra and panties off me." I laughed.

"Crimson, I don't want to hear all that shit come on."

Chapter-17

Keondra

Bitches couldn't keep my name out their fuckin' mouth to save their fuckin' life. My phone has been blowing up since last night. Griff and his new bitch were the talk of the hood and I hated it. Everybody and their mammy were in Central Station at Maria's party. Fuck all that. I'm known to check a bitch. It's this one bitch BeBe everybody and their mammy was texting me about. I had a long night last night. I didn't get the chance to pull off with Baine. Somehow Danielle ended up leaving with him ugh. She had him on lock too. I despised him when I watched him carry her to his car.

IKE, he was the next best thing. He's Baine's right-hand man and he's paid too. Ike and I fucked all night long. He got us a room at the Sheraton Presidential Suite. Ike was fine as hell too. Tall, dark, handsome dope swag. Dark brown eyes low fade with deep waves. His dick was long and thick. I bit my bottom lip just thinking about him. He took his time with me and I don't know why? I tried to tip toe out early this morning. I took a long hot steamy shower. Ike snuck in behind me to finish what we started. He asked why I was sneaking out without letting him know. It was just a fuck to me. Nothing more nothing less. He claimed he wanted to see me again today. We'll see. I'll have to check this bitch before I get my day started. I grabbed my phone off the nightstand.

"HELLO," she yelled through the phone and sucked her teeth.

"Yeah what's up BeBe? I heard you've been gossiping in the hood about me and my nigga? I don't give two fucks about the little dusty ass bitch that he's supposed to be fuckin' with? She ain't weighing up to me and neither or the hoes that's gossiping. Keep my name out your fuckin' mouth. If you got something you want to say to me, you know where to find me and you got my fuckin' number." I argued and sassed. I'm sick of hoes running their mouth about me and my fuckin' business. Find something else to talk about. Talk about you're dope fiend ass momma.

"Gossiping Keondra? Bitch it's free fuckin' game hoe. If a bitch said I said anything don't ever question that, because you know I fuckin said it. I ain't never had a problem repeating my fuckin' self twice. Out of all the bitches that's running their mouth in the hood about your husband or should I say EX HUSBAND. You got the balls to address me about your business? Bitch do you really want to address me, BeBe hoe? I ain't got nothing but fuckin' time today.

I don't argue over the phone with no bitch period about a nigga I'm not fuckin', YET. You know where you can fuckin' find me at. I'm in Decatur hoe, posted up on Flat Shoals and since you and Griff ain't together, LET me be the FIRST BITCH to tell you. If given the chance, I'll ride his BIG BLACK DICK the first chance I GET. YOU HEARD IT FROM BEBE HOE." I had to pull my face away from the phone, because this bitch was getting beside herself. She got me fucked up. A bitch always wants something that they can't have. Griff ain't up for grabs.

"BEBE LOWER your motherfuckin' voice hoe. EX HUSBAND BITCH I'M STILL MARRIED TO HIM. HE AIN'T FUCKIN' DIVORCED ME. I'M STILL CAKED

UP. NO MATTER WHAT HE DOES. I ain't scared of you. I'll address any bitch that got my name up in their mouth. Bitch you got me fucked up and, I'll show you just how fucked up you got me." I argued. She doesn't put any fear in my heart.

"Do I Keondra? If so BITCH, pull the FUCK UP or shut the FUCK UP HOE." BeBe was talking some big boy shit. I couldn't wait to get at this bitch.

"ON YOUR DOPE FIEND ASS MOMMA; BITCH I'M A DRAG YOU FROM FLAT SHOALS TO GRESHAM ROAD HOE."

"PUT YOUR MONEY WHERE YOU MOUTH IS HOE, I'M WAITING. ME AND MY DOPE FIEND ASS MOMMA BITCH." She argued and hung up the phone. I'm not even about to argue with a bitch like BeBe. I know how she gives it up. What I will do is shoot a bitch like BeBe! I swear I'm so tired of Griff making me look like a fool in the streets. Our breakup was perfect nobody knew nothing about us not being together. The moment he ran across that bitch Crimson Rose Tristan, he wanted the world to know we're done and he's with someone else.

I despised him for that. To make matters worse he cut my fuckin' water off. What you won't do is fuck up my cash flow because you got a new bitch. Nope, Griff gone fuckin' pay me in cash or pay with his fuckin' life. I can't even get my lashes done without a bitch laughing at me or my marriage being the topic of their discussion. Every time I log on Facebook it's a picture of Griff and Crimson from Maria's party last night. It had over 300 likes. His aunt had the nerve to tag me in that shit being messy. I politely untagged myself. I did save the picture to my phone to bring to the divorce hearing to show my attorney; I have proof that Griff was cheating on me long before, the video tape surfaced.

I called Arielle to come to the house to do my hair and lashes. I got something for BeBe's ass, she thinks I won't pull up, but bitch I will and I'm on my fuckin' way because I'm sick of her disrespectful ass. All it takes is for me to shut one bitch up and the rest of these bitches will be on mute. I knew she was around a crowd of people that's why she was showing off. I'm not a punk bitch. If she wanted to put on for the hood, WE CAN.

I might can't beat her ass but bitch we can fight and if I lose, bitch I'll shoot YOU. Win lose or draw I'm demanding my respect. I had to pull up on BeBe before I got my hair and lashes did. See that's the problem with these bitches now days they think because you're cute and well-kept you won't do shit. It's too bad because KEONDRA ain't that bitch. I grabbed a pair of Griff's grey sweat pants out the closet and I threw on a grey wife beater to match. I slid my feet into my Jordan's Air 11 Retros Low, Medium Grey/White-Gunsmoke. It's going down.

I grabbed one of Griff's guns that I stole from him. I knew this would come in handy to bad I'm not using it on him. If Griff wants to divorce me, he's going to have to pay me more than $200,000.00 to sign any fuckin' papers. I'm not a cheap ass bitch so I'm raising the fuckin' stakes. Catching a body with his gun is one of them. He better be prepared to pay like he weighs.

Crimson Rose Tristan is another bitch that's going to see me. A bitch can't flex with my husband without any repercussions. It's levels to this shit and Crimson doesn't want to get on my level. My phone has been ringing off the hook for the past few minutes. I grabbed my phone and it was Jermesha. I rolled my eyes because I didn't feel like talking to her. She called right back, so it had to be something important.

"Hello," I yelled when I answered the phone. I don't know why her broke ass was calling me, bitch find you a job or a nigga that can pay you for your time.

"Keondra bitch, where are you? Bring your ass to my grand momma's house right now? I was at the Chevron on Candler Road and BeBe was running her mouth about you. You know I'm not going for that shit. I had to check that hoe. We had a fight in the store, the only thing she did was pull my fuckin' tracks out and scratch my face up. Her momma had the nerve to beat me in my back with her cane." She argued. I swear I hated to laugh in Jermesha's face but damn.

"Jermesha, stop please," I busted out laughing. I couldn't even catch my damn breath.

"Keondra, are you laughing at me. Bitch that shit ain't fuckin' funny. I'm going to see if I can apply for a disability check. I think she fucked my shit up. Ms. Carolyn's metal cane could've fuckin' paralyzed my back.

You know I need my back in case I need to turn a trick or two." She laughed.

BeBe's momma, Ms. Carolyn ain't no fuckin' joke. All the dope she smokes you would think she'd be out of it, but nope Ms. Carolyn is always on go. Anytime BeBe's popping off, her momma is right fuckin' behind her. I swear to God I'll shoot those bitches. Gawd better bless those bitches before I do.

"I'm here. I'm listening. You should've grabbed a beer bottle and went to work on them. Jermesha, I'm on my way. I appreciate you. I'm not thinking about BeBe and her DOPE FIEND ASS MOMMA but on my MOMMA, I wish the two of the them would. I'll see you in a minute let me finish getting dressed. I have a hair and lash appointment later." I explained.

"Okay." I couldn't stay on the phone with Jermesha all day. I had shit to do and a few hoes to check. I finished getting dressed. My pixie cut was in shambles but I'm still cute. I couldn't wait to let Arielle do my hair. I may add a little color to it.

I finally made my way to the Eastside. I picked up Jermesha and Mia. I don't know what it is about Mother Dear but for some reason she can't stand me. I just blew the horn and they knew it was me. I spoke to her old ass and she just rolled her eyes at me. I don't know why I even continue to speak to her. I can't dwell on that right now.

I had other things to worry about. Jermesha and Mia hopped in running their mouths about what happened earlier. Traffic was heavy. I stopped by the store to grab me a Vanilla Coke and something to snack on. Jermesha paid for my stuff with her EBT card. It's the least she could do, she ain't doing shit else. I need some groceries too.

🖤

I pulled up on Flat Shoals about twenty minutes later. BeBe and her crew were still posted up. I threw my car in park and hopped out. I grabbed my keys out the ignition. I saw Ms. Carolyn at the end of the block. Jermesha and Mia were still sitting in the car. "What the fuck did y'all want to ride for if y'all wasn't getting out?" I asked and yelled. Jermesha must have gotten her ass beat. I wasn't tripping because if I didn't beat her ass, I was shooting her. BeBe's friend Niesha and Kadee turned around and tapped BeBe on her shoulder to let her know I was coming. BeBe was so ghetto she could never pull a nigga like Griff. I shouldn't have let her get to me. She's a motherfuckin' fan.

"Oh, Keondra pulled up? I got something for your ass believe that." she asked and laughed. She was clapping her hands. She thought I was bull shitting? BeBe handed Niesha her purse and Bud light Lime. Kadee grabbed her phone. BeBe grabbed the scrunchie off her wrist and placed her braids into a ponytail. Everybody knew what time it was. BeBe had to be running her mouth because everybody on the block was following right behind her, they were ready to see a fight. The niggas that were shooting dice behind the white house that was boarded up on the corner, came from the back to watch. JR done the bird call to let a motherfucka know it was going down. I wasn't even about to argue or entertain BeBe. I came to fight and that's it nothing more nothing less.

"Keondra, I want you to have that same fuckin' energy you had a few hours ago; when you called my phone on that rah-rah shit be prepared to get your ass BEAT." The joke was on her. I ran up on BeBe's ass. I was done talking hours ago when she referenced, she would fuck my husband. I started busting her in her face. We were going toe to toe and blow for blow. People were yelling "WorldStar!" I knew they were recording us, and I was prepared to put on a show. I noticed BeBe spit something out of her mouth. It was blood. I started punching her in stomach even harder. She punched me back in my stomach.

The next thing I know I felt something sharp pierce my arm. I looked at my arm and blood started pouring out. "You cut me bitch." I looked at her and she smiled.

Oh, she thought this shit was funny. She wanted to fight dirty. "Take this ass whooping that you were bragging about giving HOE. BeBe you got me fucked up. On your DOPE FIEND ASS MOMMA BITCH, YOU GONE REGRET IT." I cocked my fist back and aimed for her eye and it connected. I cocked my fist back again and aimed for her chest. She stumbled a little bit. I kept going in. The crowd was screaming "Damn Keondra!" They were adding more fuel to the fire. I kept tagging that hoe in her face and eye.

"BEBE don't let NO BITCH BEAT YOUR ASS in your fuckin' hood. I swear I'll beat your ass my damn self," her mother Ms. Carolyn yelled. I heard Ms. Carolyn sniff her nose; which means she just snorted some coke.

I turned around and spat blood at Ms. Carolyn. "FUCK YOU AND YOUR DAUGHTER." I yelled. As soon as I turned my back. BeBe ran up behind me and hit me in the head with a brick. I stumbled and fell to the ground. I tried to regain my composure, but as soon as I was about to stand up. I felt a metal object beat me in my back. I heard the crowd yell "Ms. Carolyn put the cane on that hoe." Everybody was laughing.

I couldn't get up, those bitches ganged me. "Y'all hoes had to gang me?" I yelled. I felt my back giving out. It hurt so bad. I prayed I had enough strength until they stopped. I covered my face up. I couldn't let a bitch fuck my face up, this is all I got. No ass, but titties and my cute ass face. I grabbed the gun from back so it wouldn't fall out. Hopefully they'll stop soon. I couldn't fight back if I wanted too. They finally stopped. I heard BcBe yell.

"DON'T YOU EVER COME TO MY HOOD and THINK YOU WON'T GET YOUR ASS BEAT BECAUSE YOU WILL HOE." She argued and laughed. I picked myself up off the ground. I dusted myself off. I had the gun in my hand. BeBe was so busy running her mouth she didn't see it.

"BeBe." I yelled and laughed. She turned around like I knew she would. As soon as she turned around to see what I had to say. I shot that bitch in her shoulder.

The only sounds that could be heard was "Pop, pop, pop." Everybody was looking yeah, I was the bitch with the gun. The bullets pierced threw her shoulder. She fell back instantly, and her eyes were bucked. I shot her three times in her shoulder. I wasn't trying to kill her. I was sending a fuckin' message.

"IT AIN'T NO FUN BEBE when Keondra got the gun." I laughed. Ms. Carolyn ran up on me and yelled.

"You shot my baby. Call the fuckin' POLICE" She cried. Fuck that bitch.

"You want to call the police now, but when you and your daughter jumped me you didn't think to call them? Bitch please." I shot that bitch in her fuckin' knee. I was looking for Niesha and Kadee. I had about five bullets left in the chamber and their names were written on them.

"Where the fuck did Niesha and Kadee go?" I yelled. I wanted them too.

"Aye Keondra, get out of here the police are on the way." He explained.

"Good looking out JR." I ran back to my car. Jermesha and Mia were standing right beside it. I hopped in and locked my door. I had to wipe this gun off before I dump it. I pulled off. Jermesha and Mia weren't riding with me. They can use their feet to get home. They could never ride with me again. As soon as I got to the corner. I threw the gun out. I'll call the police so they could find it. It's registered to Griff they'll pick his ass up. I grabbed my phone to call it in.

"Dekalb 911 Dispatch."

"I like to report a crime. I just saw a man throw a gun out the window on the 3700 block on Flat Shoals at the red abandoned house on the left." I swear Griff's going to learn about playing with me. I will ruin his whole fuckin' life.

"What type of car was the individual driving," the dispatcher asked?

"I couldn't see ma'am he was driving so fast. I knew it was something suspicious. I just wanted to report it." I explained.

"Thank you I'll call it in. May I have your name and a contact number?" She asked. I think the fuck not. I hung up in her face.

Chapter-18

Griff

Crimson Rose Tristan is finally ready. I knew last night would seal the deal. I swear I can't wait to dive deep off in that pussy. I'm looking forward to that. I had a busy day ahead of me. The only thing I was looking forward too was making love to her. I had to meet up with Baine and Ike in an hour to see what the fuck was up with the two of them trying to setup up shop in my hood? I'm taxing niggas. It's not going down like that at all. You can do it my way are you can learn the hard way. It's only one way out when it's comes to me and my paper and that's death. I got a crazy cash flow and I don't want any fuckin' interference.

If anybody wanted to setup shop on another block that I control it had to be my niggas and that's it. I had to meet with my attorney so Keondra and I could finalize our divorce. I can't wait for that. I gave my attorney the cashier check for $200,000.00 last week. I'm ready to put everything that happened with Keondra behind me. I had a bright future ahead of me and the last thing I needed was being married to her holding me back. I wasn't scheduled to do that until 4:00 p.m. Rashad was riding shot gun with me. My nigga Slap and D-Man was posted in the cut waiting for us to pull up. They called Rashad and told him Baine and Ike just pulled up.

"Aye nigga you got me in the dog house with Crimson because of the stunt you pulled last night." I argued. I had a strange feeling that Crimson was about to stop fuckin' with me behind that. Rashad looked at me and laughed and waved me off. I was serious I wasn't bull shitting at all.

"Man, whatever. Danielle knows she still wants me. The only reason she put me out was because Baine bitch ass showed up. You can't be too much in the dog house because you're picking her up and making plans to eat that pussy again." He chuckled.

"Fuck you Rashad. I need you to stop ear hustling. Look when we meet up with Baine and Ike let me lead this shit because I already know it's still some static between the two of you from last night. I already know how you give it up.

I'm not trying to have a blood bath on my hands today, but just in case I have Paco and Gustavo on standby to clean up your mess, because a nigga like me I got shit to do and I'm not trying to get my shoes or my hands dirty." I explained. Crimson and I had plans tonight. I got to handle this business and make sure I get everything ready for tonight.

"Damn Griff, I'm not that bad, am I? I'll let you lead but if that nigga looks at me the wrong way or even acts like he wants to do something. I'm doing what I should've done last night. A nigga can't try me twice." He argued. I looked at Rashad sideways. He had some explaining to do. "You heard what the fuck I said Griff. Straight up, that's how I'm coming." I knew shit was about to go left as soon as we stepped in the room. I could feel it. Rashad could say what he wants, but for some reason he was playing for keeps when it came to Danielle? It's always best to play your position right to avoid being in a fucked-up situation. I don't see this ending well because Baine and Rashad are two head strong individuals.

I don't cheat on females. It's not my thing. I haven't been honest with Crimson about Keondra because our divorce is almost final. I want a few daughters myself and when they look at me as their father, they'll know how a man is supposed to treat woman. We pulled up to the warehouse right off Lithonia Industrial. Baine and Ike were posted up right beside Baine's Maserati. I looked at him and just shook my head. I had money but I didn't want anybody to know I had it. I wasn't a flashy ass nigga. Never would I ever pull up to the spot in a Maserati. You never know who could ride through and mysteriously spot you.

It's cool though because I don't keep any of my work here. It's just a spot where I conduct business. No work is distributed from here at all. I threw my right hand up and flagged Ike and Baine over so they could come on. I didn't have all day. I had shit to do. Rashad and I made our way into the warehouse. Baine and Ike were following right behind us.

Security checked those niggas at the door. I wasn't worried about them trying anything. If nigga had the balls to try me while my back was turned. I can guarantee you their head would be lying on their mother's porch within two hours. I have snipers wherever I go. It's always a red beam on a nigga pointing at a nigga skull.

"Damn Griff, we're good. The fuck these niggas always searching us like we're informants and shit," Baine ask. I noticed he gave Rashad and icy glare. I swear these niggas need to dead that shit. It's bad for fuckin' business on all levels.

"For all I know you might be? Niggas always switch up. It's good to see you too Baine. Fuck all the formalities let's get straight to it. I heard y'all niggas are renting a house on my block to trap out of? I'm the governor. Y'all can't sell shit on my block without my consent. Rashad did you okay this shit," I ask. Rashad snarled his face up at me. I knew he was heated. I could look at him and tell. I was giving Baine and Ike the heads about where this conversation was leading too.

"Never THAT GRIFF. Why even question that? I DON'T fuck with these niggas like that." He argued. Rashad was looking at Baine instead of Ike. It's some tension in the room.

"Griff, no offense but stepping on your toes isn't our thing. The house we're renting it's on the Fulton County line; NOT the Dekalb County line, so I didn't think it was problem?" Baine asked and explained. I busted out laughing because that shit was funny as hell. I ran my hand across the tip of my nose. I can't believe this nigga said this shit.

"I don't give a fuck what line it's on. It's still East Atlanta which is my shit. You can't setup shop in East Atlanta. I got a house by Westlake High School, can I setup shop out there?" I asked. Baine and Ike turned snarled their noses up. "Exactly so we shouldn't even be having this conversation business is business. Don't fuck with mine and I won't fuck with yours is that understood?"

"Come on Griff, it's not like that at all." He explained. He'll have to come better than that.

"I know it ain't, but it wasn't going down like that. Come on Baine, our fathers ran this business this way for years. We might not see eye to eye but damn you're fucking up boundaries that have been put in place for years, but for some reason you want to swerve? I feel like you tried the fuck out of me?"

"Come on Griff. We don't see eye to eye on a lot of shit that's neither here nor there, but just off the bond our fathers had I wouldn't try you like that. It was a fuckin' mistake.

I'm not trying have any issues with you." He explained. "Oh yeah one more thing Rashad stay the fuck away from Danielle. That's me right there. That's my territory, with my name is on that. I know she's your EX and we gone keep it at that." He argued.

Baine just had to have the last word. I looked at Ike and he looked at me. I knew shit was about to go left. Rashad wiped the bridge of his nose and cracked his knuckles. He stepped in Baine's personal space.

"Aye Baine don't make this shit about Danielle pussy ass nigga. You pulled down on me yesterday, but today it ain't going down like that my nigga. Danielle is grown as fuck, but if she's in a relationship with you she'll tell me." He argued.

"Ain't shit pussy about me Rashad. You heard what the fuck I said, that's me right there. Danielle ain't got to tell you shit, you heard it from me. She belongs to me. That's my bitch. I put my name on it." He argued. Rashad pushed Baine. Baine pushed Rashad. Ike grabbed Baine and I grabbed Rashad. I didn't have time for this shit. Ike and Baine were finally out the door. Rashad pushed me off him.

"Why the fuck did you break it up? Griff I'm sick of him. I'll fuck around and kill him and that's fuckin' law. I don't give a fuck about the bond your OG and His OG had. It's loyalty over royalty. It's not about Danielle, but if she's his fuel, I swear I'll light his ass up."

"Rashad, you're tripping for real. He came for you. I saw it. Baine ain't built like you. If you beat his ass, he would be ready to shoot. Danielle is free game, but let that shit go. If she's fuckin' with him let them be. If you don't give a fuck about Danielle, then it shouldn't even be a problem." I argued. Rashad couldn't even look me in my eye, when I said that. He didn't want Danielle and Baine together. Rashad and I made it to the car. Slap and D-man hit up Rashad and told him they cleared it. I said what I had to say. I was done talking.

"Griff, I don't need you preaching to me and pointing out shit that doesn't need to be addressed. I ain't tripping off Danielle she knows what it is." He argued.

"Do you know what it is? Rashad that's why I don't cheat because if we end up together, it'll never be because I'm cheating. It'll be because they cheated." I explained.

"Griff, I ain't perfect. I ain't never proclaimed to be. I know I fucked up and I don't need you high lighting my mistakes. Trust me I'm paying for it every day. I care about Danielle a lot. More than she'll ever know.

I don't want to see Baine with her, but that's some shit I got to deal with when the times comes. But right now, he's not talking about shit. I got to holler at Danielle. I don't need her pillow talking about me. I heard her when she said they weren't together; it's the only word I'm going off." He argued. I couldn't go back and forth with Rashad. I had to get to this divorce attorney to finalize this paperwork. I dropped Rashad off at his spot in Midtown. My attorney's office was downtown in Atlanta off Peachtree Street right next to Wells Fargo.

I finally made it to my attorney's office. As soon as I made it in. I dapped it up with my attorney and grabbed a bottle water. Keondra was late as usual. Her attorney was here grilling me, but she wasn't. I'm sure Keondra fed her a bunch lies to make herself look good. We've been waiting almost twenty minutes. I told her attorney to call her because I'm ready to get this shit over with. I don't want to be married to her for another minute.

Keondra finally walked in looking like my fuckin' money. She looked at me and I nodded my head at her. My attorney and Keondra's attorney were talking. She took a seat in front of me and I wasn't paying her any attention. Crimson Rose Tristan was the only female that had my undivided attention. She kicked my feet under the table. I didn't even acknowledge her. She did it again, she knew she was pissing me off. I snarled my face up at her.

"Griff." She cooed.

"What Keondra? What the fuck do you want? You're already late and my time is fuckin' valuable," I argued. I'm not trying to hear nothing she's talking about right now.

"I'm sorry Griff. Some shit came up. I tried to get here as fast I could. Are we about to do this Griff? I don't want a divorce. I still love you. Do you know how I felt seeing you with her last night? Are you fuckin' her Griff and giving her something that belongs to me," she argued and cried?

Keondra was really pulling out all the stops. Her attorney rushed over to her to see what was up. I could tell they were on some girl power shit. I'm not mad at them. My attorney looked at me to see if I could give him any insight as to what happened. Keondra was putting on a show. Keondra's attorney was whispering something in her ear. Keondra finally stopped crying. Her attorney handed her some tissue. She's really putting on for these folks.

"Mr. Griffey my client would like to make a counter offer with the divorce settlement. She wants two million dollars instead of the $200,000.00 dollars that you were originally offering. She submitted proof of adultery prior to your allegations." She argued. Two million dollars over my fuckin' dead body. She ain't worth the $200,000.00 that I'm offering her. Her attorney pulled out photos of Crimson and I from Maria's party. Damn I knew Keondra was low but this low. My attorney looked at the pictures.

"I'm not giving you two million dollars. Keondra EXCUSE MY LANGUAGE but BITCH YOU AIN'T WORTH IT. I ain't never called you out your name but today I'm going to give it to you straight. You know I ain't never cheated on you. I should've and I had plenty of chances to do so, but I'm not that nigga and you know that. You want to talk about adultery? Let's talk about the nigga IKE DELEON you fucked last night?" I argued. I drained the life out of Keondra's face when I said that. She couldn't even look at me. Even though we weren't together I still had eyes on her. My eyes were always on Keondra.

I couldn't believe she was out here fuckin' off like that, but that's who she was. I just didn't know it. The video came through last night with her and Ike on tape getting it in. He couldn't even look me in my face earlier because he knew he fucked my wife. It's cool. He can have Keondra because I don't want her. I didn't even want to look at the video, but I had it just in case this bitch wanted to get beside herself. Thanks to Rashad he told me to always be two steps ahead of her.

"Dick got your fuckin' tongue Keondra? I swear I'm not even trying to go there with you, but since you want to take it there, we can. I'm not giving you shit. Not even a hard dick. The money is off the fuckin' table. You don't fuckin' deserve it. Sign these fuckin' papers before I make you sign them. I tried to do by right by you, but you fucked me over every chance you got, but it stops here." I argued. I gave my attorney the USB drive of Keondra and Ike last night.

He plugged it into his laptop. Keondra tried to put her head down. I was starring a hole at her. I wanted her to feel me. I didn't want to see it. I looked at her to avoid looking at the video, because I'm liable to break her fuckin' neck. She can have Ike.

"Excuse Mr. Griffey but you didn't have permission to record my client. It's not permissible." She argued. I swear if this chick doesn't sit the fuck down, I'm going to have my auntie to beat her ass straight up. I'm not trying to hear none of this shit.

"I don't give a fuck. I just need a divorce and since she wants to play games, she can pay her own fuckin legal fees." I argued. Her attorney started looking crazy at me, yes, I'm the nigga with the bankroll. I snatched the divorce papers out of my attorney's hand and pushed the papers in front of Keondra.

"Sign this shit right fuckin' now. I don't have all day and you're not worthy of my fuckin' time. I can't believe I wifed you." I argued. I'm tired of going back and forth about this shit.

"Excuse Mr. Griffey but you can't handle my client like this," she argued.

"Again, I don't give a fuck about how your client feels. I'm not even trying to be rude. I'm sorry I just want these fuckin' papers signed." I argued. Keondra signed her name on the dotted line. My attorney grabbed the papers and placed them in his brief case. Keondra and I were done officially. There was a knock at the conference room door. My attorney opened the door and it was two Dekalb County police officers. I was looking at them sideways. What the fuck where they doing here and why? The sheriff that was with them had on a Fulton County uniform.

"We have an arrest warrant for Carius Deon Griffey. A gun that's registered to you was used and left at a Crime scene on Flat Shoals Road today. Two females were shot but none of them can identify you as the shooter.

Your gun was left at the crime scene, so we need to take you in for questioning. It happened today around 2:00 p.m."

"What type of gun was it," I asked?"

"Glock 9. We received a tip from and unidentified female that advised you were leaving the scene and told us the exact location of where to find the gun," the officer explained. I looked at the officers as if they were crazy because how did they know to find me here?

Keondra couldn't even look at me. I knew she had something to do with this shit. I left a Glock 9mm at her house. LJ and Juice already hit me up and said Keondra was fighting BeBe and Ms. Carolyn. If you got the balls to shoot a bitch in broad day light take your fuckin' charge.

Keondra is going to make me murk her ass. I wasn't tripping because I had these cops on payroll and Keondra didn't need to know that. They carried me out in hand cuffs, and she had the biggest smile and smirk appeared on her face. I knew she was behind this shit I could feel it. I haven't been anywhere near the hood today.

I wasn't tripping because we're divorced. That's the only thing that matters to me. The officers ushered me out the building and into their police car. Officer Thomas removed the cuffs off me. I needed to call Rashad so he could pick my car up.

"Aye Officer Jones, how long is this going to be? I need to make a few phone calls to my partner and tell him to pick up my car. I need some food also because I got shit to do today. I need y'all to make this transition quick as possible."

"Look, sit tight Griff. We got you and don't talk too much in this car because it can be bugged. Everything you need is lying right underneath your feet." Officer Jones explained and looked at me through the rear-view mirror. I looked underneath my feet at the paperwork that was on the floor. I grabbed the papers to read them. It was the witness tip. It was a phone underneath it, telling me to press play. I placed the ear piece in my ear, and it was Keondra's voice was on the recording.

Damn she really set me up after all the shit I ever did for her ungrateful ass? My mother warned me about her ass, and I refused to listen. I should've listened. She fucked two niggas that I know about. It's not a female out here that can say I fucked them or entertained the thoughts of fuckin' them while I was with her.

I placed the paper work and the phone back on the floor. I looked up and Officer Jones and Officer Thomas both looked at me and shook their head. Keondra was gone see me behind this shit. All because she cheated. I sent Rashad a text telling him to pick up my whip and to meet me at Dekalb County Jail in about three hours. I swear this bitch has fucked my day up and set me back. I don't even call females bitches but Keondra deserves to be called that.

I had plans to wine and dine Crimson Rose Tristan all night. I had to handle this crazy ass girl. I haven't even had the chance to call Maria to get everything ordered that Crimson wanted. I wouldn't even be able to see her tonight because I had to handle this shit. Keondra will learn the hard way about fuckin' with a nigga like me. I grabbed the phone to call Crimson. She might not even answer because she doesn't even know the number. Surprisingly she answered the phone.

"Hello."

"Hey baby, what's up?"

"Nothing, I'm on my fifteen-minute break going over some notes for class. What's up and whose phone are you calling me from," she asked?

"Crimson, I'm not going to be able to come through tonight. I'm headed to Dekalb County Jail right now and I don't know how long I'll be here. Hopefully I'll be out in a few hours. I got one call to make and it was to you and Rashad. I didn't want you to think I was standing you up. Some shit happened in the middle of me handling my business." I explained.

"Are you okay Carius? Do you need me to do anything," she asked? I could hear the sincerity in her voice. She was a real one for sure and she deserves the world. I plan on giving it to her if she plays her cards right.

"I'm good Crimson. I always take the good with the bad. I'm just a little pissed that our plans are pushed back. We got plenty of time to get to that. I'll hit you up when I get out of here if it's not too late, I'll be by to scoop you."

"Okay Carius, be careful. I'll be up waiting on your call. I'm praying for you and I love you," she stated and hung up. I started to call her back. I wonder why she said that and hung up. She loves me. I can't think of the last time

I heard someone tell me they love me. Damn I wish my mother could've met her. I'm going to hit Keondra where it hurts.

Chapter-19

Keondra

Griff got me so fucked up. On HIS DEAD ASS momma, he gone fuckin' feel me one way or the other. If I got to hit up every trap house and stash spot to get my fuckin' money that's rightfully owed to me, I FUCKIN' will. I'll recruit a team of niggas to take him down. I'll be the head bitch in charge to execute the shit. If I got to tip the fuckin' FEDS off about his drug empire, I FUCKIN' will. All bets are fuckin' off now. It ain't no limit to what I'll do to get paid. I hope he didn't think he could walk away from our marriage without giving me anything because he's in his feelings? It's not going down like that.

Give me my fuckin' money or you're going to pay me with your life. I swear to God I will have him fuckin' murdered behind the money that he owes me. He'll be lying next to his fuckin' mother. Why did he think it was okay not to pay me? I know I pulled some fuck shit, but the $200,000.00 was guaranteed if something ever happened between us. He would still give me that and the house we shared. We wouldn't even be going through this if he would've given me another chance. He wanted to say fuck what we built and move on because I made one fuckin' mistake. I fucked the wrong nigga and I'll admit that. I'm not perfect and I'm a little disloyal so what?

Dekalb County picking him up was just the beginning of his demise. My heart dropped when he revealed that he knew I fucked Ike last night. I wanted to fuckin' die. I swear it felt like I was setup. I swear the next time I decide to fuck anybody it's going to be at my spot and on my terms. Ike took me down through there, he didn't seem like the type of nigga that would record a female without her permission. My attorney looked at me with so much disgust. I pay you to fight for me in court not to judge my lifestyle. I don't appreciate him man handling me in front of my attorney the way he did. I hate him. We're divorced but this shit is far from over.

Why did he have somebody following me anyway? If I would've known, he still cared I wouldn't have fucked IKE last night. I was peeking at him out the corner of my eye to see if he was looking at the video. His eyes were trained on me the whole time. I know he wanted to fuck me up. Griff has never laid hands on me before, but I could feel the anger and rage coming from him.

I rode Ike's dick last night like I had something to prove and I did. Ike had a bag that I wanted a piece of no matter the consequences. He was looking for me in the day time. He's been blowing my phone up all morning. I haven't given him a response yet. My phone was ringing, and it was my mother. I answered on the first ring because my mother has been sick, and God forbid something happened to her I would go insane.

"Hello mommy," I cooed. My mother is my weakness. In her eyes, I was perfect and couldn't hurt a fly but that was far from the truth.

"Keondra don't fuckin play with me. What the fuck you have done? Griff had the Sheriff at my house, and he put me the fuck out of my shit? I thought you owned this house? To make matters worse some bitch name BeBe and

Carolyn came over here and busted out my car windows. They shot up my fuckin' house and said they owed you one?" She argued. Oh, hell no they got me fucked up. I don't give a fuck what we got going on, leave my mother out of it. She's fuckin' off limits. If she ain't touched you don't touch her.

"Mommy let me explain. Griff and I are going through a divorce right now and it's ugly. He's not trying to give me anything. I can't believe he kicked you out of your house. I did own the houses they were in his name. We didn't have a prenup. The houses were guaranteed and the $200,000.00 in spousal support, but he took that off the table because of some false accusations." I lied. I couldn't tell my mother the truth. Admitting that I fucked my marriage up was something that I couldn't do.

"Keondra Lashay Terry, stop all the fuckin' lies. I know you better than you know yourself. I carried you for nine months. I hate to say it, but you're just like your father, evil and conniving and always scheming." She argued. I hate to hear my mother reference me that way.

"Mommy let me explain, -" I cried. It was all I was able to get out before she cut me off.

"Keondra, I don't give a damn if you don't want to hear it or not. Listen to me when I fuckin' talk. The streets are talking, and my ears are always to the fuckin' streets. I heard all about your little sex tape floating through the hood. I raised you better than that. If you can't keep it real with yourself about what's going on, then you can't keep it real with nobody else.

Admit you fucked up your marriage? You know right from wrong? Griff is a good man. Shit, he's nothing like his father. His father would fuck a different bitch Monday through Sunday but not him. You want to know how I know. It's because I was one of those bitches that had a date with Big Griff every week. Tuesday was my day of the week. My pussy was only worth $1000.00 a week to him. I couldn't compare to his wife. Shit, I wanted to be wanted, but I couldn't compete where I couldn't compare.

Griff married you. Anybody can look at him and tell he loved you. Whatever you did Keondra, you didn't have to do it. He wanted you for you.

Don't ever make permanent decisions on temporary emotions. I've been in the streets for a long ass time and just because I'm not in them heavy doesn't mean I'm not in the loop with shit because I am.

Oh my God, I was so happy when you brought him home to meet me. I knew he was the one. I was so happy when he decided to marry you. I was thrilled to know that nobody could say they were fuckin' my daughter's husband. I was pissed when I heard a few niggas say they were fuckin' my daughter and she was married to Griff." She argued and explained.

"Mommy I'm sorry I fucked up and I made a few mistakes along the way and I'm paying for it every day. He won't forgive me. I wasn't ready to be a wife. I still had a lot of living to do." I cried.

"Stop fuckin' crying Keondra because you should've told him that. I'm so disappointed in you. Do you know how many of niggas I had to fuck to provide for you and pay my way through school? A lot. I sold and busted my ass to make sure you didn't have to do the shit I did to survive.

You only had to fuck one nigga and that was Griff. But he wasn't good enough for you. Keondra, what the fuck are you going to do now with yourself? You're a smart girl. You were with Griff for years, I hope you saved plenty of money and have more to show besides clothes, shoes, and jewelry?" She asked, argued and explained.

"Mommy why didn't you tell me any of this. I have some money saved. Not much, but I do have something. I feel so bad that I've failed you," I cried. My mother couldn't talk about me. She's the reason I'm like this. Just maybe if she would've told me some of these things, I would've turned out different.

"Stop crying Keondra because you haven't cried about none of the shit you've been doing. BeBe and her momma told me you shot them. Next time you shoot a bitch you better kill them and cover your fuckin' tracks. All it takes for them is to give your name and your whole life is thrown away and for what? Bitches are going to talk regardless. Let them talk. If a bitch doesn't touch you it doesn't mean shit. Protect yourself by all means

I didn't tell you how I was living because; I never wanted to glorify what I did. Who I did and why I did it was to provide for you? I never wanted you to follow in my fuckin' footsteps. I'm your mother and it's my job to provide for you by any means. My past plays apart to my future but that's just a small glimpse of my reality. Every mistake I made I learned from it. Your father was the biggest mistake, but I wouldn't trade you for nothing in this world." She explained.

"Mommy I'm sorry I swear to God I am. I hate to use God's name in vain. You can come and stay with me. I know Griff won't throw me out, but I can't have you out on these streets. BeBe and Ms. Carolyn got me fucked up. They ganged me so I had to shoot them. It was self-defense. You can stay here in my mother-in-law suite." I beamed.

"No Keondra I'm good. Thank you for everything. I spoke with Griff and he agreed to let me stay here for forty-five days and he's getting my car fixed. I've been offered a traveling nurse position in California and Las Vegas so I'm leaving Atlanta baby girl and I want you to come with me?

I can't leave you out here by yourself and I'm over three thousand miles away." She asked and explained.

"Mommy Atlanta is home and all I know. I'll come and visit but I can't impose on you. You deserve it. I'll be fine. Don't pass up and opportunity because of me, but I will come out there to help you get situated for a month or so."

"Okay I'll take that but please stay out of trouble Keondra. Trouble is easy to get into but hard to get out of," she explained. My mother and I finished talking and hung up.

Chapter-20

Griff

Never in a million years would I think Keondra and I would've been here? Where the fuck did, we go wrong? No, where the fuck did, she go wrong; because I've done everything that I possibly could for her? I wouldn't have thought loving her would lead me behind these bars. I wouldn't be behind these walls on some bull shit if it wasn't for her because she's in her feelings. Keondra was out to get a nigga but why? All because she cheated. Thank God my grounds keeper at the warehouse in Lithonia can account for my time. Trust me if my time wasn't accounted for, I wouldn't have walked out these doors today.

Crimson Rose Tristan telling me she loved me was the only thing that kept a nigga sane. I reported the gun stolen. I was kept in a holding cell for about three hours. My mind was in a million places. I know I had to do shit differently. Rashad and I have already switched up our whole operation. Keondra knew something but she didn't know a lot. My mother always told me to never pillow talk with my partner no matter what. The less she knows the better. She knew where we trapped because I met her on the block. Lately, I've been switching everything up, bank accounts, stash spots.

I can't really say if they know Keondra did it, but they knew I didn't. I'm not a rat no matter what she did to me. I would never drop the dime on her. She will hang herself, but I won't. I checked the time on my time piece. It was a little after 7:00 p.m.

I could still see Crimson Rose Tristan if I wanted too, but I had to put my hands on Keondra first. I'm sick of her playing with me. I'm a ruthless ass nigga and I never wanted her to see that side of me. The worst thing Keondra can do is a poke a beast. She keeps poking and fucking with me. Rashad was already waiting for me. I hopped in the whip with him and we pulled off.

"Gawd damn nigga you fresh out Dekalb County. The next time you want to light up the block, let a nigga know something," he laughed. Rashad and I slapped hands with each other.

"Fuck you nigga, you know I didn't do that shit," I argued. Rashad looked at me and laughed. "Drive, you already know the location." I was ready to get this shit over with and put this shit behind me. I called Maria and told her everything that Crimson wanted, and she was cooking it for us. My Auntie Kaye was setting the house up for me. I wanted shit to be perfect. I had plans to take my time with her.

"Say less." He already knew what the play was. The moment Dekalb County cuffed me and took me into holding. Rashad had eyes on Keondra. I wanted to call Crimson Rose Tristan and let her know a nigga was out them gates, but I couldn't right now because I had to focus. D-Man and Slap were posted up outside guarding the old house that Keondra and I shared. They hit Rashad up and advised that they didn't see any movement. Keondra's been at home all day since she left the court house. Our house was ducked off in Conyers, Georgia.

It took Rashad about thirty minutes to get to our old spot. Traffic was heavy as fuck even the back roads was fucked up. I've been debating rather or not I wanted Keondra to keep this house, because she doesn't deserve shit from me, but I wouldn't put her out on the streets. Her mother couldn't stay in my house because Keondra and I aren't together and out of respect for Crimson she had to fuckin' go. Rashad finally pulled up to my house. I hopped out quick. Rashad grabbed my arm. I looked at him like he was crazy.

"Aye don't do shit crazy fuckin' with this girl. I need you out here in these streets with me. Don't put your hands on her, because we already know what type of female she is. She won't hesitate to call the police," he argued and explained.

"I know Rashad, I'm not going to touch her. Officer Jones is at the corner in case she does decide to call the police. They'll be the first ones on the scene."

"Good looking out. Smart move, I like that shit." I dapped Rashad up and headed into the house. I used my key because I'm still paying the bills here. Our house wasn't like I left it. Keondra wouldn't clean up shit. The living room was a mess. I could tell she's been shopping. Clothes and shoes were everywhere.

The kitchen had a shit load of dishes in the sink, she was fuckin' my house up. She could move. I'll get her a

Condo or a town house before I let her fuck up this house. I finally made my way upstairs. She was in our room standing in front of the mirror naked as the day she was born. She looked up at me. I could tell she was headed somewhere because her make-up was done, and her clothes were laid across the bed.

"Are you going somewhere Keondra," I asked?

"I am Griff, but what brings you by here? Last I checked we're divorced remember?" She asked and sassed. Why answer a question with a question?

"You know why I'm here, but I'm asking the fuckin' questions, not you. Damn Keondra what the fuck type of shit is you on? I'm your enemy all sudden? You shot BeBe and Ms. Carolyn and set me up to take the downfall? I told you about touching my fuckin' guns. The police know I didn't do that shit. BeBe and Ms. Carolyn were ready to give you up, but I told them not too. Gawd damn I've always been a good man to you, despite all the shady shit you've done to me. I know you stole from me, but I overlooked that shit because I loved you and what's mine was rightfully yours, so I didn't give a fuck. You hate a nigga that bad; you want to see me fucked off and caged up like an animal?" I argued.

"I made one fuckin' mistake Griff and it's over? You never gave me the benefit of the doubt to try to make shit right between us. You ain't no better than me. So how dare you come up in here and fuckin' judge me. It didn't take you long to find another bitch, but you ain't never cheated on me? All niggas cheat and you ain't no fuckin' different. You just did a great job covering your tracks. So, miss me with that shit Griff. You said fuck me? So, it's fuck you," she argued. I walked up on Keondra. It took everything in me not put my hands on her, but my mother taught me better than that. If it ever comes to a point where I'll have to put my hands on her it's time for me to leave.

"Aye watch your fuckin' mouth for real. Don't ever call Crimson a bitch. She ain't got shit to do with why you and I aren't together. It's fuck me now, because I divorced you? It's your fault because you couldn't keep your legs fuckin' closed. You're the cause of all of this. You created this shit. Own up to it. You're still fuckin' different niggas.

I don't regret marrying you. It was a lesson I learned. I should've listened to my mother when she told me not to marry you. I loved you enough to go against her word. I went against my mother for you. It was a lesson and in the midst; of the lesson, I received a blessing. I wasn't looking for Crimson. The only thing I was focused on was divorcing you and being alone, but one of my guardian angels had other plans for me. I haven't even blessed her with this dick yet, because I couldn't break her off while I was still married to you.

You know what Keondra, I put this shit on my OG. You don't want to be an enemy of mine because KEONDRA, I will burn you every fuckin' time and I mean that shit. I'm selling this house find you somewhere to fuckin' move too. Since you hate me so much. You don't need shit from me. Tell Ike and the nigga in the video to support your life style because I'm not doing it. I'm not your cash cow anymore. I hope you saved all the money you stole from me. You can keep it. I want you out of this fuckin' house by the end of the month. You can have everything here." I argued. Keondra swung at me, she tried to hit me. I moved out the way. I swear she wants me to put my hands on her, but I'm not that nigga. I will never put my hands on a female. "Aye keep your hands to yourself."

"Fuck you, Griff. You ain't shit but a pussy ass nigga. I don't even regret cheating on you now because a pussy always shows his true colors. I'm glad I stole from you and this is the reason why. Fuck that bitch too. I know it's because of her why you want to take everything from me? I ain't never wished bad on a nigga before, but I can't wait until the day your empire falls and the bitch that you think is so much fuckin' better than me, leaves you for another nigga with a bigger bank roll than you," she argued.

"Real niggas do real things. It was never about her. It was always about you. No matter what you say about me Keondra, you can never say I wasn't good to you. I don't give a fuck about the money. I don't care about the material shit that comes with living this life. I could lose it all today and not give a fuck. I'm hustler baby and I can hustle anything rather it be drugs or hoes. You can't take that from me. It's not a nigga or bitch out here that's going to stop me from eating. I swear I was blind when I was fuckin' with you. I don't even know how I missed the signs.

I guess the saying is true huh, love is blind? It was all about that bag for you huh? I'll never deny how much I loved you. Guess what, I didn't give a fuck about blowing stupid cash on you. It's crazy because I was a fool for you. I did everything for you. I Thank God every day he revealed the real you and I don't have to toss and turn laying next to you. These past few months I've been uncomfortable as fuck laying next to you. I knew it was a reason the pussy felt extra loose, it's because I wasn't the only nigga fuckin' you.

I can't even compare Crimson to you because Keondra, shawty, you don't even weigh up to her. I brought her a Maybach just because I wanted too. You know what's crazy. She demanded I take that shit back because she didn't want it. She told me to stop spending my money so reckless and to invest in stocks and bonds. I did that shit too. I'm making legit money off stocks too. I haven't even been with her for a month, but damn she's bringing more to the table than you ever could. I want to give her the world, but she doesn't want anything from me but me. I thank God every day for her. I swear to God I'm going to cherish her." I explained.

"Blah Blah Blah Griff, I'm glad you got you a new bitch that's as lame as you. You ain't the only nigga out here with a bag. As you can see, they ain't hard to fuckin' find. It's plenty of niggas out here checking for me. Your new bitch ain't weighing up to me. If you think you're going to leave me assed out without nothing your sadly mistaken. Everything you've built I can guarantee you it'll fall. Get the fuck out my house and I'll leave this bitch when I'm good and gawd damn ready. I hope you die when you leave this bitch. I swear I'm not gone cry." She argued. I sent Rashad a text from my phone giving him the okay to tell the movers and officers to come on.

"If I die today it'll be a Trap Holiday." I chuckled. It was pointless to even have this conversation with Keondra. She wasn't listening to shit I had to say, but if she kept talking, I would do something that I wouldn't normally do. I had officer Kilgore and Jackson to escort Keondra off my premises. I couldn't let Jones and Thomas do it. I didn't want her to know they worked for me. The movers were coming through the door packing up all her stuff. I swear I hate it came to this, but she forced my hand and disrespected me for the last time. She started grabbing all her clothes and whatever she could to take.

"Griff, I swear you gone regret this shit." She argued and threw her phone at the mirror. She started kicking the walls and destroying the house. I wasn't even about to respond. She wanted a reaction out of me, and I refused to give her anymore of time and energy.

Chapter-21

Crimson

The moment I got the call from Griff and he stated he was headed to Dekalb County Jail my heart started hurting. I swear I wasn't prepared for the pain I felt. I wasn't prepared for the words that slipped from his mouth. I still can't process that. My mind was filled with a bunch of what ifs. The thought of not seeing him again hurts. I love Griff. It's crazy because we just met, but you can't put a time limit on love. The time we've spent together I can honestly say that I love him. I wasn't ready to lose him. Life is a gamble and my feelings are in shambles. I hope he makes it back to me. I've been checking my phone for the past few hours with no calls or text messages. It was just a waiting game. I heard my room door open and it was Danielle. I sat my phone down beside me to see what she wanted. She took a seat on my bed right beside me.

"What's up Crimson, what's wrong with you? You've been quiet since we left work, and don't fuckin' lie because I know you. It's written all over your face," she argued and explained. I couldn't lie to Danielle if I wanted too. She's more than my best friend, she's my fuckin' sister.

"I'm stressed out. It's Griff. He called me while I was on my break and canceled our date because he was headed to Dekalb County Jail because something popped off. He didn't get into the details. I told him I loved him. Danielle what if I never see him again?" I pouted.

"Crimson, you know I'm riding with you right or wrong? I love Griff for you, but sis Griff is a street nigga. His name rings bells in these streets. The less you know the better. Him going to jail comes with the life style he lives. If you're going to be with him, I'm not saying you're weak but sis you got to toughen up and roll with the punches.

If he gets cased up and then you'll have to decide if you want to ride it out with him and be prepared to visit him. Shit, you got that niggas' black card. The moment he laid eyes on you it's been about you. You're falling in love with Griff. I can see it all over your face. That glow is everything. What did he say when you told him you loved him?" she asked.

"I know Danielle and I'll ride it out with him, he hasn't given me a reason on why I shouldn't. Yes, I'm falling in love with him. I can't even lie if I wanted to. He took my heart and held the moment he got in my good graces. How can I not? He's so perfect and attentive. He's everything I ever wanted and dreamt about in a man. I feel so safe and secure with him. I didn't give him the chance to say it back. I hung up before he had the chance to. I just wanted him to know that I loved him in case I don't see him again." I sighed. I held my head down because I didn't like the way Danielle was looking at me.

"Crimson Rose Tristan, girl you got it bad. I'm not even mad at you. Hold your fuckin head up when speaking about your man. It's nothing to be ashamed about. You know I would never judge you. I swear to God I'm so happy for you and I'm blessed to experience this with you. Griff loves you and I saw that the night we were out. He didn't give a fuck about me and his coward ass friend being in the room. He was all over you. I want that one day I swear I do. Don't ever doubt for one minute that he doesn't love you because he does." She beamed and smiled.

"Thank you, Danielle, for always keeping it real with me and having my back through everything. I wouldn't trade you for nothing in this world. What would I do without you? Lord knows I don't ever want to find out. Real friends are hard to find, and I thank God every day we found each other." I cried.

"Crimson cut all this mushy shit out. I swear I'm not trying to cry. I just did my make-up. I have a date with Baine tonight and he's been on me so tough since the Rashad shit. I think you're more upset that you won't be getting that cat busted open tonight," she laughed.

"Whatever Danielle! Have fun and behave."

"I am. I swear he better not piss me off." She argued and laughed. We finished talking. I curled Danielle's hair. Baine pulled up early to. My date was canceled. I was sitting by the phone waiting on Griff to call me. I decided to brew some tea and read a book.

Griff

"Aye Griff was everything cool back there. What the FUCK happened." he asked? I nodded my head no and ran my hands across my face. Rashad was my brother and there were no secrets between us. I trust him with my fuckin' life and my ex-wife. Today has been one of the worst days of my life. It was supposed to be special because the divorce was finally finalized. Keondra and I were finally going our separate ways and I could move on with Crimson how I wanted too, but Keondra had other plans for me.

I fucked around and got arrested and almost caught an attempted murder charge because she wanted to be mad at everybody because she fucked up. I know Ms. Carolyn and BeBe didn't play fair, but damn to shoot up the block and toss the gun and call the cops with my fuckin' gun. She knows those crackers can't wait to hide a nigga like me.

"Man Rashad, Keondra showed her motherfuckin ass. She was feeling herself talking about she was glad she cheated on me and stole from me. I started to put my hands on her but she ain't worth it. She fucked Ike last night. I almost knocked her ass out giving these pussy ass crackers a reason to hide me. She got to go. I had to cut all ties with her. I know hurt people hurt people, but it's not going down like that. A bitch can't hurt me or fuck off on me and think she can spend my cash. It ain't fuckin' happening.

She's a fuckin' liability. I try so hard to keep the beast in me calm, but she's begging me to put my fuckin' hands on her and let that beast roam free. I won't change who I am because of what the fuck she did to me. When my OG died you know these streets weren't fuckin' safe. Every fuckin' block was yellow taped behind mine. I don't want to be that nigga anymore, but I fuckin' will if she keeps fuckin' with me.

The whole time we were together I never cheated on her. It didn't even cross my mind. I went against my mother for her. The last words my OG told me about Keondra was the milk ain't clean. Rashad that shit fucks with me. She was warning me all alongKeondra wasn't it, but I was a dumb ass nigga not trying to hear that shit." I argued and explained and banged my fist on the dashboard.

"Aye Griff let that shit go! You live and you learn. Ike couldn't even look you in your face because he knew he fucked your ex-wife last night. I don't trust those niggas Griff, and it ain't got shit to do with Danielle. Now Keondra. I don't like the way those niggas are moving. I swear I'll put those motherfuckas to sleep without you giving me the okay. Fuck the truce Big Griff and Mahone had back in the day. We got to switch everything up now because she'll try hard as fuck to give them niggas our blue print. I'll do what you won't do and the cover that bitch in the dirt when it comes to my paper and my family.

It was better to cut ties with her now than later. Don't even sweat that shit. We've taken plenty of losses and bounced back every time. We'll add her to the list. I'm glad you're done with that bird. I hate to say I told you so, but I knew Keondra was a hoe because of the company she kept. Come on Jermesha, Tasha and Mia all those bitches are hoes. I don't give a fuck how fine they are. Slap, D-man, and Juice ran a train on all three of those hoes at the trap on Glenwood. I had to nip that shit in the bud. Take those hoes to a room. I didn't trust those motherfuckas around our money and work.

Auntie Kaye called and she said everything is done. She and Maria just left your house. Go pick up Crimson and take her home," he explained. I couldn't believe that shit. I'm not surprised though. I never understood why Keondra still wanted to hang with them and she was married? Now I know she was still hoeing around.

"I know Rashad, we've been switching shit up already. Trust me we're two steps ahead. I'm ready to cut ties with them niggas and if we go to war than it is what it is. They want war anyway just off the shit they pulled by renting that spot. It's whatever and I mean that shit. Baine ain't his OG and I'm not my OG. We grew up together but he ain't you.

I care about Crimson a lot she's different. It ain't about the bag with her. That's why I'm fuckin' with her. My street status means nothing to her. She ain't never had it so she doesn't give a fuck about getting it. I want to spoil her, but she won't even let me. It's something about her and whatever that something is has my nose wide the fuck open. I'm addicted." I explained and smiled.

"I see. Trust me, my nigga, I see! On some real shit Griff, that's a good look for you. Crimson is a good girl. Danielle always spoke so highly of her," he laughed and smiled.

"Rashad you know you fucked up with Danielle man? I swear you need to make shit right with her. You know shawty is going to be around because of Crimson and I don't want shit to be awkward all the time when you guys are in the same room with each other?"

"Griff, I know I fucked up. Stop reminding me of my fuck ups. Trust me I know what the fuck I did. Danielle and I ain't got shit to do with you and Crimson. If she's going to be around, then I'll move around. I'm cool on shawty. I did what I did. Yeah, I was a dog ass nigga because I couldn't shake old girl, but she should thank me for leaving her the fuck alone instead of dragging her along while I was fuckin' off. I was man enough to leave," he argued. I raised my hands up.

"Aye, I'm going to leave it alone." Rashad and I finished chopping it up. He dropped me off at Maria's because my car was parked in her the garage. I was headed to get Crimson Rose Tristan. A text message appeared on my phone from Crimson.

Crimson Rose Tristan - Carius Deon Griffey! I can't stop thinking about you. I hope you're okay. Jail isn't the place for you. I miss you, Griff I swear to God I

do. When I told you I loved you earlier, I meant it. I said a prayer for you earlier. I hope God grants it. Since I met you, I've been addicted to you. I don't know how to take being away from you. If I don't hear from by tomorrow morning. I'll be at Dekalb County Jail demanding a visit to see you. For some odd reason, sleep won't find me. I know why. It's because I'm so used to lying in your arms. If you so happen to get this message before I wake. I just wanted you to know that I was thinking about you before I lay it down.

I kept reading the text message over, and over again. A nigga couldn't stop smiling. Crimson Rose got my nose wide the fuck open. She was missing the shit out of me, and I was missing her too. She keeps me sane. I love her too and she knows that shit too. I couldn't wait to show her how much I do. If she was asleep, I couldn't wait to wake her. I can't wait to see the look on her face when I pull up. It needs to be a big ass smile because she has a nigga showing all thirty-two.

Crimson

Griff has been on my mind heavy. I've been looking at my phone waiting on him to call. I wish Danielle and Rashad were on good terms, so she could call him for me to see what's up. Danielle has been gone for a few hours. I brewed a cup of hot tea and took a hot shower. I knew I needed to eat, but I didn't have an appetite. I couldn't go to sleep for anything. I've been tossing and turning all night. I finally looked at the clock and it was only 9:00 p.m. I wanted to read a book, but I couldn't. I opened my kindle and closed it. My nerves are bad, and I've been biting my nails. I miss him. Right about now I would be with him. I was complaining about not being able to enjoy being in my own spot. Be careful what you wish for. I guess I had to make the best out of it. I don't want to be here right now. I feel helpless. I wish I could do something, but I can't. Griff didn't give me any details. He was very discreet. I would rather be somewhere laid up with him. I miss him, please free him.

I killed the light on my lamp and sat my phone on my night stand. I had too because I would keep looking at my phone waiting on him to call. I cut my TV off because I needed complete silence. I threw my covers over me. It was freezing in here and I could feel my eyes getting heavy. Thank God sleep was finally ready to take over my body. I guess I could get used to this for tonight.

I drifted off to sleep. I wasn't a hard sleeper. I heard someone knocking at my door. I wasn't expecting anyone. I looked at my phone. I didn't have any missed calls. I grabbed my robe to see who was at my door. I was sleeping good too. I wiped the sleep out the corner of my eyes. Danielle probably left her key. I don't remember her grabbing it. Baine was all over her. They look cute together.

"Who is it," I yelled and ask. I didn't hear anybody respond. Whoever it was they continued to knock without answering my question. I'm tired and sleepy.

"Who is it," I yelled and asked again? I wasn't opening this door without confirming who it was behind it. Shit somebody could be trying to break in. We just moved in too, they probably know I'm at home all alone. I grabbed my bat out the hall way closet. This time the knocks got louder.

"Who is it?" I yelled. I looked through the peep hole and it was covered I couldn't see anything. It's been a lot of home invasions

"Open up the door and find out," they yelled. It was muffled. I couldn't really make out who it was or what they were saying. I was taking a chance on opening this door. I hope I don't regret it. I hope it wasn't Rashad because Danielle was gone, and I didn't have time for his shit if Danielle and Baine popped up.

I opened the door and my face lit up. It was Griff. I was so happy to see him. He pulled me in his arms, and I wrapped my arms around his neck. He picked me up and I wrapped my legs around his waist. He closed the door behind him. I swear I didn't want to let him go. Oh my God, I missed him so much. He bit my neck. I balled my face in his chest. I swear his touch alone sent chills through my body.

"Why you didn't text me back? You should've told me you were free. You had me worried about you." I pouted and beamed. He was holding me so tight. He smelled so good. I kept inhaling his scent. I loved this man.

My nerves were a wreck. Thank God he's free. My mind can finally be at ease.

"I know, I'm sorry. I wanted to surprise you. It's funny because as soon as the text came through, I was headed your way. You know I had to see you. If you were asleep, I had plans to wake you, so here I am baby, in the flesh." He explained. I tilted my head back away from him and cupped his face. I've been waiting all day to kiss him.

"I missed you Carius. I'm glad you're free." I whispered. Thank you, God, for answering my prayers.

"I see. Grab your bag so we can get out of here. We still have a date tonight." He explained. Griff grabbed my hand and led me to my room. My bag was already packed sitting by the door in my room. I hung my robe up in the bathroom. I grabbed a face towel to wash my face.

"You messed the sheets up without me," he asked and laughed? I walked out of the bathroom to see what was so funny. I know my sheets didn't look that bad. I can't stand him sometimes, but I love him.

"Don't start with me. I couldn't sleep, how dare you make fun of me." I pouted. Griff walked up on me and cupped my chin. I gazed in his eyes to see what he wanted. Every time I looked at him in his eyes, I felt loved.

"I'm sorry Crimson. Come on baby and let's roll. I'm just fuckin' with you." I knelt to grab my bag out the corner. Griff snatched it out of my hand, and I hit the lights in my room. Griff grabbed my hand and led me to the living room. I grabbed my key off the counter so I could lock up. He snatched the key out of my hand. I popped him in the back of his head.

"Stop, snatching stuff from me." I pouted and laughed.

"Let me play my position and you wouldn't have to worry about me snatching things out of your hand." He argued and explained. I rolled my eyes at him. I missed him but I didn't miss his smart-ass mouth.

"You can play your position. I never said you couldn't. I'm sorry I'm just used to doing things by myself. It's taking me a minute to get used to you doing it." I explained. It's the truth. This relationship shit was new to me. I didn't depend on Griff to do stuff for me, but everything he's done is a blessing and I appreciate it.

"I know you can, but as your man, it's my job to do a lot of the stuff that you're accustomed to doing. I'm supposed to lighten your load and spoil the shit out of you even if you don't want me too." He explained. I didn't respond because no matter what I said Griff was going to do what he had to do anyway. We finally made it to the car. He opened and closed the door for me. We fastened our seatbelts and we pulled off. I connected my phone to his Bluetooth. My song was coming on by Future and Griff cut it down I was so mad at him.

"Griff, why did you that?" I asked and pouted.

"Because I got some better shit to say besides what's playing on the radio," he explained.

"Okay Griff, I'm listening," I stated. I turned around to face him to see what he had to say. He grabbed my left hand and held it.

"I've been thinking about you all day. I was caged up in a holding cell for three hours before they finally decided to set me free. I swear the only thing that kept me sane was you telling me you loved me. Did you mean it Crimson or were you just saying it to calm me?" He asked.

Griff took his eyes of the road for a minute and stared at me.

Why was he putting me on the spot right now? I didn't have anything to hide. Shit, I do love him. I couldn't hide it or mask it if I wanted too.

"I've been thinking about you too. My nerves have been a wreck since the moment I got the call from you. I knew then that I didn't want to be without you. Damn, I'm addicted to you. I love you, Griff, it wasn't a façade. I really care about you. It's crazy because I just met you.

I wanted you to know that just in case I never got the chance to see you again. Tomorrow isn't promised but today is. I refused to hold it in. My heart wouldn't allow it. I wouldn't be able to live with myself if I kept my true feelings to myself." I explained. Damn, I just confessed how much I love and care about him. I tried to lightly put my head down because I was embarrassed. Griff cupped my face.

"Crimson, I love you too. You got my heart. I think you know that? If you don't, I don't have a problem showing you. I got a big heart and some people will take advantage of that, but I don't get that feeling from you. It's one reason why I'm so open and honest with you. I swear I was good on love until I met you. I'm not going to hold back when it comes to loving and spoiling you. I get it from my mother. Damn, I wish you could've met her. I know she would've loved you. I love hard and I've been addicted to you." He explained. I'm speechless.

"What am I going to do with you Carius Griffey," I asked?

"You know what to do with me. You've been doing it since the moment you met me. Don't ever switch up on me. I need you. You're the only things besides Rashad and my immediately family that seems real to me." He explained and looked at me.

I took everything in that Carius was saying. I could feel it. I swear I could love him forever. Damn, he's perfect. I've never prayed for a man before, but with him, it'll be an everyday thing.

Chapter-22

Griff

We finally made it to the house. Traffic was heavy coming through the city. I couldn't wait to make it home and make love to Crimson. I thought I could wait, but shit if she was ready it was going down tonight. It's crazy seeing Crimson in her element and finally, being honest and open to me about how she feels. The whole time I was zooming through traffic I kept catching glances at her. I was breaking her down slowly but surely in a good way. I had other walls that I was anxious to break down.

My day was fucked up, I can't even lie but being with Crimson had me looking toward the sky. Things were looking up for real I can't even lie. It took me longer than usual to get to the house, but as soon as I hit the gate and entered the garage. I could smell the aroma of the seafood boil and steaks that my Auntie Faye and Marie hooked up for us.

Maria sent me pictures of the bathroom setup. Rose petals and candles were everywhere. There was a masseuse table setup in my room. I wanted shit perfect for her. I grabbed Crimson's bag out the back seat. We headed in the house and my stomach started growling instantly. I haven't eaten all day and I was hungry as fuck too.

"Griff it smells really good in here, how did you have the time to do all of this," she asked?

"I make shit happen remember that. I'm about to take your bag upstairs fix our plates and I'll be back to join you." Auntie hooked the table up. It was covered in a few candles. I had to light the candles quick before Crimson walked in here.

"Griff, what you want," she yelled and asked?

"Everything." I headed upstairs to check the setup Maria and Auntie Kaye had put together. It was cool. I hope she likes it. The rose petals were everywhere. They over did it.

I made my way back down the stairs. My eyes locked with Crimson and she was starring a hole in me. Her hands were rested on her thick hips. Her breasts were spilling out of her tank top.

"What I do baby, why are you looking at me like that," I asked

"Carius what's all of this? Everything I wanted to eat. It's already cooked and prepared. If you went to jail how the fuck did this happen?" She asked and argued. I walked up on Crimson and invaded her personal space. I ain't trying to lose Crimson that's why I made sure my divorce was finalized before I really took it there with her.

"Calm down. I did go to jail. Why would I lie about something like that? I make shit happen I told you that. I had Auntie Kaye and Maria do this for you. Did I commit a crime Crimson? If loving and spoiling you is a crime, then charge me, baby." I explained. I bit Crimson's bottom lip and stole a few kisses. "Come on and let's eat. Stop being mad at me. We got a long night ahead of us."

"I'm not mad at you. I just find it odd everything I wanted to cook is already cooked and laid out in front of me. Thank you. The setup is beautiful," she explained and beamed.

"You don't have to thank me for doing shit I'm supposed to do. My day was fucked up Crimson, but I wasn't canceling our plans because of it. The moment I walked out of those doors I made some calls to get this done for us. The night's still young and we have a long night of head us.

"Carius, I have manners and I appreciate you, so I'll always thank you regardless of what you say. Get used to it." She sassed and explained. Crimson took a seat at the table. I grabbed her hand and said grace. It didn't take me no time to get to it. The food was good. I shot Maria and Auntie Kaye a text and told them thank you. I had to throw them something extra for this. Crimson started yawning.

"I'm tired and full Griff. Hurry up I'm sleepy," she yawned. I need her to wake up she can tap out later. I hope she doesn't have to work tomorrow. I made plans to change the forecast for the weekend.

"I'll put you to sleep later, let's put this food away and the dishes in the dishwasher. I got a few more surprises before I allow you to go to sleep." I explained.

"You know how I feel about dish washers. I'll wash the dishes and clean the counters and you can dry them," she explained.

"What if I didn't want you to help me? I just want you to sit here and keep me company." I knew she would try to wash them, but we don't have time for that.

"You know I can't do that, especially after you've done all of this for me? Team work makes the dream work," she beamed and explained. I swear Crimson was hard headed as fuck. I just wanted her to sit here while I cleaned the kitchen. She's trying the fuck out of me. I know she's just trying to help but I got it. As soon as she ran the dish water and grabbed the sponge. I politely cut the water off and grabbed her hand. I picked her up and sat on her the island so she could have a seat.

"Sit down Crimson, tonight is about you and I don't want you lifting a finger, I explained. Crimson had a problem with pouting and whenever she didn't get her way. Crimson wasn't talking about shit. I wasn't about to wash all these pots and pans. I'm using the dish washer. If it's not clean to her liking, then I'll wash them in the morning. I washed our plates and dried them. Crimson was giving me glares when I was loading the pots and pans in the dish washer. She better be glad I didn't throw them away.

"Griff. I would've washed those if you would've allowed me too."

"I know you would've, but I want to get our night started." I dried my hands off and pulled the blind fold out of my back pocket. I approached the island where Crimson was sitting and stood in between her legs. I pulled her close to me. Damn, I couldn't wait to get her up out of these clothes.

"Come on and put these on, so we can get our night started."

"Why do I have to put a blind fold on Griff?" She sassed and huffed. I bit the crook of her neck and gripped her ass.

"Because I said so. I got a night full of surprises planned, that's why." I put the blind fold on Crimson and led her upstairs to my room. The tub was filled with rose petals. I cut the water on and placed Crimson's hand inside.

"Is this warm enough to your liking?" I asked.

"Yes, it's fine, when can I take this off," she asked. She was pressed to get the blind fold removed.

"When I'm ready for you to take it off. I'll let you know." I explained. I sat Crimson on the toilet in the bathroom and started undressing her from her head to her toes. I massaged her feet. A few soft moans and hisses escaped her lips. "You're tense. Do you like how that feels?" I asked.

"Yes," I swear her pussy was sitting up talking to me, begging me to free it. I pulled her shorts down and lifted her shirt over her head and unfastened her bra. Her breasts touched my chest. The tub was almost full. I cut the water off and removed the blind fold. I grabbed Crimson's hand and led her to the tub.

"Griff this is beautiful," she beamed. I knew she would like it. It seems like some shit that she would like.

"I know I told you I wanted to surprise you. That's why I didn't you want you to see the setup." I poured Crimson a glass of wine in the champagne flute. I took a shot of Don Julio to the head. "Take a sip. It's Moscato. Maria said you'll like this. It's a girly drink. I'm sure you can handle it." I started undressing. I took my Rolex off and climbed in behind Crimson and started massaging her shoulders. She tilted her head back on my chest. Crimson got to be the one because she got me doing shit I ain't never done. I ain't never did this for no one. I ain't tripping though because I know she's worth it.

"Carius, why are you so quiet? What's on your mind?" She asked. Lately, I've been keeping a lot of shit to myself, but Rashad knew it all. I feel like I could let Crimson in a little bit.

"What makes you think something is on my mind? I'm just enjoying the moment. You good," I ask. I was tired. I felt Crimson's body shift. I opened my eyes. She wrapped her arms around my neck and stroked my goatee. She placed a kiss on my lips. I returned the kiss and wrapped my arms around her backside and gave it a tight grip. "What's up?"

"Griff, if you're tired, we didn't have to do this. It could've waited. I appreciate you so much, but I don't want you to be tired trying to surprise me. I care about your health, and you need to get some sleep. You've been on the move for a few days now," she explained.

"I'm good Crimson if we got plans nothing is going to stop me from keeping them. You're special to me I ain't gone never disappoint you. If I tell you I'm going to do anything for you my word is bond and that's the only thing that I'm standing on."

"I swear Carius, you never cease to amaze me. Sometimes I trip on how we met. My routine has never changed. I'm always at the store on the first of the month shopping for Mother Dear and I ain't never ran into you. What were you doing there and why didn't you have any groceries with you?" She asked. I swore I thought we moved passed that.

"Does it matter why I was there? It really doesn't matter now is because we ran into each other. I was supposed to be there to find you. Since you want to be nosey, I was there looking out for someone who I shouldn't have been. I was supposed to grab her a few things. I guess my guardian angel knew my focus needed to be on you, but I lost my train of thought when my eyes landed on you. I had to have you. I was determined to get to know you. My determination landed you here, so I think we were meant Crimson." I explained. Damn, I miss my mother. I miss my

OG too. A tear escaped my eye just thinking about the two of them. My father wasn't the best man to my mother, but he was a real ass nigga to me. He showed me the game and gave it to me for free. Crimson wiped my eyes with her thumbs.

"What's wrong baby," she asked? She cupped my face in the palm of her hand forcing me to look at her. I swear she notices everything about me. She pays attention well. It feels good not to be the only one in the relationship.

"I was just thinking about my mother. I miss her like crazy. I need to go see her. I was supposed to go by there a few weeks ago, so I could tell her about you, but I haven't made it by there yet." I explained. My mother would be tripping if she saw me right now. My mother always brought a smile to my face. I know she would've loved Crimson for real.

"Carius, I want to see some pictures of her. What's her name? I can tell that she's special to you, because every time you speak of her it's this sparkle in your eye, and it's this expression on your face. It tells a story that I want you to tell me one day. When you do decide to go see her, I want to go with you so I can introduce myself." She explained. I felt that for real.

"Cayleigh Griffey I'll take you with me when I go. Don't flake out on me? I'm holding you to that." It speaks volumes she wants to meet my mother.

"Cayleigh that's a beautiful name. I may have to use it one day. Why would I flake out on you? If I didn't want to go with you, I wouldn't have asked. She's special to you so of course, I want to meet her, even if it's not in the flesh. You were blessed to have a mother and a father. I had none of that just, Mother Dear, but I wouldn't trade her for anything in this world. I swear to God I wouldn't." She explained.

"You're blessed too Crimson. I didn't have any grandparents, but I got plans to steal Mother Dear from you if you would allow me too. I'm taking her anyway rather or not you give me the okay. My mother was a good woman and my father was a real ass nigga. I'm sure you'll be a wonderful mother one day."

"Whatever, Mother Dear isn't up for grabs, she likes you though and that's a good thing. I forgot to tell you Jermesha and I got into a few days ago. I swear I almost beat her ass in front of her kids and that ain't me. She took me out of my element. She was talking reckless about you and me. Mother Dear vouched for you. She swore I had sex with you already. I told her when I did, she'll be the first to know, so her accusations would be true." She explained. Fuck Jermesha I know why she was hating, but Keondra and I are divorced.

She ain't got to prove shit to nobody. They know what it is with us, they can see it. I don't give a fuck about what she says. I'm done with that. She didn't deserve a nigga like me. She better give thanks to God she didn't give me shit or else she would've been lying in dog shit.

"I told you she was jealous of you. Don't even touch her, she ain't worth it. She ain't on your level. You got too much to lose baby. You're going places that she can only dream about going too. If she thinks she's mad now, she hasn't seen anything yet. It's just the beginning. Come on and let me wash you up because this water is about to get cold and as you can see, we can talk all night, but your cousin is irrelevant."

"I know Carius, but nobody can tell me about you, but you. I don't go fishing for information about your past because that has nothing to do with me. I couldn't let her disrespect me in front of her friends. I don't bother anyone I'm tired of her coming for me. It's only so much I could fuckin' take and I'm way past my boiling point." She argued. I don't do female drama, but I'll check Jermesha. Keep my name out your mouth because you don't fuckin' know me. You know of me. I can't stand messy as females. She's already on my shit for coming at Crimson sideways. I'm not feeling that. Keondra is just like the company she keeps. I don't know how I didn't see it. Hoes always flock together.

"I hear you. Always defend yourself. I want to take you to the gun range, with me in a few weeks. I want to teach you how to shoot." I explained. I grabbed a wash towel and started washing her up. I felt her body tense up with each part of her body I touched. "Be still I'm not going to bite you yet. I need you to get used to this. We have plenty of nights like this ahead of us."

"Griff, what would I need to learn how to shoot a gun for-," was all she was able to get out. Crimson wanted to say something about that, but it wasn't up for debate. I put my hands over her mouth because I didn't want to hear her response. I'll never put her in harm's way. If something ever happens to her and I'm not around, I want her to be able to lay someone down and defend herself. I finished washing Crimson up and I was about to start washing myself up and she snatched the towel from me and did it for me. I rested my hands behind my head because I enjoyed her hands on me.

"Aye be careful down there I don't want my snake to bite you," I laughed. She rolled her eyes and didn't respond.

"Raise up and turn around so I can wash your back and neck," she yelled.

"Who are you talking to like that?" I asked and laughed.

"You, who else. It ain't nobody in here, but you and me," she sassed and laughed. She finished washing me up. I let the water out the tub and Crimson tried to rush up out the tub without me. I had to stop her because I wanted to dry her off and put the blind fold back on her.

"Griff, what are you doing now?" She pouted and huffed.

"I need to dry you off and put this blind fold back on." Crimson started huffing and puffing. I swear she's spoiled as fuck if shit doesn't go her way.

"Look you can dry me off, but I'm not putting the blind fold back on. I'll close my eyes and not peek. Is that cool with you," she argued and sucked her teeth.

"It's not cool with me. The blind fold is going back on, but only for a few minutes. Come on and stop being defiant before I give you a few reasons to pout." I finished drying her off. She had a few flowers stuck between her ass. I swear it was a beautiful sight to see. I smacked her on her ass when I was finished.

"Ouch you can't be smacking people like that and I just came out the tub. It hurts," she whined and pouted. Crimson finally decided to oblige. I put the blind fold back on her. My hands roamed every inch of her body. Her nipples were erect from my touch and a few chill bumps appeared on her skin. I grabbed her hand and led her to the bedroom. I picked Crimson up and laid her on her back side on the masseuse table. Damn, I wanted to dive in head first.

"Griff, what are you doing," she asked? I swear Crimson was nosey as hell. She wants to know everything. I got her and I need her to trust me and follow my lead.

"You'll find out! I got you and never doubt that. I'll never let anything happen to you." I removed the blind fold. Crimson raised up and took in the scenery of the room. Roses and candles were everywhere. It was a full moon tonight. I had the blinds opened and the moon light mixed with the candles light were shining through the windows.

"It's beautiful Carius, thank you, baby," she beamed.

"I know. That's why I wanted to surprise you. I wanted to see your beautiful smile appear on your face. Lay back on the massage table so I can handle my business." Crimson laid back on the masseuse table. I grabbed the massage oil and started massaging her feet. Crimson's feet were pretty. Her toes were painted white with some glitter shit on it. It looked good against her toffee colored skin.

My hands moved their way to her calves and thighs. I swear her pussy was singing to a nigga. Fuck me was the tune. I massaged her thighs and gave them a tight grip.

"Damn you thick as fuck." My hands massaged her thick ass and hips. She was looking at me out the corner of her eyes. I grabbed her breasts with both of my hands. Her nipples were hard as fuck. I placed both, of them in my mouth and sucked them. My tongue was having a field day with her nipples. I traced my tongue down her stomach. My face was eye level with her pussy I dived in head first.

"Mmm," she moaned and squirmed. I tongue fucked Crimson wet. Her juices were coating my tongue. It tasted like mangos and peaches. Her juices mixed with my spit were running down the crack of her ass. The sheets on the masseuse table were soaking wet. I started to snatch those motherfuckas off. She has a tsunami between her legs. I hope she doesn't drown me. Her legs were shaking, so I knew she was on the verge of an orgasm. Soft moans and hisses were escaping her lips. Crimson ran her hands through my waves.

"I want you to fuck my face." My teeth latched on to her nub. Crimson locked her legs around my neck and started bucking her hips wildly. I lifted the bottom of her ass shoving her pussy in my mouth. She tasted good as fuck.

"I'm about to cum," she moaned.

"Go ahead. I want you too." I felt Crimson's body jerk a few times. I licked all of her juices up. She had made a fuckin' mess on this masseuse table. I tapped her on her legs, and she raised up and looked at me. I motioned with my hands for her to come a little closer. I grabbed a face towel and wiped my face clean. I picked her up and tossed her on the bed. Her body bounced a little bit. I can't wait to murder this pussy.

"You know it ain't no turning back after this?"

"I know Carius. I want it," she mumbled and explained. She bit her bottom lip. Turning me on even more. "Take it easy on me Carius." I climbed in between Crimson's legs. Her thighs were so fuckin' thick. I knew she was a virgin. I ate her pussy just to loosen her up some. She was beautiful as fuck. Her hair was a mess, I had plans to fuck it up some more. "Wait we need a condom," she pleaded. I snarled my nose up at Crimson. She was tripping for real. I wasn't using a condom.

"Crimson, God doesn't make any mistakes if we go half on a baby then it was meant to be. I'm not using a condom I need to fill all of you. I'll take care of you and my seeds until eternity. I mean that shit. The only thing I want to do is take care of you and spoil you." I leaned in and took Crimson's bottom lip in my mouth. I shoved my tongue down her throat. The kiss we exchanged was passionate. You could hear our hearts beating at the same tune.

She raised up and wrapped her arms around my neck. Her nipples were touching my chest. She was looking a little uneasy. She wrapped her legs around my waist. I slid the tip of my dick in. I tried to pull out and slide back in, but her pussy was too wet, and her walls had a death grip on my dick. Crimson was tight as fuck. Her walls were pulling me in and gripping my dick. "Shit, damn!" I couldn't even move. I felt the nut already rising toward the tip of my dick. I had to take it slow because I wasn't ready to bust just yet.

"It hurts Griff," she moaned and whined. I wasn't trying to hear that shit because it had to hurt first before it felt good.

"I'm not even in all the way Crimson. It'll hurt at first, but it'll stop." I explained. She started moving back toward the headboard trying to get away from me. I already told her it was too late for that. It ain't no turning back. I closed the small gap between us. She started grinding her hips making herself more comfortable, giving me more access to her. That was my cue.

I slammed my dick inside of her pussy. She moved back a little bit. I stroked her long, deep and hard. My dick and her pussy found their own rhythm. The only sounds you could hear throughout the room were her moans and hisses and my dick pounding her pussy. Sweat was dripping down my forehead and the beads were landing on her chest. I noticed a few tears in her eyes. I wiped them with my hands and continued to pound her pussy.

I had too it's the only way she'll get used to it. I tried so hard not to look at her because I'll fuck around and take it easy on her.

"It's too big and it hurts Griff," she moaned and cried. I continued pounding Crimson. I was knee deep in her pussy. I whispered in her ear.

"You got to get used to it, Crimson sometimes love hurts, but this is a good hurt. Turn around and arch your back. I want you face down, ass up." I grunted. She did as she was told. I started pounding her from the back. Her juices were sliding down the crack of her ass. I gave her slow death strokes. It was time for me to take my time with the pussy. Her hair was a mess. I grabbed a hand full of her hair pulling her toward my chest. She looked over her shoulders giving me a faint smile. I was almost at my peak. My hands were rested on her breasts. I slammed her down on my dick three times. Using her body for support. I shot my seeds in Crimson I couldn't help it. I fell on my back she drained a nigga. She fell with me. I placed soft kisses on her neck.

"I love you Crimson Rose Tristan."

"I love you too," she stated. I raised up and made a warm towel with soap. I had to clean us up. I rolled Crimson over and removed the sheets so we could lay it down. Crimson couldn't even open her eyes after our session. I laid down right beside her and pulled her in my arms and drifted off to sleep.

4 WEEKS
LATER

Chaper-23

Crimson

The moment Griff and I first had sex six weeks ago, we haven't been able to stay away from each other. He had my body reaching peaks that I never could reach. If I wasn't at work or school I was at his house. I haven't been home in weeks, but today I kept losing my balance at work, so they sent me home early. I had to leave class early because I couldn't keep my breakfast down and I kept running out to throw up. It's almost flu season maybe I caught something at school or work? I can't even think of the last time I've been sick.

I didn't even tell Griff because I knew he would be worried and telling me to quit my job, because he didn't want me working. He just wanted me to go to school and that's it. I loved the fact of having my own money. So, whatever he did for me was extra. Danielle brought me home to our apartment. The whole way home she's been eyeing me. I knew she had a few things she wanted to say to me since class. I haven't seen much of her either because she's been with Baine.

"What's wrong with you Danielle? Say what you got to say." I sighed. I really didn't feel like being lectured today. I just want to lay down and relax without any interruptions.

"Crimson you've been sick for a few days. I didn't want to say anything but are you pregnant?" She asked. I looked at Danielle as if she was crazy how dare she ask me that. I can't be sick without someone assuming I'm pregnant.

"No Danielle, I'm not pregnant. I just caught a little bug that's all. Besides the nasty patients, we see at Walgreens and the people we go to school with, I caught a cold or something that's it. Griff pulls out." I explained.

"Yeah okay," she mumbled and gave me the side eye.

"What the fuck is that supposed to mean?" I asked.

"Crimson you just started having sex. How do you know that he's pulling out? Have you seen him pull out? What does his cum look like? I'm just keeping it real with you. I think you're pregnant? I brought you a pregnancy test at work. I know you better than you know yourself. You never get sick because you're always eating ginger and garlic. It's morning sickness quit being in denial," she argued and explained. I didn't even respond because she made some very valid points.

"Bye Danielle." She handed me the pregnancy test and dropped me off at home and headed back to work. I climbed inside of my bed and I sent Griff a text and told him I was at my apartment. He always pulled up on my lunch break. My phone rung instantly. I hope I wasn't pregnant. I wasn't ready to have a child.

"Hello." I yawned. I swear if Griff didn't pull out like he claim he did. We're about to have some problems. I don't care about how much money he has because he knew I wasn't ready.

"What's up, baby? What's wrong why did you leave? I thought we were having lunch," he asked?

"They sent me home from work because I can't keep my balance and I can't keep anything down," I explained. I knew he was about to trip. I feel it. He's so protective over me it's crazy.

"Are you okay I'm about to pull up, do you want me to grab you anything to eat," he asked?

"I don't have an appetite." I sighed.

"Alright if you say so. I'll make you some chicken noodle soup when we get home. I'll call Auntie Kaye to the house she's a nurse. She'll examine you to see what's going on. I'll be there in about twenty minutes." He explained.

Twenty minutes for Griff was more like ten or fifteen minutes. I'll close my eyes until he gets here. I need a few minutes by myself because I know he'll be under me and I won't be able to relax.

Griff

My schedule was busy as fuck today. I had to meet up with Baine and his father today regarding business, but if Crimson was sick then I'll have to reschedule. Rashad could handle it, but I'll never send my nigga into a blind situation without me on hand. I told Baine I had to reschedule. I couldn't be out here in the streets and Crimson was sick. I got to take care of home first and then get back to this money. I called Auntie Kaye and she advised me that'll she'll meet me at the house in about two hours she has another client and then she'll stop by.

I pulled up to Crimson's spot. I jogged up the steps and let myself in. Crimson was in her bed asleep. I climbed in bed right behind her. I ran my tongue behind her ear lobe. She started stirring in her sleep and turned around to face me. She was running a fever too; her body was extra warm.

"Why didn't you wake me up?" She asked and yawned.

"I was about too but you were sleeping, and I wasn't ready to wake you up just yet. You're sick Crimson and you're running a fever. Come on and let me get you home so I can take care of you."

"I feel fine Griff," she yawned. Crimson was sick and she didn't even know it. I grabbed a towel out of the bathroom and wiped her face. Her cheeks were red.

"Come on so we can get up out of here." I grabbed Crimson's hands and helped her out of the bed. She threw on a tank top and some jogging pants. I grabbed her water out the refrigerator, handed it to her and locked the door to her townhouse. Crimson and I made our way to the car. I noticed she didn't say anything the whole time we've been driving. I turned down the music to see what was up. She looked over at me.

"What's wrong with you baby, you haven't said anything since we pulled off? Do you need me to pull over and get you something?"

"I'm fine, can I ask you something," she asked? She turned around to face me. She had a smug look on her face. I'm not going like the next thing that comes out of her mouth.

"Sure, what's up?" I asked. Crimson was sucking her teeth. I knew she had an attitude because she was sick, but I haven't done shit.

"Have you been pulling out," she asked? Damn, she caught me off guard with that one.

"You want me to be honest? I slipped up a few times Crimson and I didn't pull out. I'm sorry do you think you're pregnant? If you are, abortion isn't even a thought. You know I got you so don't even trip because I'm going to take care of you and my child regardless." I explained.

"How do you slip up and you know I'm not ready for any kids yet?" She argued and explained.

"Crimson God doesn't make any mistakes. If you're pregnant it was meant to be. I got you. Sometimes things happen that we can't control. I'm going to take care of you and my child regardless. I'm sorry what more do you want me to say," I asked?

"I feel so stupid because not once have you told me that you slipped up a few times and didn't pull out. I might be pregnant because I'm trusting you to do the right thing and you couldn't even do that. You know what take me back home Griff." She argued.

"Look Crimson I fucked up, by not telling you that I didn't pull out okay. I'll admit that. So, if you are pregnant trust me that I'll take care of you and my child. I'm not taking you back home so you can dead that shit. If you're sick and you're pregnant with my child, it's my job to take care of you. Let me do my job and take care of you." I argued and explained.

"Griff, I don't even want to be around you right now. Don't say anything else to me and I mean it."

"What the fuck is that supposed to mean," I asked?

"I don't want to be pregnant. I still have things that I want to do in life. I didn't give you permission to plant a kid inside of me," she argued and explained.

I wasn't about to go back and forth with her. It wouldn't get us anywhere. I turned the music back up and headed to the house. Whatever she wants to do in life I don't have a problem helping her do it all.

Crimson

Tears were flooding my eyes. I tried so hard to hold in my sobs and sniffles, but I couldn't. I wiped my face with the back of my hand. Griff kept stealing glances at me and trying to hold my hand, but I didn't want him touching me at all. I swatted his hand away. I wasn't ready to be a mother to a child. I know he'll take care of us but that's not what I want right now. As soon as he pulled the car in his garage. I hopped out and slammed the door. I grabbed a plastic cup out the kitchen and went upstairs. I could feel Griff staring a hole in me, but I don't care he's wrong and he knows it. I locked the door behind me. I meant what I said.

I swear I feel so stupid and naive because I know better, and I still was so fuckin' careless. I can hear Mother Dear's mouth now. Why did Danielle have to be right and why did Griff have to be wrong? I don't know the first thing about being a parent. Hell, my momma didn't even raise me. I know I would never be like her, but still. I guess that's what I get for going with the flow. I'm so scared to even pee on this stick, because I don't want to know the results. Griff and I haven't even known each other long enough to be expecting a child together. I'll do it later I haven't had my cycle and I didn't think anything of it. I just brushed it off. I climbed in his bed and hid under the covers. This is where I wanted to be, but not with him in this room.

It didn't take long for sleep to take over my body. I was drained mentally and physically. I was so over today. I woke up because somebody was lying beside me that shouldn't be. His cologne invaded my nostrils and his hands were rested on my stomach like he knew something was there. I tried to get out of his grasp, but I couldn't. I had to throw up. I shoved his arms out of my way. I jumped up immediately because I had to throw up.

I ran to the bathroom and emptied my stomach in the toilet. I hated throwing up. I didn't want to eat anything because I was afraid this would happen again. Griff walked up behind me and grabbed my hair and put it in a ponytail. He grabbed a face towel and washed my face. He wrapped his arms around me and held me. I threw up again.

"Are you okay Crimson? I know you're mad at me, but I got to make sure you're straight. I made you some homemade chicken noodle soup. I need you to eat and drink something even if you can't keep it down. My Auntie Kaye is downstairs. She's a nurse and she came to examine you." He explained.

"Okay give me a minute. I need to brush my teeth." Griff stood in the door waiting on me. I slammed the door in his face. I wasn't even mad at him anymore. It's just the principal. When were you going to tell me that you've been slipping up? I brushed my teeth and washed my face. As soon as I opened the door, he was standing right there grilling me. I tried to walk past him, but he wouldn't let me. He pulled me in his arms and held me.

"I'm sorry Crimson. Talk to me. Tell me what I have to do to make things right between us?" He asked. It's a lot he must do.

"We'll talk about us later Griff depending on what the results are." I went downstairs with Griff right on my heels to see Auntie Kaye. I would prefer Mother Dear to be here because she's a registered nurse also before she retired, but I don't have the balls to face her. Auntie Kaye was sitting in the living room with her nurse scrubs on and medical equipment setup.

"Hey Crimson, it's nice to see you again. I hate it's under these circumstances, but my nephew cares about you a lot, so I'm making a house call," she explained.

"Thank you. It's good seeing you too." Auntie Kaye gave me a hug. She was nice. I liked her a lot. Griff and I had Sunday dinner at her house a few weeks ago.

"Griff let me borrow Crimson for a minute," she stated. Griff gave us our privacy. I know he wanted to know what was going on. If I was pregnant, he'll be the first to know. I wasn't going to abort my child. I just wasn't ready. Auntie Kaye started asking me questions. When she asked about my menstrual, we both started laughing.

"I can't wait to see what we're having." She laughed.

"Auntie Kaye don't say that I'm not ready." I pouted.

"Well, you should've of thought about that before you had unprotected sex. It'll be alright. Griff is going to be a great father. I swear it's like history is repeating itself. You remind me so much of his mother. The day she found out she was pregnant with him I had just graduated from college. Big Griff called me over to the house to see what was up with her. He wanted to see if all the money he paid for me to go to medical school paid off? Let's just say it did. Twenty-five years later and I'm still doing what I love," she explained and laughed. She got a urine sample and a blood sample.

Now it was a waiting game for her to confirm the unknown. She was waiting for the results to come back from the pregnancy test and the blood sample. I went in the kitchen to fix me some of the chicken noodle soup that Griff made. It smelled so good. I walked right past him and didn't say anything. He walked up behind me and wrapped his arms around my waist. He rested his face in the crook of my neck. I love him, but I'm mad as fuck at him.

"Crimson I'm sorry. I'm not used to you giving me the cold shoulder. I want you to be the only woman that bears my children. Would you have my child Crimson if you're pregnant?" I swear he won't give up. Go on. I can't even be mad at him in peace or eat this soup. He knows he fucked up. Why do you want to ask me now, if I would have your child? WHY? You should've asked me before you decided to slip up. Auntie Kaye walked in and interrupted us. Thank God because I wasn't ready to have this conversation with him.

"Crimson and Griff I have some good news for the two of you. You don't have the flu virus, but you are expecting. You're four weeks to be exact. I know a great OBGYN doctor you could see. I'll give you the information and you can call to setup an appointment. You're dehydrated, so you need to drink plenty of fluids. I'm sending over a prescription to Publix for some prenatal vitamins and iron pills. It'll help with the morning sickness.

Crimson you're in the first trimester please take it easy, no lifting, and no over working yourself. You have a bundle of joy growing inside of you. I want a healthy niece or nephew. Griff take care of her." She explained. I don't even know how I feel about this. Griff reached in his pants and gave Auntie Kaye a wad full of cash. She gave it back to him and yelled.

"It's on the house." Griff helped Auntie Kaye pack up. I went to the kitchen to finish my soup. I can't believe I'm pregnant. I'm about to be a mother to a child. I finished my soup and headed back upstairs. I didn't lock the door behind me. I just wanted to go to sleep in peace. I know that wouldn't happen if Griff and I were mad at each other. I climbed in the bed and hid under the covers. My mind was in a million places. I heard footsteps in the room and my body tensed up. I knew it was him. I felt Griff pull the covers back. He climbed in the bed right behind me and wrapped his arms around my waist. He started whispering in my ear.

"I love you Crimson. I swear to God I do. I messed up but I'm sorry. I got caught up in the moment. I know it's an excuse, but it's the truth. I love you and I'm in love with you. I'm a stand-up guy and I'm going to take care of you until I die. I want you to have my child. I know you'll be a wonderful mother. It's nothing in this world that I won't do for you or my child. I know you don't want to hear it, but I want you to move in with me. I want to wake up to you every morning making sure that you and my child are straight. I don't want you working or standing on your feet all day. I'm buying you a car tomorrow no matter what you say."

"I love you too Carius. I forgive you but I'm still mad at you. I'm scared because everything is moving so fast. I don't want you to think that I tried to trap you because that isn't the case." I cried.

"Stop Crying Crimson, before you upset my baby. Get those thoughts out of your head. We know what it is between us and that's all that matters. I got you. I'm your man and your child's father for a reason. Whatever you want, I'll do anything in my power to make sure you and my child have it. You still haven't answered my question yet. I want you to move in with me. I want to give my child a two-parent household."

"Do I have choice, Griff?"

"You do but you're here every day anyway. I want you to move in because I got to make sure you're taking care of yourself and my child properly. If something was to happen to you and I'm too far to reach you I'll be pissed. I want to make this big house our home."

"Okay, I'll move in with you."

3 MONTHS
LATER

Chapter-24

Jermesha

Christmas was always my favorite Holiday of the year. It's the season to be jolly and I was always showered with gifts. This Christmas might be the best yet. I've been paying Mother Dear to keep my kids and I haven't had to sell my food stamps or steal anything. I was able to buy her and my mother a few things. I guess that's why I loved it so much. I brought my kids a shit load of stuff. I didn't have a new man, but I was able to come up on a few tricks for the season.

I had a couple of niggas in my pocket that didn't mind bussing down. All my tricks were very generous and I'm very thankful for that. Mother Dear and my mother were in the kitchen cooking. A lot of our family members were in attendance with us. Mother Dear always cooked a big dinner for Thanksgiving and Christmas. All her brother and sisters always came through. She cooked ham, turkey, and fried chicken. You name it she fuckin' cooked it. Her desert menu was stupid. Cooking wasn't my thing. I was more of the host. We had a small bar setup with eggnog and a few mixed drinks. It was a cool little setup. I had a few drinks in me and I was feeling good.

My kids were sitting around the tree opening their gifts. I couldn't wait to shit on Crimson. Danielle came through with Baine earlier on her arm. I can't believe she snatched him up. Baine was a hoe too. So, him settling down was odd to me. She dropped Mother Dear and Ms. Glady's off their Christmas gifts. I despised both of those bitches.

You can't tell me Crimson and Danielle ain't no hoes. I eye fucked Baine the whole time he was here. I saw him lusting after me. I bet I could fuck him, and I would let

Danielle know I did it. Keondra couldn't fuck him anyway since she fucked Ike.

I knew Crimson would be coming through here sometime today. I got my hair and nails done. I made sure I was dressed to kill. I copped me a bad ass Chanel jump suit out of Nordstrom's. I had the pumps to match and one of my tricks brought me a cute little wristlet that has my wrist shining. Keondra already told me about all the shit Griff brought her. I was glad my bitch got her man back. I couldn't wait to rub it in Crimson's face. I told that bitch that she was the side bitch, but she didn't want to believe me.

Speak of the devil. The front door opened, and it was her. She was smiling with her dimples showing and all thirty-two of her fuckin' teeth. She was dressed casually and plain like I knew she would be. Basic ass bitch could never pull a nigga like Griff. She couldn't compete with Keondra if she wanted too. I stood up and headed to the door. I wanted that bitch to see me. She had the nerve to tell motherfuckas I was wearing her dirty panties. Bitch I got too much ass and hips to squeeze in her shit. If I did do it, it's my fuckin' business. I got a few pairs of panties that

I couldn't wait to throw his way. I guarantee you one sniff of this pussy and he'll be coming back.

I couldn't wait to knock that smile off her face. I haven't seen her in a few months. I must have talked that bitch up. She just walked in the house and Griff was right behind her. I had to do a double take. He grabbed her jacket, and something looked different about her. Her face was fuller, her hair was longer. Her hips and ass were both spreading. She was glowing. Her shirt was oversized. I couldn't really tell, but I think I see a baby bump. Oh, hell no I got to call Keondra over here right fuckin' now. Please tell me she's not pregnant by this nigga. I can't hold water. I ran to my room and bumped Crimson on my way up the stairs.

"You better watch yourself Jermesha," she yelled.

"No bitch, you better watch yourself. Give me a few fuckin' minutes." I argued. My momma couldn't wait to watch me whoop Crimson's ass. I grabbed my phone off the charger. I had a few missed calls from my tricks.

Mia and Tasha wanted to know if I was coming out tonight. Of course, I was one of my tricks got me a rental for the weekend. We were going to Blue Ridge. I'll call them back later. I had to call Keondra. She answered on the first ring.

"What's up Jermesha? Are you ready to get out tonight?" She asked. "I'm not far from Mother Dears. I can pull up and scoop you in about twenty minutes. I'm picking up a few things from my momma."

"Bitch, I'm ready but I need you to pull up right fuckin' now. Griff and Crimson just walked in. Don't quote me on this but I think she pregnant. Get over here right now and bust this cheating ass nigga. How dare he cake up with you but he's here with her. Set the record straight for this hoe before I do," I argued.

"Jermesha, bitch, you lying. I'm on my motherfuckin' way. I'm not going to make a scene at your grandmother's house, but I'm about to show my face card." I need her to pull up right fuckin' now to shut this shit down with Crimson and Griff. I know it's our families Christmas Dinner but Keondra needs to nip this shit in the bud.

"I don't give a fuck what it is. Let Crimson know he's your fuckin' man. She might have had him once, but bitch, you got him all the time." Keondra and I finished talking. I couldn't wait for her to pull up and get this motherfucka jumping. I hate to rain on Crimson's parade, but it is what it is. If she was pregnant by Griff, she'll lose her baby today. Griff was a bold ass nigga too. Crimson is so fuckin' dumb and stupid to actually think he wants to be with her.

He's been playing her this whole fuckin' time. I grabbed a pair of panties from my drawer they were brand new. I sprayed a little perfume on them. I couldn't wait to stuff them in Griff's pocket. Keondra sent me a text and stated that she was pulling now and to meet her at the front door. Say less I was headed that way.

Mother Dear might be mad, but she needs to see what type of man little Miss. Crimson Rose Tristan was dealing with. She also needs to see that Crimson was a hoe just like I've been saying all along I saw right through Crimson. Bitches like her always play the innocent role. You're Mother Dear's precious Crimson but you're fuckin' somebody else's man.

Get your own man. I walked down the stairs and Crimson and Griff were standing by the bar. I pressed up against him from behind. My breasts were touching his chest. I slid my panties and number in his back pocket. He turned around and grilled me.

"Excuse me I was trying to get through, I argued.

Keondra

Damn I wish I wouldn't have answered the phone when Jermesha called me. Something told me not to answer it. I should've trusted my first instinct. I knew we were supposed to link up tonight for the Christmas Party they were throwing at the Opera. I thought she was ready to pre-game. I knew she had a few coins. That's the only reason I answered the phone for her. She's been treating me to lunch and different little shit. I wasn't tripping because she needed to buss down. I did shit like this for her on the regular. If I had it, she did too. Now I got to show my face at her grandmother's house. If Griff got this bitch pregnant, I'm showing the fuck out. How could you give this bitch something that I wanted so badly?

I haven't been honest with Jermesha about Griff and I splitting up because it was nobodys business but mine. I moved out of the house we shared by force. Despite my actions and tantrums, he still brought me a small ass two-bedroom town house so I wouldn't be on the streets and $100,000.00. I was grateful for that, but it still wasn't over between us. I move in silence and Griff would never see me coming. It's not over until I say it is.

I know I said I wouldn't show out at her grandmother's house, but it was for Griff's sake and not mine. He better keeps shit cordial because I still have a few wounds from our break up that were still open. I know I said some shit and he did too. Jermesha walked up to my car and opened the door. I looked in my mirror to make sure my makeup was on point.

"Girl come on. You look cute. You're killing it. Crimson just has on a t-shirt. She's not weighing up to you. I don't know what Griff see's in her." She sassed and explained.

"I know but you know how I am." I checked my teeth to make sure I didn't have any food in my teeth. I checked my dress to make sure I didn't have any cum stains visible. I just left Ike a few hours ago for a quickie and a few racks. He wanted to lay up, but it was too early for that. I started to apply the cover stick on my neck, so Griff wouldn't see the passion marks, but I wanted him to see the passion marks. He knew I was fuckin' Ike. He didn't give a fuck about sparing my feelings, so I wasn't sparing his.

Jermesha looked cute too. Her new tricks must be breaking her off nice. My friend has leveled the fuck up. Chanel this Chanel that. Ice on my wrist, bitch. Damn, if she got to fuck three niggas to get it I ain't mad at all. We made our way into Mother Dear's house. The food smelled amazing, but his cologne trumped everything. It invaded my nostrils. I could smell him from a mile away. I used to long for his scent. My eyes scanned the room for him and there he was posted up in the corner with her sitting on his lap and his hands were rubbing her stomach. Jermesha nudged me and we headed in that direction.

"Dinner is ready. You can come into the formal dining room to eat. Jermesha I fixed your kid's their plates. It's on the kitchen table." Mother Dear yelled. She looked at me and cut her eyes. Crimson stood up and grabbed Griff's hand and led him to the dining room. They had to walk pass me to get to the dining room. He looked at me and snarled his face up.

Jermesha grabbed my mink coat so she could hang it up. I couldn't wait to drop the top on this mink. She grabbed my arm and led me into the dining room. She had us a seat right in front of Crimson and Griff. He was mugging the fuck out of me. I ran my tongue across my teeth. I ran my feet up Griff's leg. I was reaching for his dick. He kicked me with his feet, and I kicked him back. I hope my heel scratched up his leg. He's a disrespectful ass motherfucka. I swear I'm going to kill him.

"Griff, baby, what do you want to eat?" She asked and smiled. I wanted to bash her head in so fuckin' bad. It's not even about her. It's between me and him. I grilled his ass. I know he could feel it. I wanted him too. He acts as if I don't fuckin' exist. I don't think I could hold my composure. I'm about to act a fuckin' fool. I can't even help myself right now.

"What do you want to eat? I got to feed you and my baby? I'll go fix it?" He asked. I know he just didn't say what the fuck I thought he said. We've only been divorced for a few weeks and he's taking this shit to a new fuckin' level. Pregnant? I got heated instantly. My legs started shaking.

"Crimson are you pregnant?" Jermesha ask. Mother Dear damn near broke her fuckin' neck to hear her answer. I was waiting for her to confirm it. Jermesha was grabbing my hand. She knew I was about to reach across this table and fuck him up.

"You heard what my man said? Do you have a problem with it Jermesha," she asked and smiled? Jermesha grilled me and elbowed me. I raised the fuck up.

"Bitch, you ain't gone say shit?" Jermesha clapped her hands and asked me. Griff gave me an evil glare and Crimson was looking at me like she wanted to say something. I wish Griff and his bitch a would try me today.

"Is she gone say what Jermesha? Do you know me, because you're the same bitch that sent me a drink in the club? I'm curious as to know why you're here and you're not family?" She argued. Griff stood up behind her and whispered something in her ear.

"I invited her here Crimson. She's not related to you, but she's family to me. Why are you getting so upset? You must be guilty of fuckin' somebody else's man?" Jermesha argued and asked?

"The apple doesn't fall far from the tree. She's just like her slut ass mammy that didn't want her motherfuckin' ass," Jermesha's momma chimed in. I knew it was about to go down. I wish Jermesha wouldn't have said that. I shouldn't have come. Crimson's face turned red. I don't know what Jermesha's problem was with her cousin. Griff was heated. I knew shit was about to go left.

"Keondra and Jermesha y'all got her fucked up. Excuse me Mother Dear this ain't even my thing. I'm not trying to ruin your Christmas dinner, but your granddaughter has an issue that I don't mind clearing up. Jermesha long as I'm living ain't nobody ever going to disrespect her. When you see Crimson Rose Tristan, that's me and I don't give a fuck who knows it. Keondra, do I fuck with you? Since you got Jermesha thinking otherwise let's clear that shit up right now," he argued.

"No, we're not together anymore," I sighed. I stood up and grabbed my shit. I was ready to go. Mother Dear stopped me as soon as I was about to leave. Mother Dear never liked me. I could tell the way she put her hand on my shoulder. It was firm with a mean grip. Jermesha was looking at me sideways. I don't know why she was so pressed to be in my fuckin' business anyway.

"Sit Keondra. Don't fuckin' leave because you've been busted out. You wanted to be messy and fuck with

Crimson because of something you used to have. We all miss a good thing sometimes. I don't know what Jermesha's lying conniving ass told you but this ain't motherfuckin' that. You stepped in the motherfuckin dungeon when you walked through my doors.

Jermesha, why are you so fuckin' jealous of Crimson? I don't fuckin' get it. She ain't never did shit to you. That's your fuckin' blood but look how you treat her? The moment she walked in the door you've been mad at her. That's why she's blessed, all because of your demise. Get that hate up out your heart and Sherrie you're too old to even entertain your daughter. Be a mother for once in your fuckin' life instead of trying to be her damn friend.

Stop fuckin' lying all the time. Cheree didn't fuck your man, you were fuckin' hers; if you want to be technical. State facts instead of stating lies. Your daughter is just like you. Vindictive and fuckin' conniving. I can't stand it."

"Mother Dear I don't mean to cut you off but if they're that mad now, then they ain't ready for what's to come." He argued and explained. I wanted to leave so bad. I couldn't take it. I couldn't take him professing his love for her in front of her family. I wasn't ready to live in my truth. Admitting that Griff and I aren't together is what hurts the most. I tried to raise up and leave again but Mother Dear pushed me down in my seat. I feel so fuckin' defeated right now.

"Ain't nobody jealous of Crimson. What the fuck do I need to be jealous of her for? She ain't no fuckin' body. She ain't weighing up to me. Look at her and look at me? Just because she trapped Griff with a baby don't mean shit. She's a home wrecking bitch and I don't give a fuck, blood or not. I'm calling shit how I see it. I don't like her and that's my fuckin' opinion. If she died today, I wouldn't give a fuck." Jermesha argued. I don't know what the fuck I walked into, but I wish I hadn't. Mother Dear smacked Jermesha in her face so damn hard I fuckin' felt it. Everybody was shocked and Crimson busted out laughing.

"Mother Dear I'm leaving and I'm taking Griff and I a plate to go. I'll see you later." Crimson sassed. Crimson grabbed Griff's hand and she was about to lead him somewhere and Mother Dear stopped her.

"Sit your hot ass down Crimson. You ain't going no fuckin' where; you or Griff. I know it was the reason I hadn't seen you. It was because you're pregnant and you didn't want me to know? Why I told you months ago I wanted some grandchildren from you, and I had the dream about fishes I knew it was you. Griff, I like you but don't for one-minute think, she's about to be having your babies without the ring," she sassed and laughed. Crimson was blushing. Griff asked Crimson to raise up and she did.

"Mother Dear come on now we talked about this. I love Crimson I swear to God I do, and she knows it too. I don't want her to be my baby momma. She didn't trap me if anything, I trapped her. I'm in love with her," he explained and laughed. He knelt on one knee. I know he was not about to propose to her. I got heated instantly. I felt my chest cave in. I used my hand as a fan to cool me off. I started shaking.

"I hear you Griff but are you listening to me? You're on one knee for what," she asked him? Mother Dear was baiting Griff meanwhile looking at me the whole time. Jermesha was looking at everything but the two of them.

"Crimson Rose Tristan, will you marry me? I want to wake up to you and my daughter every day. I want to spend the rest of my life with you. I want you to be my wife," he ask

ed and explained? A daughter, really? She was crying. Tears were running down her face.

"Griff yes I'll marry you. I love you so much," Crimson cried and smiled. He wiped her tears with his thumbs. I wanted to throw up everything I just ate. Mother Dear couldn't stop me from leaving this time. I had to go. As soon as I reached the exit of the dining room. Mother Dear stopped me. I swear I'm trying so hard to respect my elders but I'm about to lose it.

"I love you Crimson and Jermesha these panties you slid in my back pocket being slick, you can have them. I don't fuckin' need them. I don't cheat. Did Keondra tell you that?" He asked. Crimson handed Jermesha back her panties. How dare this bitch give my ex-husband a pair of her panties. I knew she wanted him.

"Keondra, leaving so soon? You haven't eaten yet? Griff gave us desert already did you enjoy it? Let me make some shit clear to you. Whatever beef you got with

Crimson Rose Tristan you better dead that shit now because I'm her fuckin' keeper. I won't hesitate to put any bitch to sleep behind her. Not even my granddaughter or my daughter." She explained.

"Is that a threat?" I asked.

"I don't make threats I make fuckin' promises. You heard it from me." She argued. I swear this was the worst fuckin' Christmas ever. How dare Griff propose to that bitch in front of me like I didn't mean shit to him. I swear it's not over between us. I might not get his ass today or tomorrow but when I do, I guarantee you I'll be the last bitch to see him take his last breath. I should slice his fuckin' tires. I rode up beside his car and hopped out. As soon as I knelt, I felt somebody tap me on my shoulder. I looked over to see who it was, and it was Grimo. Griff's henchman. I mugged his big ass. Fuck him too.

"Keondra, I don't want no fuckin' problems but you need to take your ass on. I don't want to have to air you out right here. We're better than this Keondra. Let that shit go." He argued. I raised up and hopped in my truck and pulled off. I can't wait until the day Griff gets his. I couldn't even drive because tears clouded my vision and my eyes were burning. I called Ike from the Bluetooth in my car.

"He answered on the first ring.

"Hello," he yelled through the phone. I broke down crying. I couldn't hold it in anymore."

"Keondra, what the fuck is wrong with you? Where you at shawty, I'm about to pull up," he argued and yelled.

"I'm driving Ike," I cried.

"Pull over and text me the address. I don't know why you left anyway," he argued.

"I'm sorry Ike." I cried.

"Sorry would've saved you some tears."

Crimson

What a fuckin' Christmas? Never in a million years has it gone down like this at Mother Dear's house. I swear I couldn't wait to get up out of there. Staying away from my family might be a good thing. I can't believe Jermesha and Sherri, those bitches ain't no fuckin' cousin or aunt of mine. I'm not even surprised. Damn your own family hates you more than motherfuckas that don't even know you? I never forget faces. I recognized that bitch the moment she walked in the door looking. I knew she was trouble, but whatever she and Griff had going on, it has nothing to do with me.

He let it be known that he wasn't fucking with her. She also let it be known that she wasn't fuckin' with him. I can't wait to have my daughter. I got to let Jermesha feel me because I'm sick of her ass. If I had never known before how jealous she was of me, I know now. I know now Griff proposing only made it worse because the diamond that flooded my finger could light up a dark cave. Her friend used to fuck with Griff, that's why she was mad. Griff and I took us a plate home to go and said our good byes to everybody.

Mother Dear prayed over our union and our unborn child. Griff escorted me to the car. I can't believe he proposed. I sent Danielle a text telling her I was engaged and what happened at Mother Dears. She was now on her way. I told her to stay put because I'm headed home. Griff pulled off and grabbed my hand and raised it to his lips and kissed it.

"I'm sorry Crimson about that bullshit that happened back there." He explained.

"What are you apologizing for? You didn't invite her and whatever doubts I had about the two of you. You confirmed all of my suspicions."

"I know but I'm sorry they came for you. I don't like your cousin. She's trifling as fuck. I told you she was jealous of you. Stay the fuck away from Mother Dear's if I'm not with you. If something happens to you or my daughter, I'm murdering every motherfucka over there besides Mother Dear and your uncle. I don't give a fuck and that's not a threat. It's a fuckin' promise." He argued.

"I know Griff but that's last thing I want to do is stop going over to Mother Dear's house. After the little argument that we had a few months ago. I haven't been over there because I don't like their energy. I don't want you going to jail behind somebody that's not worth it. So, I'll keep my distance until you're able to go over there with me."

"Whenever you want to go, I'll take you over there. You and my daughter come before anybody. I'll stop what I'm doing just for you." He explained. I love him so much. I can't wait to get home and show him how much. Things are finally looking up for little ole me.

6 MONTHS LATER

Chapter-25

Griff

Crimson hasn't been feeling well these past few days. I know Cariuna has been giving her hell. I told her it'll be over soon and just to be patient. She'll meet our princess when she least expects it. Today is her due date. We went to the doctor yesterday and she's only dilated two centimeters. We've been walking every day and Cariuna ain't budging. She's stubborn just like her mother.

I don't know who wanted to see her more her mother or me. It's a little after 2:00 p.m. and it's time for our afternoon walk. I haven't been in the streets to heavy because my baby is about to have my baby, so home was the only place I wanted to be. Crimson needed me because she's about to bring our first child into the world. I wanted a child for the longest. I can't wait to spoil my princess.

"Griff," she yelled and whined. I ran upstairs to see what was going on. I've only been gone for a few minutes to make her a sandwich, some fruit, and water. I think she likes to whine just because she likes to see me sweat. Crimson was leaned over, and a puddle of water was in between her legs on the floor. I know that's not what I think it is? It can't be.

"I think it's time Griff. Your daughter is ready to make her presence known and these contractions are picking up. We need to go now," she screamed. Damn, I'm right here she doesn't have to scream. I hope It's time for our daughter to arrive because her hormones and mood swings are driving me crazy.

"Calm down before you upset my daughter. Come, on let me clean you up. Crimson, you can't go to the hospital like this. Your bag is already in the car." I argued.

"Griff, I don't care about the mess that's in between my legs. I just want her out and I want to see my baby." I just shook my head at her. I grabbed her hand and led her to the bathroom. She can't go anywhere like this. I don't care if she's had a shower or not. "Griff, I don't have time to take another shower. I need to get to the hospital to make sure my daughter is okay," she argued.

"Calm down Crimson your water just broke. She's coming but you ain't leaving this house until I clean you up and change your clothes. If it's that serious I'll call Auntie Kaye and Mother Dear they'll deliver my daughter." I argued. Crimson started pouting but she knew I was telling her the truth. I don't care about any of that whining shit. I cut the shower on and adjusted it to her liking. I smacked her on her ass and told her to "Get in." I climbed in right behind her. I had to feel the pussy one last time before she gives birth to my daughter.

"Griff, are we really doing this right now and my water just broke? Sex can wait it's how we got here in the first place." She argued. I can't believe she's tripping off that and here we are nine months later. What's done is done and it ain't no turning back.

"Crimson chill out. A few strokes ain't gone hurt. It's going to speed up the process. I want two more kids from you and I'm cool. I got needs and wants too. Last time I checked I handled all of your needs and wants."

"I know Griff and I'm very thankful for everything that you do for me. I don't have a problem giving you another child, but can I get this one out first?" She asked.

"Okay, I told you, you ain't got to thank me for nothing I do for you. It's what I'm supposed to do. I know you appreciate me. Let me bust my nut since I won't be able to do that for a few weeks. You get what you want, and I get what I want."

"Griff, I can't believe you right now. Hurry up and make this shit quick. I'm trying to meet my daughter and she's trying to come into the world. Her father doesn't give a fuck." She argued.

"I do care. I'm just trying to shorten your time in labor. I care about you and my daughter. Don't ever say that I don't. You two are all I have. The two of us arguing isn't going to solve anything. You know I hate when we argue about small shit?" Crimson arched her back. I took my time with the pussy. She was already extra wet, and I didn't want to hurt my daughter. I tried to make this as quick as possible. Crimson clamped her pussy muscles on my dick making me bust instantly. I heard her do a faint laugh. She knew she drained a nigga dry.

"Can I shower in peace?" She argued and huffed. I handled my hygiene and let her do her thing. I called Auntie Kaye and Mother Dear and told them to meet us at Piedmont Hospital because Crimson's water just broke. Mother Dear said she'll beat us there. I sent Rashad a text and told him it's time. He's my daughter's Godfather. My nigga had to be there for the arrival of my daughter. Crimson finally came wobbling out the shower.

"Griff, can you dry me off, please? I can't dry my legs off, she asked and pouted.

"I thought you didn't want my help since you wanted to shower in peace." I taunted.

"Just because I wanted to shower in peace doesn't mean that I don't need you. I just didn't want to have long sex session with you, and we need to get to the hospital. I can't wait to meet her and see who she looks like. I've been waiting forever. I'm anxious and excited. I'm a little nervous too." She explained.

"I feel you." I nodded my head in agreement with Crimson. I grabbed a handful of her mango Shea Butter and applied to her legs and stomach. Crimson had some gray Polo cotton shorts and a white wife beater lying on the bed. I grabbed that and her sports bra. I swear Cariuna has her mother's breast big as fuck. I didn't like her wearing those shorts because her pussy print was too visible, and they fitted too tight. I wasn't tripping because after today she wouldn't be wearing these anymore.

"Griff, can you put my shoes on," she asked? I grabbed Crimson's Air Max's and slid them on her feet.

"Is there anything else you need?" I asked.

"I need you to give me a hug and a kiss. I love you Carius," She beamed.

Crimson

G riff and I made it to the hospital in about forty-five minutes. Mother Dear, Ms. Gladys, Danielle, Auntie Kaye, Maria, and Rashad were all waiting for us when we arrived. I'm excited, but I'm nervous more than anything. It's a lot of things that can happen during labor. I've been waiting on this moment since the moment I found out I was pregnant. I couldn't wait to meet Cariuna Dionne Griffey. Griff has been amazing throughout my whole pregnancy. He's a man of his word. It's nothing that he won't do for us. Literally, we have everything that we could ever need or want.

My princess means the world to me. I never had a mother, but I vowed to be the best mother I could be to Cariuna. As soon as we entered the hospital, we sat in the waiting room for a few minutes before my Doctor and Nurse Practitioner escorted us to Labor and Delivery. I changed into the gown my nurse gave me. She checked me to see how far I had dilated. I was already at seven centimeters which means Cariuna would be here in a few hours or maybe an hour. I guess Griff did know a few things. Mother Dear, Auntie Kaye, and Ms. Gladys, were smiling at me. Danielle was on her phone.

I knew she didn't want to be here because of Rashad. She must get used to being in a room with him because she's my everything and he's Griff's, right-hand man. My contractions were speeding up. I couldn't get an epidural because we got here too late and Cariuna was ready to meet her parents. Griff laid in the bed right beside me. I guess he knew I wasn't feeling good because I started banging on the wood railing of the bed, I was in. I can't take these contractions at all, they're killing me.

"Baby what's wrong, are you okay?" He asked. Hell, no I wasn't okay his daughter was killing me. I guess she wanted to see me as bad as I wanted to see her. Griff grabbed a face towel from my bag and ran cold water on it to wipe my face. I was sweating bad and I was hot.

"Not really the contractions are killing me. It's nothing I can do about it." I pouted.

"Okay, breathe like they taught you in your prenatal classes. Let me get the nurse to check you again. It might be time to meet our princess." He explained. Griff went to go page the nurse. The Doctor and The Nurse came into the room to check me. I couldn't take these contractions anymore. I couldn't do it. They hurt so badly.

"Ms. Tristan, you're at nine centimeters. It's time to get you prepped for delivery. Little Ms. Cariuna is ready to meet mommy and daddy!" She smiled. Thank God, because we couldn't wait to meet her. Griff looked at me and kissed me on my forehead. I wasn't nervous anymore. I knew this would be over in a matter of minutes or an hour. I have a low tolerance for pain, but I would have to deal with this. Griff was right by my side and he hasn't left it since we met. Our family had cleared our room and it was just the two of us now. He held and kissed my hand for reassurance.

"Crimson Rose Tristan, I love you and thank you for having my first child. I got you and I'm not going anywhere." He explained.

"I love you too baby." The Doctor and The Nurse finished setting up the room. I squeezed Griff's hand for support because I needed him.

"Ms. Tristan on the count of three push for me. 1,2,3." I started pushing. My doctor instructed me to push again. I started pushing.

"One more push." My doctor yelled. "She's coming. One more push Ms. Crimson. I think she's a little bigger than we expected." I had to push one more time. Hopefully, this is the last one. "She's coming." My doctor yelled. Thank God. I don't think I had to many more pushes in me.

Cariuna came out hollering. She had a set of lungs on her. I hope she could sing because baby girl had loud pipes. She weighed in at nine pounds and three ounces. Griff cut her umbilical cord. My doctor and nurse started cleaning me up. It was blood everywhere. I haven't had a cycle in months, and I was looking forward to one. I don't think I've ever been this happy to see blood before. Cariuna was so beautiful she looked like her father.

The only features she had of mine were my eyes, lips, and dimple in her left cheek. Other than that, she looked like her father. I couldn't wait to hold and kiss her. I'm ready to hold my daughter I can't wait to shower her with kisses.

SOME ODD
YEARS LATER

Chapter-26

Keondra

Patience is a motherfucka! Vengeance is a given because it's real when you're fuckin' with a bitch like me. Evil is my middle name and I'll do anything for the price of fame. Conspiracy will never be the case, but I won't hesitate to catch a body today. Money makes me cum, and any nigga with a big bag excites me. If a motherfucka ever gave me anything and took it back from me its hell to pay. I'm a calculated ass bitch. I may not get you when I want too, but I will get you; when you least expect. I will have the last fuckin' laugh. I bet a bag on it.

Any motherfucka that ever tried to play me and think they can live to tell about is sadly mistaken. I let shit die down and wait until shit gets old until I make my presence known. I love motherfuckas to get comfortable. I love to bring motherfuckas out of their comfort zone. I've been waiting patiently on this moment. I could taste it. It's time to cash in and cash this nigga out the right way and rightfully take back what was mine.

I had about six hour's tops to handle this. My husband was gone to Florida for the day and he wouldn't have a clue to what I was up to in his absence. Besides the early morning head that he gave me for breakfast and our maid joining in on a threesome I was a little spent.

"Keondra, you taste so good," she moaned. The only sounds that could be heard throughout my room were my moans and her slurps. My adrenaline rush was at an all-time high. I couldn't wait to cum. I would cum even harder after I take this nigga out. I heard a faint knock at my door. I didn't pay it any mind because I was trying to cum a few more times.

"Boss Lady we got the drop on this nigga. Let me know when you're ready to make a move," my lil shooter Dace ask. I jumped up immediately and threw the covers over me. Daisy was still between my legs sucking my fountain dry.

Dace shook his head at me. I didn't want anybody to know that I had a small fetish for women. Daisy crept back upstairs to finish our sex session as soon as Ike was gone. I wasn't expecting Dace here until 10:00 a.m. I looked at the clock and it was only 9:15 a.m. Why is he here so early? Her head was stuffed between my legs and my hands were snatching her scalp bald. I fucked her face with no remorse. My legs had a death grip around her neck. Each time she ran her tongue down the crack of my ass I came.

The moment Ike decided we needed a maid to keep our home clean without consulting with me, I knew something was up. He started complaining about every little thing I did. He hired help without even running it by me first? One day I decided to come home earlier than I normally would. I always beat Ike home. I thought it was odd for a week straight he would beat me home and he was always tired. I'll never forget it. One Tuesday morning he left before I did. I pulled off about an hour after him. I parked two blocks over. I walked back to the house and crept in through the basement. I caught that bitch fuckin' my husband and I went off. He told me he always wanted a threesome, but he was scared to ask me? She came on to him and it just happened.

He was familiar with her body. He fucked that bitch raw with no condom. He ate her pussy like it was mine and I could tell she was used to it. My heart caved in. It's the same pain I felt when Griff and I split. I wasn't buying that shit. A bitch ain't just coming onto you just because and you end up fuckin' her in our home and disrespecting me, and she's our maid all of sudden. You and that bitch had something going on and you didn't give a fuck about disrespecting me to satisfy her needs. I couldn't believe him.

I did a little digging myself. I followed him one day when he thought I was going to California with my mom for a few days. I asked him to come with me and he declined. It was business as usual. I wasn't surprised. I followed him and he was parading this bitch around town.

Places that we frequented. I even saw the two of them on a few double dates with Baine and a bitch that wasn't his wife. I snapped a few pictures. I couldn't wait to let the cat out the bag.

The only thing Daisy could do for me was eat my pussy and lick my ass clean. Whenever Ike wasn't home her face stayed between my legs. She wanted to fuck my husband up under my roof and think she could have her hands in my bag! It wasn't going down like that. I nipped all that shit in the bud if she wanted to stay here and fuck him. He wasn't paying her. She could stay here for free and eat pussy and suck dick all she wants for free. Ike's bag is mine and I'm the only bitch that's going to secure it. He felt some type of way about it, but I didn't give a fuck. We argued for weeks about it, but I didn't care. Eventually, I won. It wasn't going down like that.

I fucked up when I married Griff without a prenup. I wasn't going out like that with Ike. Thank God he wasn't as smart as Griff. I had him right where I wanted him too. In due time this nigga and his bitch will be gone. He can count his last fuckin' days. Dace clapping his hands broke me out of my thoughts.

"I thought I told you to never walk in my room without knocking," I argued. I don't know why he thought he could barge into my room without knocking? Last I checked Ike paid him and I did too. He needs to follow my commands. I noticed Daisy was eye fucking him when she raised up and scooted her ass behind me. I had a thing for Dace, but we couldn't cross that line until we finished our business and then we might be able to do something.

"What the fuck I got to knock for? I know you're fuckin' the maid when Ike is gone. I just want to know; when can I fuck-," was all he was able to get out. I cut him off before he could say anything else.

"Aye, you can't fuck Daisy, ain't that right baby?" I smacked her on her ass to play it off. Daisy wasn't my bitch. She was Ike's. So, no I don't tell her my plans or any of my moves. My husband was her motive. His bag was mine and I wasn't about to let his side bitch fuck it up for me because of Dace.

"Dace, can you please leave? I don't feel comfortable with you in here while I'm naked," I ask.

Daisy already heard too much so that bitch had to go. It's always no face no case.

"I've seen pussy before," he laughed. I didn't find that funny at all.

"Go take a shower Daisy you're rolling with me today." I smiled. If she only knew what I had in store for her ass. She pushed me back on the bed. I bounced a little bit because our bed was huge. She tongued fucked my pussy wet. She was putting on for Dace. His eyes fucked me lustfully the whole time. I could see the huge print in his pants rising. He was turned on. My hands were gripping Daisy's ass checks. He walked over to us and dropped his pants to the ground. I gave him an evil glare. He stroked his dick a few times. He dropped his dick off in Daisy. He started pounding her from the back.

I was so heated with him. I couldn't even watch. He grabbed my face forcing me to look at him. Daisy was so into him fuckin' her. She stopped eating my pussy just to enjoy him fuckin' her. She looked at me and smiled. I politely removed myself from the two of them. Dace cupped my face roughly forcing me to look at him. He leaned up toward me, and we were mouth, to mouth. His hands were on her head, covering her ears so she couldn't hear what he was saying. His pounds were getting louder. Her ass smacking up against his torso were pissing me off. I could smell the fresh mint on his breath. He whispered where only I could hear him.

"Stop fuckin' playing with me. I don't want to fuck this bitch, but I don't want to watch my bitch fuck another bitch in my presence. How the fuck, do you think I feel? Her pussy ain't even all that. What you mad for?" He argued and snarled his face up at me. My tears were threatening to seep through my eyes. I used my hands to fan my eyes so they could dry my tears. I hated when he was hard on me. Dace didn't have a problem putting me in my place. He pulled out of Daisy and nutted on her ass. I grabbed the sheet to cover myself up. I stomped to the bathroom to take a long hot shower.

Today was the day I was making a boss move. My life was about to change forever. It was time for me to level up. I've been plotting this come up for years and now that I have my plan fully executed. It's time to make my move.

I know Ike would hate me forever, but it is what it is. He crossed me and for that, he would have to pay. I took a long hot steamy shower. My mind had to be in the right place to go through with everything I had planned. Dace came into the bathroom while I was still inside. He pulled the curtain back and watched me. I cut the water off because I know I was in here longer than I should have been. I grabbed a towel and dried off. He watched me very intensely. I refuse to even acknowledge him. I didn't have anything to say to him. I grabbed my thongs off the toilet and knelt to put them him on. He grabbed my pussy and attempted to finger fuck me. I swatted his hands away.

"Don't touch me. We got shit to do. Last time I checked I was paying you. It's not the other way around. You just got a sample of some pussy, you're good," I argued. He held his hands up surrendering. I finished putting my clothes on. I was dressed in all black. Daisy knocked on the bathroom door.

"I'm ready," she stated. I told Dace to go in my room to entertain her. I brushed my teeth and coated my lips with a purple matte lip. I walked out of the bathroom and Daisy was up in Dace's face begging him to fuck her again. I heard him curve her. I motioned with my hands that I was ready to go. They followed me downstairs to the garage. Daisy was riding with Dace and I was riding by myself with Jacque another one of my shooters in Ike's truck. I slid my black leather gloves on making sure I didn't leave any traces of me being in here.

I left my cell phone at home. Jacque gave Dace the signal. We followed behind Dace and Daisy. Jacque looked at me and I looked at him. I bit my bottom lip. He grabbed my thigh and ran his hands across my pussy. I opened my legs wider giving him easy access.

"Not now we got plenty of time to do this." He explained.

"Yeah, we do." I sighed. I wanted him in the worst way. I kept my freaky thoughts at bay only for the moment. I closed my eyes reminiscing, about how he fucked me. Late nights, long strokes and intense choke holds. A loud moan escaped my lips.

Yeah nigga, this shit real out here running through the red light

Looking through your rear-view Nigga might just sneak up on the car

and try to spray you. We're playing for keeps,
down here in the A

Future's Red Light was blaring through the speakers. We finally made it to our destination. I rubbed my hands together like Birdman. We pulled up on the block. It wasn't a lot of movement. Ike's truck blended in with the regular cars on the street. Nobody suspected anything. I've been watching this nigga for years and he hasn't switched up his routine yet. It was a bad thing for him and a good thing for me. Out of all the years I've been watching him and casing him out, today was the fuckin' day that I made my move. She had his heart, but he was my prey. I checked my watch and it was 11:11 a.m. he walked out the back door of the trap as usual and hopped in his black BMW 550. He had a big duffel bag on his shoulder. I knew it was over a million dollars in the bag itself.

As soon as he pulled off. Jacque looked at me and I looked at him. It was showtime. He did something on his phone. He looked to the left of the street and gave Saye a head nod. We waited about three minutes for him to pull off and bust a left at the stop sign.

As soon as he made his complete stop and turned left. Saye and Jacque both hit the gas and sped up to catch up with him. Dace came from the other direction. Saye and his hitters had the windows raised down with AK's pointed in that direction. Dace was on his ass bumping the back of his car. He was trying to get away from him. Dace bumped the back of his car again and he hit a pole. Saye and his six shooters lit up the BMW. They aired that motherfucka out. It was loud and it sounded like a fuckin' marching band with over a hundred round drum. Bullets and glass were everywhere. The BMW was spent. Dace and Daisy hopped out. I hopped out right behind them I pulled my ski-mask down over my face. Jacque looked at me and I looked at him.

"Stick to the fuckin plan," he argued. I hopped out the truck. Dace pulled the driver's door open and fired multiple shots. He reached over and grabbed the duffel bag out the backseat. I couldn't even recognize his fuckin' face. This job was worth every fuckin' penny I spent.

I reached in his back pocket and grabbed his wallet. His license was visible. I dialed 911 on the burner phone and gave it to Daisy. We had to make this shit quick. I don't hear any sirens yet, but they were coming.

"I need you to call this murder in," Dace explained to her.

"What do I got to do," she asked. Dace gave her the instructions. We had to make this shit quick. A lot of people were looking. I dialed 911 and shoved the phone in her hand.

"Dekalb 911 Dispatch."

"I like to report a homicide I just witnessed. The victim I think he's dead. I pulled him out of the car. He has identification on him," she cried and stated. I shoved the gun in the back of her head, I wasn't for the games and shit.

"Calm down Miss what's him name," the dispatcher asked. It was showtime.

"Carius Deon Griffey." She stated. As soon as she stated his last name. I pulled the trigger and shot her in the head. Jacque was right on my heels and shot Dace in the head also and grabbed the duffel bag out of his hand. We pulled off in the car Dace and Daisy were in and left the burner phone and Ike's truck on the scene. Finally, I pulled this shit off. I couldn't get excited just yet. I had one more move to make. Jacque shoved the other burner phone in my hand. I dialed 911 and got the recording ready on the spare burner phone.

"Dekalb 911 Dispatch." The dispatcher stated. I pressed play on the recording.

"I like to report a homicide I just witnessed."

"Go ahead mam what's the location?" The dispatcher asked.

"Glenwood and Columbia drive. I recognized the killer getting away."

"Ms. calm down do you have a name or description," the dispatcher asked?

"Yes, it was IKE DELEON. He fled the scene, but his car is still on the scene." I hung up and busted out laughing.

CHECK MATE

Pushing Pen Presents now accepting submissions for the following genres: Urban Fiction, Street Lit, Urban Romance, Women's Fiction, BWWM Romance Please submit your first three chapters in a Word document, synopsis, and include contact information via email @pushingpenpresents@gmail.com please allow 3-5 business days for a response after submitting.

Book Bae Basket Giveaway! I Wanted to Announce It Here First. Read, Review on Amazon and Goodreads! Tag Me in Your Review on Facebook (Nikki Taylor) or Instagram (WatchNikkiWrite) Twitter (WatchNikkiWrite) Email Your Entry to NikkiNicole@Nikkinicolepresents.com. The First 50 Reviews I Get I'm Going to Draw A Name and Ship You A Basket. I Do Things in Real Time! I'm Not Holding It Until the End of The Month. If I Get 50 Reviews on Day 1 Of This Release. I'll Draw A Name the Next Day and Ship the Basket the Following Day. I'll be 33 in March! I'm Giving Away 3 Baskets Pick Your Series and I'll Handle the Rest.

CPSIA information can be obtained
at www.ICGtesting.com
Printed in the USA
LVHW031931120319
610380LV00002B/125/P

9 781798 602300